Fight FOR YOU

A STRIPLING WARRIOR NOVEL

Fight FOR YOU

A STRIPLING WARRIOR NOVEL
BY
MISTY MONCUR

EDEN BOOKS - UTAH

Published by Eden Books, Stansbury Park, UT

ISBN-10: 0989895904
ISBN-13: 978-0-9898959-0-3

Moncur, Misty Leigh, 1978-
Fight For You / Misty Moncur
Summary: Keturah must gain the trust of her fellow warriors to fight beside
them in battle. She is ready to fight the Lamanites but is not prepared to fight
the battle in her heart.

ISBN: 978-0-9898959-0-3

Library of Congress Catalog Control Number

2013949208

To Tom and Elsie

For hours and hours spent reading my words.
(I can count to a million. Want to hear?)

Acknowledgements

I want to say thank you to Dave.
It takes a freaking awesome person to be married to a writer.
Thanks for picking up all the pieces that I drop and pretending
my pretend people are as real to you as they are to me.
And even though you can't just order a plain pepperoni pizza,
thank you for feeding the kids.

A special thanks
to my readers for making me feel like I'm kind of a big deal.

And finally, it is long past time I said
Misty is better than Chad.

Chapter 1

The shouting started when Reb made his first stab at me with the spear.

I blocked the stab and returned it. Reb blocked it easily, but I could see he had lost his good grip on the spear already, so I cut, jabbed, flipped the weapon from his hands, and got the tip of my spear to his chest.

The shouting stopped abruptly.

When Seth and Gideon returned from their council meeting with Captain Helaman, where they had presumably obtained our orders for the day, a crowd of boys had gathered to watch the sparring. I had already beaten Reb, Cyrus, and Mathoni, and by then the boys were biting their thumbnails and yelling out suggestions to Corban.

He jumped back, but not quick enough, and I scored a final point on his ankle. Giving me a disgusted look, he threw down his spear and hobbled away through the commiserating jeers of the crowd.

I tossed my spear toward Ethanim who caught it easily with one hand. "I need a break," I told him. I didn't, but I felt like I was making a spectacle of myself. Were they all letting me win?

Was I just a big joke to them?

My hair had come loose during the fight with Corban, an errant lock falling over my eyes, so I slipped out the leather binding, smoothed back my long, dark hair, and retied the tether. When I looked up, I saw a lot of the boys in the sparring circle were still watching me. Hadn't they ever seen anyone tie her hair back before?

I could feel their eyes on me as I walked away—varying degrees of mistrust and skepticism—nothing that even bordered on admiration. But I stood tall and held my head high as I looked to Seth, my chief captain. His kohl-rimmed eyes held both amusement and exasperation.

He clapped his hands together, raised a fist into the air, and yelled to get his men's attention. "Gear up!" he bellowed.

As the crowd dispersed, I caught Gideon's eye. I wondered what he thought of the sparring. I had done everything just as he had taught me, but he was frowning deeply. He glanced toward Corban, and as I followed the direction of his gaze, I knew he was disappointed that I had injured one of his men. I gave a small shrug and bit back a smile. He frowned for another moment, then rolled his eyes and turned away, probably to hide a smile of his own.

My unit consisted of ten boys, each around sixteen years old, and me, the only girl in Helaman's army. Already, boys from other units were ribbing them hard, making jokes about me and smirking. It would only get worse as time went on, too, with privacy and modesty concerns to consider. Each of these boys would have to make adjustments and concessions in order for me to be here, to live and fight beside them in the army. They didn't like it.

Lib, our unit leader, went to Seth to get instructions and Ethanim brought his gear and came to stand beside me. Lib and Ethanim had been shadowing me all morning. I doubted they would admit it, but I was sure one of our captains, Seth or maybe even Helaman, had assigned them to be my friends. It was kind of humiliating.

"You did great," Ethanim said, gesturing to the place the sparring circle had been.

"They were trying to embarrass me."

He winced. "Everyone here has something to prove."

Me more than anyone.

We both knew it was true, and the thought sat heavily between us. "Hey, where did you get that?" he asked into the uncomfortable silence.

"Get what?"

"Paint." He made a sweeping motion with one finger under his eyes, referring to the black paint I wore under mine.

"Oh!" I couldn't help but blush when I thought of how my best friend, Zeke, had smeared the dark paint under my eyes early that morning. But I had my own jar of it. I rummaged in my satchel until I came up with the jar and then handed it to Ethanim. "Help yourself."

He took it and smeared some under his own eyes to reduce the sun's glare as we traveled. I motioned to the group of boys that surrounded us, and he took the little jar and began passing it around.

As I strapped on my travel pack, tent, bedroll, weapons, and water skin, I looked toward the large stone platform across the field where Captain Helaman stood. He was tall, broad-chested, and smiling. He was a prophet of God, not a military man, but he had agreed to lead us into battle, and we all believed—really believed—that God would keep us safe. Helaman knelt to offer a prayer, and the rest of us followed.

As I bowed my head, I found myself kneeling between Lib and Ethanim, my new best friends, who exchanged a glance over my head. I tried to catch Lib's eyes, but he wouldn't look at me.

When the last amen had been uttered from the farthest on the field, Helaman stood and began giving directions.

Excitement rolled through the lines as we marched off the training ground toward the West Road which we turned onto and followed south through the foothills. By midday we had traveled to the southern border of the land of Melek without stopping.

Gideon eased up beside me, edging Ethanim over. He pointed to a large green field in a small valley down below us to the west.

"My family's farm," he said.

I looked in the direction he pointed. "It's pretty."

He watched it for a moment as we marched by. Then he cast me a glance and a small, sad smile. I noticed he wore some of my black paint under his eyes.

"Yeah," he said, "I guess it is." There was a sadness in his eyes he didn't bother to conceal.

"Do you miss it?" I asked.

Something about the way he turned his eyes forward and gave me the sharp edge of his profile made me feel that he had been glad to leave it.

"Not really," he said.

"Who will bring in the harvest this year?"

He turned to look at me. "My father," he said. "The other men of the town will help him, and he will help them with their sons' work. I have two younger brothers still at home. They are strong, but they are only boys. And then there is my mother."

"You feel guilty."

He sighed, ran a broad hand through his chestnut-colored hair. "I have responsibilities at home. We all do. Who will bring in your family's corn?"

"Our neighbors and others of the village, I suppose. Hemni—Zeke's father—will take care of it."

"That's kind of him, but don't you feel responsible to bring it in?"

I laughed and shook my head. "I hate the harvest. It

4

makes my back ache." I fingered the axe at my belt. "I'd rather face Lamanites."

"You don't feel bad that your mother will be burdened with the work?"

"Oh, Mother is coming with us. You know she is a healer. She feels it would be wrong not to come."

His eyebrows rose. "So you have entrusted your entire harvest to Hemni?"

"Sure. His wife has been my mother's best friend since they were little girls. My family has lived near Hemni and Dinah for my entire life. Longer even. He took care of us after my father died until my brothers could work. There is no question Hemni will tend our fields and see to our flock as if they were his own. He intends to bring the harvest to the troops."

"That's a lot of extra work for him, don't you think?"

"He's a man. He can shoulder it," I tossed out blithely.

That garnered a long assessing look from Gideon, one I was not sure I liked.

"Keturah," he said. "If you seek equal rights, you must also accept equal responsibilities. Privilege does not come without a price. You think men have life so easy because their work is fun for you, but it is still work, and not all men enjoy the work they must do."

"You sound like Zeke."

The mention of his name brought an uncomfortable silence with it.

We passed by his farm, and he didn't even glance back over his shoulder at it. We were gradually descending into a large plain, and in the very far distance I could make out what appeared to be a city. Beyond it the glimmering Sidon River snaked through the valley.

Gideon had trained me near a stream that my brothers said flowed into the Sidon to the north. I had never followed the stream that far nor seen the main branch of the river.

Gideon pointed. "Zarahemla."

A thrill shot through me at being so near the capital city. I had never been there. I wished our journey was taking us in that direction, but we were going south to assist our allies in a city called Judea.

"I didn't realize you lived so close to Zarahemla," I said.

"So do you," he replied. "We are not yet a full day's journey from your home. And anyway, it would still take another three days to walk there."

"It took Micah weeks to travel there and back when he went to ask Helaman to lead us," I pointed out.

"Not everything your brother does is for his family's ears." Was he deliberately avoiding my eyes? "And anyway, he had to wait for Helaman to make his own arrangements before he could leave his home and family, his public duties, and his ministry."

Micah had responsibilities I didn't know about? I pondered this for a while in silence and finally concluded that Micah was entitled to keep some things private from me, his little sister.

"Don't you worry about your mother?" asked Gideon suddenly. "Traveling with the army?"

I knew what he meant. The reason, the whole reason, we were marching to the battlefront was that our parents couldn't do it. Twelve years ago they had made an oath to God that they would never again shed the blood of man. Ceremonial sacrifices, murders, unjust punishments, waging war—they were ashamed to have such customs in their past. To break such an oath, even though our enemies, the Lamanites, were conquering the cities that formed the southern border of our lands, would be grievous indeed.

Many of the men had considered breaking their oath in order to help our Nephite allies. These boys, the ones who surrounded me on all sides as we marched, were young and

6

inexperienced, but they had not made any such oath, and they would not let their fathers break theirs.

"My mother would hide, prevent coming in contact with the enemy in any way she could, but you're right—she won't even touch weapons." I thought of how she had shied away from my father's dagger, the look in her eyes, on that evening she had given Father's weapons to my brothers and me. "She has her tools—her little knife to cut roots and slice meat—but she would never raise it in defense of her life."

"That doesn't worry you?"

"Of course it does," I said. "My brothers too. Kenai was teaching me to defend both myself and Mother when you found us in the meadow that first day."

Gideon caught my eye. That hadn't been the first day we had met—the morning I had tossed the moonflower in with the shards of black obsidian, the morning Gideon had picked it up. From the way his eyes flicked away from mine, I knew he was thinking about it too.

"You planned to come with her, even if you weren't in the militia?"

"I wasn't going to stay home alone," I pointed out.

"You could have stayed in Zeke's home," he suggested. "If you are so close as family."

I definitely detected the jealousy in his voice.

"I didn't want that," I said quietly. And Gideon knew it. I wanted the army.

Zeke was my oldest friend and my family's choice for my husband. My relationship with him and Gideon's feelings about it were not topics to discuss in front of the other boys.

"You might have become betrothed and lived there legitimately."

"I didn't want to be betrothed," I said more forcefully. Gideon commanded these boys. It would not do for him to say these things, so I changed the subject. "Do you worry about your own parents?" I challenged. "Being so close to the wilderness?" Dangerous bands of Lamanites were known to camp in the wilderness.

His jaw tightened.

"Gideon?"

"We've been...attacked before. Plundered. Many times," he admitted quietly.

"Attacked? Do they steal your grain? What do your parents do if they won't fight?"

"Do they steal our grain?" His laugh had no humor in it. He lowered his head and put his lips near my ear. Did I imagine that Ethanim leaned closer? "My younger brother—the oldest one at home now who helps my father with the farm—is not my father's son."

I turned to look at him. His head was still bent to mine. I swallowed hard. "Well, there's a little family secret," I said.

"Oh, it's no secret. He doesn't look like any of us."

"I'm sorry," I said. "For your mother, for all of you. Why don't your parents leave and move into the town where it's safe?"

"Is anywhere safe?" he asked.

I thought back to the Lamanite raid in Melek a few days ago. I had killed a Lamanite warrior to save Leda, a girl from my village. There was no safe place. That was why we were marching out to assist the armies. I frowned and shook my head.

"My brothers and I are the only protection they have," Gideon said. "The only protection they have ever had."

I was slowly realizing why it had bothered Gideon so much when he had not been able to save Leda's parents. He had not been able to save his mother, either. And he wasn't there to protect her now.

"Anyway, I don't want to talk about the farm," he said, clearly closing the topic to further discussion.

"Okay," I said, eager to end the topic myself. "All I need to know about that farm anyway is that it gave you those beautiful muscles."

I heard a bark of laughter from down the line of boys. Obviously, they could all hear our conversation.

I glanced at Gideon, mortified, as Reb made kissing noises with his fat lips and Noah feigned gagging. Lib snorted but tried to hold back his laughter. I turned and slugged him in the arm, making sure to use my knuckle.

"I meant, you know, the barley." My cheeks were burning hot, and I couldn't look at Gideon again.

"I know," he said. And he did. He knew how it frustrated me to be unable to build muscles like a man could. I was getting stronger, but not as strong as I wanted. I worked harder than any of these boys. It was not fair. Gideon had once told me he had built his strength by threshing and throwing sheaves of barley all his life, which had inspired some of my own training practices.

But with all the other boys around, calling Gideon's muscles beautiful was more than unwise. I sighed. After that, I kept my mouth shut. Gideon continued to walk next to me, but after the break for the midday meal, he didn't reappear at my side, and I didn't blame him.

We marched for several more hours after the break, taking only short rest periods, until the sun was a hand's width above the mountain peaks to the west.

"Make camp!" Seth had come up behind me and bellowed above the chattering boys. He instructed us to move a distance off the highway into the forest, fan out, and set up our camps in the same basic formation in which we had marched.

An army of boys scattered, but Lib lingered near me, and when we found our unit making camp against an outcropping near the stream, he said, "I'll help you set up your tent."

Most of the boys had tents, but very few set them up now. It was hardly worth it for one night. "Won't it be kind of conspicuous if there are Lamanite spies about?" I asked Lib uncertainly.

He looked around. "I think two thousand boys sleeping on the ground would be a little more conspicuous than one tent."

I dropped my pack to the ground and had to brush Lib's hands aside when he would have set up the tent for me. As I unrolled it, I glanced around and saw units of tens setting up small camps tucked in amongst the trees.

"I can't earn respect if you do my work for me," I told him. "Don't treat me like a little girl."

He watched me for a moment. I glanced up at him and saw he had his hands on his hips.

"You don't have to prove anything to anyone, you know. Everyone saw you fight."

"You'll make me look helpless, Lib. None of these boys will fight by me if they can't trust me. And I can't fight by them. Let me take care of my own needs."

Lib was gnawing on a fingernail. He didn't like it, but he agreed. "Okay, but I'm not going to just sit and watch you do the work."

"So get the fire started."

He groaned, probably irritated with me, and turned to fetch kindling from the woods.

My unit had been lucky to snatch a place next to an outcropping of rock against the hilly terrain. A stream flowed past our campsite, but I soon saw the problem with this piece of luck.

Units of boys came to the stream to fill their water skins, and they all stared at me as I crawled around on my tent, lashed it to the poles and prepared it for setting up. Some milled around in small groups obviously prolonging their time at the stream much longer than it took to get water. Some pretended to be busy or to talk to one another. Others just crossed their arms, hitched a hip, and openly stared at me.

I was glad when Lib returned.

"You would think none of them had ever seen a tent

before," I remarked as I gazed warily over my shoulder at the boys.

He coughed. "They are not looking at the tent."

I rolled my eyes.

"They've never seen a girl like you before."

I snorted un-prettily and went back to my work. "Well, they will just have to get used to me being here."

"Or you will have to get used to the staring." He gave a half-hearted wave to send the boys on their way, which didn't have much effect on any of them. "Can I borrow your flint?" he asked.

"Sure." I toed my satchel toward him.

I pulled on the poles, tugged a little, staked down the ropes with a rock, and my tent was up.

"Whoa-ho!" I heard Lib exclaim, followed by a low whistle.

I leaned over and peered at him from behind my tent.

"Did you carry this all the way from Melek?" he asked.

I looked at what he held in his hands. It was a good-sized cloth sack rounded with whatever was inside.

"Where did you get that?" I asked.

He gave me a curious look. "From your satchel."

"No, that's not mine," I said. "And I think I would notice something that size in my satchel all day."

I walked toward him and looked inside the sack as he opened up the tie. Corn flour. I hadn't packed that. I had planned, like the rest of the troops, to either eat from the forest on the way to Judea or supplement with some dried venison, nuts, and fruits.

"Your mother must have tucked it in when you weren't looking."

I reached out and hefted the sack from him. "This weighs half a stone, at least. I'm telling you, I would have noticed that in my satchel. Where did you really get it?"

He raised his brows.

I frowned. "You didn't put it there?"

He slowly shook his head.

I peered again at the ground corn in the bag. I shrugged, reached for my pack and pulled out a clay bowl. After dipping some water from the stream and mixing the corn flour into it, I said, "I'll be back," and set off into the forest to find herbs and perhaps some oxalis or plantain leaves to accompany my meal.

Chapter 2

Noah and Zach brought back a rabbit and five fish from the forest. Corban, who had been such a big baby about losing the sparring to me, filleted the fish very capably with a wicked looking blade.

"You're good at that," I told him after I had watched him work for a few moments. He just glared at me and said nothing. He had walked all day on a sore ankle that was my fault. I suppressed a sigh and went back to the fire.

I used the whole sack of flour for the corn cakes and made enough to share with my entire unit. They ate them, definitely enjoyed them, but tried to pretend the cakes hadn't come from me.

I shrugged off their half-hearted thanks, and I told myself I wasn't going to gain their favor in one day. But in my heart, I had hoped to win them over quickly.

After the evening meal was cleaned up, I slipped past my guards and went into the woods. I thought Lib and Ethanim let me go alone until I sensed someone quietly following me. I smiled to myself. Men of honor were so predictable.

The terrain was different here with more hills and small

valleys than at home. The ground was rockier, and growing in it were a few plants I had never seen before. I picked a few stems of each new plant and pressed them between the thick flax-paper pages of a little book my mother had given me. She might know if these plants could be useful.

I found that from the top of the outcropping, which our camp was nestled against below, I could see Zarahemla and the Sidon still far away near the eastern horizon. We had passed other smaller settlements during the day, but Zarahemla was clearly the largest.

I stood at the top of the rocks for a moment looking out over the camps below me. Then I sat at the edge and let the breeze blow my hair back from my face. After the long march, the soft breeze felt good. But the memory of Noah's words from earlier in the day made my heart sink again.

"It's not too late to go home," he had said when he had seen me wiping sweat from my forehead in the heat of the day. It was a small thing, but the sneer on his lips made it cut deeper than I should have let it.

Helaman had allowed me to come with the army, but the other soldiers weren't going to let me in.

I heard the rustle of grass behind me. "How did you get past my guards?" I asked without turning.

"Your guards are playing ball in camp."

I could see them in a circle of boys below me trying to keep a small ball off the ground with knees, feet, chests, and elbows. The reason Lib and Ethanim weren't following me was because Gideon had agreed to do it instead.

"You shouldn't be out here alone, Kanina."

Kanina was what my mother called me. It meant "little rabbit," but it was a term of endearment to me. Besides my mother, Gideon was the only other person who called me Kanina, and I secretly loved when he did.

"Every boy in camp is right down there." I gestured to the

empty space in front of me.

He snorted. "Not a safety measure. Do you know how many people would go insane blaming each other if you got hurt on a walk through the forest?"

Gideon sat down beside me, and I turned to look at him. His skin was dark with the touch of the sun. His hair was wet—he must have bathed in the stream. Recalling the curious eyes of the boys who had watched me set up my tent, I had decided to wait for the cover of darkness to wash off the grime from the march. Gideon smelled like fresh air and earth. I probably didn't smell as fresh.

"Spare me the lecture," I said and tried to surreptitiously sniff the fabric at the shoulder of my sarong.

Gideon had washed off his black eye paint but his eyes themselves were pools of shimmering black in the falling twilight. He twisted away from me and when he turned back, he held out a white moonflower between his fingers. It was just beginning to open.

Flattered beyond what I should have been, I took it from him and brought it to my nose. Moonflowers had an unmistakable fragrance, which I loved. They bloomed quickly, in a matter of minutes, and they only bloomed at night, different from all the other flowers that bloomed during the day.

Without thinking, I reached up and smoothed my finger over the scar at his eyebrow. How had he gotten it?

"You were gone, weren't you? When your mother got hurt. You weren't there to help her."

Slowly, he reached up, took my wrist, and moved my fingertips away from his scar. Frowning, he gave his head a small shake to discourage me, but he allowed my hand to rest loosely in his. He looked down at them—his hand, large and rough and hard, and mine, so small it might have been dainty but for the calluses.

"My brother and I had gone to purchase seed and

supplies. I was eight. He was eleven."

"You have an older brother?"

"Jashon fights in Teancum's ranks. He's been gone for several years already."

"He is as eager to fight as you are."

"It's not fighting that interests us, Keturah. It is freedom and peace. Safety. Justice."

We stayed quiet, listening to the sounds of the boys below. The smoke from the camp fires drifted up, and the air smelled of hickory.

I looked down at the flower in my hand, and I felt something for the boy who sat next to me. It didn't matter what. Any feeling was a betrayal of Zeke.

We got to our feet and re-traced our footsteps back to camp. The boys in my unit had stopped playing ball and were sitting around the campfire on their bedrolls, and Gideon joined them. They didn't look like they wanted my company.

I set the moonflower Gideon had given me inside my tent with my book. It would wilt before long, but I kept it anyway, and I didn't ask myself why.

I wanted to go to the stream for a quick bath. Between the humidity and the dirt the army had kicked up on the road, I felt caked in grime. I left camp and headed for the stream. When I dropped my satchel on the bank, Ethanim spoke from behind me.

"Go farther downstream so we can make sure you're not observed."

I heaved a sigh. "This isn't necessary," I called back, but it was only met with silence.

I trudged on. "Is this good enough?" I called back over my shoulder.

"Yes." I couldn't tell which one called back.

I dropped my satchel, sat beside the stream, and took off my sandals. The water was soft and cool on my tired, dirty feet.

My sandals were comfortable—Hemni had fashioned them just for me—but I had been walking in them all day, and I was glad to take them off.

I reached into the slow water, and as I rubbed the dirt off my feet I felt something soft and spongy coating the large rocks at the bottom of the stream. I scraped off a handful of the moss from the rocks and brought it out of the water for inspection. Yes, it would work. I retrieved a folded cloth sack from my satchel and placed a good portion of the spongy algae into it, then I set the soggy sack aside.

I let my feet relax in the water while I loosened the knot in my sarong and finished washing myself as best I could without removing it fully. I scrubbed my face until I was sure it glowed pink. I rinsed the cloth and started on my arms and legs, which were covered in dirt from the dusty march. Pulling my feet up and kneeling on the grassy bank, I quickly dipped my hair into the stream and rinsed it, wringing it out thoroughly when I was done and rubbing some flaxseed gel through it. I combed it and let it hang in heavy, wet strands to dry in the cool evening air. Finally, I smoothed some oil over my skin to keep the mosquitoes and biting bugs away during the night.

When I was clean, I turned and stretched my legs out to let my feet air-dry before I placed them back into my sandals, which I brushed the dust out of while I waited.

Lib and Ethanim were standing within calling distance. Lib had gone beyond me and they both had their backs to me. Their postures were identical—hands clasped in front of them, legs shoulder-width apart, heads scanning the area for possible dangers. They looked so serious. Too serious. This had to be a big joke to them—guarding the little girl from the scary forest. Giving them one last wary glance, I ducked into the bushes to complete my necessary tasks.

"Don't you two think you're overdoing it just a little?" I said when I emerged.

"No," they said in unison, and that was all they said to me until I had finished, gathered my things into my satchel, and started back toward camp. Then Lib tried to reprimand me.

"You should—"

"Tell you where I'm going, I know," I interrupted. "But I'm capable of being in the forest alone. I'm telling you, I don't need guards just to go down to the stream, and to, uh, visit the trees." Then, appealing to their sense of decency, I added, "It's embarrassing."

Lib answered, and he didn't seem particularly sympathetic. "You'll have to get over the embarrassment. You chose this for yourself. How did you imagine you would find privacy in an army full of boys?"

"I didn't."

"So why are you complaining?"

"I mean I didn't think that far. I was too busy learning to kill Lamanites."

"Nevertheless, tell us when you leave camp."

"That's not a condition of me being here," I argued. There were no conditions of me being here. I was a soldier like everyone else.

"No," agreed Ethanim. "But it's the way it is, and you don't need to make things difficult, though I'm told you have a knack for it."

"Who told you that?" I demanded.

They both laughed, and it didn't really sound like nice laughter.

Dozens of campfires lit our way as we made our way back to our camp. I could feel eyes watching us as we passed.

Before I went into my tent, I stepped up to Corban and stopped in front of him. He was sitting on his heels, as most of the boys were, and tossing twigs into the fire. He scowled up at me in annoyance. I smiled tentatively down at him. The other boys went silent.

I knelt down. "Let me see your ankle," I said.

He didn't say anything. For several moments I thought he would refuse, but he slowly shifted into a sitting position and slid his foot out from under him, extending it toward me. I felt a pang of guilt when I saw that it was discolored and swollen.

I swept my long hair to one side and slid the damp mass of it over my shoulder, its weight lessening as it dried. I shifted so I could work without my body blocking the firelight. Then I reached into the soggy cloth bag and pulled out a handful of the stringy algae.

Eyeing me, he attempted to pull his foot back, but I gripped his leg lightly.

"Let me help," I said. I took a long strip of bandage from my satchel, something Mother saw that all four of her children always carried, and used it to secure the algae against his skin over his swollen ankle. "This will help," I explained. "Keep it on all night and you'll be good as new in the morning."

I got up to leave and began to pick my way toward my tent in the shadows.

"Thanks," he said quietly to my back.

I paused and smiled back at him over my shoulder but walked on.

Lib and Ethanim had observed without interruption as I bandaged Corban's ankle. Then they followed me to my tent and instead of rolling out their bedrolls near the fire with the other eight boys of our unit, they rolled them out near the tent's entrance. I should have known.

But there was no use even complaining. It was full dark now, and I was dead tired. I knew they must be too. Nobody wanted to fight about this.

I lay on my back staring up at the top of my tent, and though moonlight filtered in at the door, it was too dark by then to see much of anything. The inside was made of leather from Hemni's tannery. I wondered if Zeke had tanned this skin. I reached out and let my fingertips brush against the soft hide. Mother's weaving adorned the outside, and together the layers would protect me from cold, heat, and rain when some of the boys would have no shelter at all. I knew I was lucky.

But that night it felt a lot like a guarded prison cell.

I wondered where Mother was. I tried to think about where we had been at midday. Mother, with the support teams, was probably camped there now. She would have done her share of the cooking and camp work. If I knew Mother, she would have tried to make everyone else comfortable before she allowed herself any measure of ease. Was she near Gideon's home? Had she seen the beautiful green barley fields?

Though I had resented his presence in my life for a long time, I was glad Kalem was traveling with her. He was probably sleeping outside her tent much as Lib and Ethanim were sleeping outside mine, but because he had long ago made the oath against violence, he would not be much protection if there was trouble.

When I said my nightly prayer, I remembered to pray for Mother and for Kalem and for all those who would not break their covenant with God, the men we were fighting for, and especially for those who were braving this journey with us. Sometimes I wished I had enough faith to make a covenant like theirs, but I knew I had my own mission to fulfill and fulfilling someone else's would not do any good.

I thought of my brothers, Micah, Kenai, and Darius. And I thought of Zeke, how his hair was mussed in the morning, how he teased his little sisters. But sleep came quickly.

The morning came quickly as well. It was still dark when I groggily slipped my head out past the flap of the tent to observe what was happening around camp. Only a few boys stirred. As my eyes scanned the camp, I saw that Lib and Ethanim slept near the fire. Gideon sat on his bedroll near my door.

I yawned. "What are you doing over here?"

"Taking my turn."

"Not you too," I moaned and ducked my head back inside to steal a few more minutes of sleep. After a moment or two, I thought better of it and got up to prepare for the day. I had worked very hard to get there, and I wasn't going to sleep it away.

Hot coals still glowed in the fire pit, though no one had fed them yet, so I tossed handfuls of kindling on the coals. When they caught, I gradually added larger pieces of wood until I had a small blaze. We would not be staying long, so I didn't allow it to get large.

After starting the fire, I decided Corban's ankle would benefit from a day of wrapping, so I went to my satchel for another bandage.

I stilled when I found another sack of corn, a sack of dried beans, and five large pieces of fruit.

Chapter 3

"**H**as anyone been in my tent?" I asked Gideon, who knelt near it tying his bedroll and gear to his travel pack.

He straightened. "When? No."

I dropped the sacks near his knee in the dirt and held up a piece of fruit.

He barely glanced at the sacks. "What's that?"

"I think it's manna," I said, only half kidding.

Lib came over, rubbing the sleep from his eyes. "More of the corn?"

Gideon finished with his pack and stood up. "More?"

I let Lib explain finding the full bag of corn flour in my satchel the previous night. Gideon raised a brow, but he said nothing.

We were all three silent for a few moments amidst the activity of the morning. The other boys were stirring now, excited to start the march again.

"I guess I'll get cooking," I said and bent to retrieve the sacks.

As the boys began to eat, I saw Kenai approach from the

south end of the camp. He wore his gear already and walked with almost a skip in his step. After he bent to fill his water skin at the stream, he scanned the area. His face lit up when he found me, and he started toward where I knelt frying corn cakes on a hot stone over the fire. He sat on his heels near me and swiped a cake from the stone.

"Help yourself," I said instead of smacking his hand away like I wanted to.

"Hey, Gid!" Kenai grinned and took a bite. "Hey Ket," he said with his mouth full.

I looked at the boys of my unit who were still waiting for their morning meal and eying the cakes. I gestured toward each one as I introduced them. "This is Noah, Reb, Corban and Josh. You know Gideon. And these are the boys who trail me like little puppies, Ethanim and Lib."

Kenai took the time to clasp arms with each of them.

I spoke to the boys. "Kenai is my brother. He serves as captain under Eli at the head of the march."

Kenai ranked as Gideon, commander of fifty, and I knew why his men had been placed at the front. He and his men were being trained as spies, and when we got to the front of the war, they would be sent ahead on scouting missions. Kenai was extremely stealthy and could disappear in any environment. He had taught me to sneak up on deer, and I suspected he could sneak up on an enemy and kill him without the man sensing his presence until the last futile second.

"Why did you bother with the tent for one night?"

"Lib talked me into it. He thought it would be an easier prison to guard."

"Ket, he's doing you a favor. Why give him such a hard time?"

"Because you're not around. Hey, have you seen Zeke?"

He shook his head. "I was on my way back to see Micah, but I got sidetracked." He took another big bite and grinned.

"Are you still planning on going back?"

He looked up at the sky. It was getting lighter but the sun hadn't cleared the eastern mountains quite yet. The horn hadn't sounded the call to line up.

"I've probably got time. You want me to take a message? And no, I am not telling Zeke you love him, and I am definitely not giving him a big kiss from you."

"Of course not," I replied, conscious of the boys around us. "Mui would be too jealous."

He placed his hand over his heart. "Ah, Mui, how I miss my little goat," he said dramatically.

I laughed with him. "Take these to Zeke and Micah," I said and handed him the mysterious cloth sack filled now with the warm, leftover corn cakes.

He saluted me and set off to the north. I wanted to go along with him, but I wasn't ready to leave. I had been cooking over the fire all morning and hadn't seen to any of my personal needs, let alone taken down my tent or tied my gear to my pack.

I fetched my satchel and hurried toward the area of the stream I had gone to last night—it was daylight now, so I needed the thick bushes far from the army of boys. On my way back, I decided to see to Corban's ankle before we left for another long day of marching.

I was pulling another bandage from my satchel as I approached him. He sat with Cyrus and Mathoni, and they exchanged the occasional comment with each other as they watched all the action around them. They were ready to go.

"How's the ankle?" I asked Corban.

"It feels fine, but I haven't taken off the wrap yet to see it."

He allowed me to unwind the bandage and assess his wound. Everyone around us drew in a breath when I removed the cloth and the dried algae. Even I was surprised.

Yesterday where a large purple and black bruise had

formed on his swollen ankle, tan skin now looked clear and normal. I fingered it. The swelling was gone and so was the bruising.

"How does it feel when you put weight on it?"

He stood and walked a distance away and back.

"Feels great."

I frowned. The algal wrap was supposed to minimize the bruise and decrease the swelling. And to be honest, I hadn't been sure it would have a very noticeable effect since the wound had been hours old before it had been treated.

"I was going to suggest we wrap it again for the march, but it doesn't look as though it needs it."

"You're a healer," he said as he tested the ankle by bouncing up and down, which reminded me of the way my little brother bounced when he was excited.

"My mother is a healer. I am but a very poor apprentice."

"Don't be so modest," Corban said genially.

"You're generous with the compliments today for someone who hated my guts yesterday," I couldn't resist saying.

He stilled and hung his head a little. "I was wrong to think ill of you," he said quietly. "I shouldn't have harbored contention. Please forgive me, Keturah."

I was taken aback by his sudden and sincere apology. He was so quick to acknowledge his own wrong-doing and repent of it. He was younger than me, I knew, and yet he had behaved so much better, for I knew that though I had not intentionally wounded his ankle, I had also not been careful in the placing of my blow. I had thought the boys were making fun of me by letting me beat them all. I had merely wished to win as quickly as possible so I could get away from all the curious stares.

"Keturah? Will you forgive me? My mother says I must always hold my temper, and she would tan my hide if she knew I had let it get the best of me." Light stains of red appeared low on his cheekbones.

I had been thinking about our pairing for too long, and Corban had begun to look worried.

"I have a temper of my own," I confided. "I will forgive you if you will forgive my carelessness. I did not intend to hurt your ankle on the first day of the march."

"Oh, I know that. I just wanted to win."

It was then that the horn sounded. We both turned to look to the road.

"Let me know if you have any more pain with that. I know the herbs of the forest that ease pain."

He nodded as we started out of the woods toward the road, followed by Mathoni, Cyrus, and the other boys.

I thought to gather my things and roll my tent as I ran to the column, but when I turned I saw Lib and Ethanim waiting where my tent had been. Lib held my pack, complete with rolled tent and bedroll, and Ethanim held out my scabbard, bow, and other weapons.

"Here. Hurry, Keturah."

"You didn't have to do this," I insisted even as they helped me shrug into my gear. "I can take care of myself."

"Then next time, see that you do."

I jerked my scabbard away from Ethanim and jogged off ahead of them. Lib wanted to see to my tent last night, but he didn't today? Whatever the two of them were doing—following me around, sleeping outside my tent like guards but looking more like men who didn't trust me, trying to be my friends but failing miserably—I wished they would stop. I could protect myself, and I had my own friends.

"Everything alright?" Gideon asked quietly when I got to the road.

I nodded as I brushed past him, knowing the hurt would show in my eyes if I looked at him.

My unit was the first row of Seth's command in the column. I could see Kenai standing about five rows in front of me to the side of his fifty. I knew Darius and Jarom marched in one of his units, but I couldn't see either one of them. Most of the boys were taller than I was which made it difficult for me to see much of anything, so I just stared at the back of the boy in front of me, a thin, light-haired boy I didn't know who had glanced at me curiously when we were lining up and to whom I had given a small smile which he had not returned.

Helaman addressed his troops from a slight rise near the road. He had one of the chief captains from the rear of the command offer a prayer and then he read to us from the words of Lehi, our first father out of the land of Jerusalem.

I glanced down the row to Corban as we began a steady pace up into the hills. He was talking animatedly to Cyrus and Mathoni, who marched on either side of him and who, I had overheard, were his cousins. He showed no signs of having a hurt foot. Lib and Ethanim were talking back and forth over my head, so I set my eyes on the light-haired boy, wondered what his name was, and marched silently southward.

By midmorning, few of the boys were still talking. I hadn't seen any more of Kenai, but I did see Micah once jogging to the front presumably to talk to Helaman about something or other of importance. Zarahemla was behind us now, as we had begun executing the wide arc of a turn toward the path of the sun, following the natural curve of the hills.

At some point before the stop for a noontime meal I began noticing the flag that bobbed above the heads of the boys in front of me. I had seen the flag before flying in Melek, waving resplendently on a pole in the main city center, an ever-present reminder of our struggle for freedom and liberty. In fact, it was called the Title of Liberty, said to wave above every Nephite holding. It waved above us now, and it was the standard that would lead us into battle.

Just as I began to feel tired—it seemed that we had marched long past midday—we halted on the road. I saw Seth jog forward to meet with the chief captains at the head of the formation, and after a while I saw a runner streak back to relay orders to the chief captains who awaited them at the rear. Seth returned and let us break our ranks. Like yesterday, when the sun had reached a hand's width to the west, we would move out again and march until we reached our camp for the night.

I emptied my water skin, swallowing the last of the tepid water inside it, and set out to refill it at the stream Seth directed us to, which lay some distance off the road. This, I realized, was why we hadn't stopped at midday—there had been no water. I was glad that I had been conservative with mine. I had always practiced a rationing of water, for though fresh water was abundant in our lands, finding it could sometimes be tricky.

While I refilled my water skin, with my two shadows ever following me, Micah called out to me. I turned at the sound of his voice and saw that Zeke accompanied him on a direct path toward me.

I broke out into a smile and waved them over.

"We'll be over near that ravine with the rest of the unit," Lib informed me and gestured to where the rest of my unit was standing at the edge of a wide ravine trying to throw rocks to the other side. He nodded at Micah and Zeke as they approached, then he followed Ethanim and left me alone with my brother and my best friend.

Glancing curiously after Lib and Ethanim, Micah gave me a smile, the one Mother said looked just like Father's. Then he tugged at my hair and bent to fill his own water skin.

I turned to Zeke with more wariness. I thought he was mad at me for that scene I had made in the mud with Gideon. It had only been spear training. I hadn't realized how it might look or that it might hurt Zeke. But he put one long arm around my waist and pulled me to his side in a kind of hug.

Zeke was my best friend. He was also my intended husband. Our marriage had been all but arranged since we were young, and until I had met Gideon that day near the obsidian, I had never thought to question my family's wishes in the matter. Mother had suggested we complete the official betrothal before Zeke left for the war, but I just couldn't go through with it. Zeke had agreed to wait and give me my time in the army. I loved him for it—and also resented that he got a say.

Micah cleared his throat. "I've got to get back to my men."

Maybe he did, maybe he didn't, but the fact was he left me standing alone with Zeke—and his approval of it—in the middle of two thousand thirsty boys. Was Zeke really going to try to court me here?

I took Zeke's water skin, nearly empty, from his belt and knelt near the stream to fill it for him. He took a knee next to me, scooped some water into his hand, and drank his fill. I noticed he wore his hair tied back with an old cloth tie I had made for him ages ago when Mother had first taught me to weave.

"Why do you still wear that old hair tie?" I asked.

He met my eyes and wiped his dripping chin with the back of his forearm, well-muscled from skinning game with his father. He didn't answer, just rose and led me back toward the road. Most of the other soldiers sought the shade near the stream, but we walked beyond the road and finally found a fallen log to sit on where we could be alone.

"Are all your men well?" I asked him, thinking of Corban's ankle. When I glanced at him he was watching me with unabashed affection in his eyes. Sometimes I really wished he would quit doing that, but after neither Gideon nor anyone else had talked to me all morning, I was glad for it, and I drank it in deeper than I had the cool water.

"My men are all fine. I don't know if I'll ever learn all their names."

"I know you—you will. Did Kenai find you this morning?"

His smile was quick. "Yes, thank you, but I think he came bearing decidedly fewer cakes than you sent him with."

"The corn flour," I confided to him, "appeared in my satchel last night and again this morning, along with beans and fruit."

His brows furrowed. "Who do you think put it there?"

"No one could have. Even if someone carried enough corn flour and beans for my entire unit to eat their fill twice and leftover for my brothers, Gideon said no one entered my tent last night."

I sensed his disapproval. His huge and sudden frown was a big indicator.

"Zeke," I said in an effort to placate him before he became angry, hating that I felt I had to. "Lib and Ethanim took the first two watches outside my tent, and Gideon woke hours early to take the third—unnecessarily. I thought you and Gideon had settled...things."

He heaved a sigh. "We have, and I have to confess the thought of someone in your tent bothers me more than the thought of Gid guarding it. Believe it or not, I actually like him. He's been a good friend to you, and it may not seem like it, but I do appreciate that."

"He has been my friend," I allowed.

"But he doesn't respect what's between us."

"I think he respects it more than you give him credit for. Besides, much of the time, he doesn't even seem to like me."

"So he doesn't try to kiss you?"

I burst out laughing, and I laughed hard, maybe a little too hard. "No!" I smacked him on his chest with the back of my hand.

But Zeke didn't laugh. "Would you let him? If he tried?"

I had limited experience with boys and kisses. Zeke had kissed me exactly two times and one of those had been in front of my brothers.

If another man tried to kiss me, I could take him down to the ground and hold my knife to his throat, black his eye, bloody

31

his nose, or maybe break his arm. But with Gideon?

"Don't be stupid," I said. "Micah would never give him permission."

"I only care whether or not you give him yours."

I turned to look into his face. Was he really looking for the truth, or did he just want me to ease his concerns?

"I don't know. I might not stop him," I said honestly, thinking instantly that it was the wrong thing to say.

But for some reason, the honest answer seemed to be the one he was looking for. Honest was the only way to be with someone like Zeke.

When he finished eating, Zeke lay on the ground and put his hands behind his head. As I finished my food, I looked down at him from where I sat, still on the fallen tree. He was chewing on the end of a blade of grass, and he rested with his eyes closed. A bee hovered over him and then buzzed away.

With a quick glance at the position of the sun, I slid off the log and knelt beside Zeke. "We should go," I said, but instead of leaving, I just studied his face. When he opened his eyes and looked up at me, I smiled.

Was this handsome warrior really the boy I had grown up with, the kid who had run wild through the forest with me, gotten into mischief with me? He had grown into a plainspoken man and stalwart disciple of God, a man for whom honesty came as easily as breathing, a man who fought only to preserve his family's freedom and who considered me already part of his family. He was a man of peace but fought as he must for what he believed in, including me.

Would I grow into a woman he could believe in?

I couldn't help reaching out to touch his brow, though I felt foolish as I remembered doing the exact same thing to Gideon. But Zeke suffered my touch as Gideon hadn't because he was honor-bound to suffer it. The thought made me study him curiously. When he had begun to court me in earnest, I had believed it was because his feelings had grown out of our youthful friendship and into love.

I thought of Mother calling out to tell me Zeke had arrived to take me for a walk in the forest. I thought of my family leaving us alone in the courtyard. I thought of Micah bringing him to me at the stream. I thought of my brothers down the trail when he had kissed me, and I had to wonder how much of Zeke's courtship was just duty.

Chapter 4

The final morning of the long march dawned with corn and beans in my satchel, and I was able to find some cattails near the stream to go with the meal. There were plenty so I stashed some of the roots away for the midday meal.

The rumor running through camp was that we would be to Judea by midday. We had covered a lot of ground on our march, and we had covered it quickly.

The pace was the same, maybe even a little faster as we all sensed our closeness to our destination, but when it still was not in sight by midday, the general morale declined. We stayed in the tops of the mountains through the morning, but after the first afternoon break, we began to descend into a mountain valley. The ground flattened into wide meadows, which I gradually realized looked more like crop fields as we walked on.

But where was the city? I thought it would be large with huge, or at least visible, reinforcements. Embattlements, moats, fences, walls—something. I craned my neck trying to see it somewhere and began taking a little hop on every other step to see over the others.

"Is this why they call you rabbit?" asked Gideon, who had

fallen in next to Ethanim.

Reb, behind me in the narrow column we had formed as we came down out of the craggy peaks, let out one of his stupid guffaws.

I threw him a look over my shoulder. He was already passing my nickname down the line.

"Thanks for that," I said to Gideon. "Where's the city? I can't see it."

"I can't either, but Seth says it's just around that hill."

"What hill?"

"You're short," he said as if he had never noticed I came only to his chin, but I knew he had noticed. He had altered my training to compensate for it.

"I'm taller than Reb," I said and not only did I shoot Reb another look, but I gave in to childishness and stuck my tongue out at him too.

Joshua smacked Reb in the chest and laughed, but I had the feeling he was laughing at me more than at Reb.

I turned back to Gideon. "So? Where is it?"

"Patience, Keturah," he said and turned his attention forward.

Presently we did come to a hill, or rather, a kind of canyon between two hills, and Judea truly was beyond it. As we marched toward the city, I could see that it was fortified with embattlements and guards.

The captains called a halt down the lines. Most of the boys took their water skins from their belts and drank. I shifted my bow to the other shoulder as I watched Micah walk down toward the gates of the city with Helaman and several others.

Probably an advance party, like Kenai's scouting unit, had been sent up hours ago to inform the city leaders of our arrival, but this would be the formal meeting between Helaman and Antipus, the commander here. Helaman's party approached the guards at the gate where Helaman talked to a group of men for a moment and then clasped arms in greeting.

Before I knew it, we were marching past the outer walls of Judea. Though tidy and open, the city looked rundown. The people looked bedraggled. Their clothes were clean and maintained, clearly with pride, but their eyes showed a weariness they couldn't hide behind the care they took of their possessions. Children peered at us, but it was clear that soldiers were not an unusual sight to them. War was all these little children had ever known.

Their mothers, however, regarded us as the peculiar sight I was sure we made. This war had gone on for years in the outer Nephite holdings, and these people had likely seen much. But despite what they had seen, they had never seen two thousand adolescents come bearing arms to help them defeat their enemy.

The soldiers' camp was a small city in and of itself, not very different from our fallow corn field in Melek, made from tents of various sizes, shapes, and colors. They stretched in long rows with cook fires in front of them, but there didn't appear to be many inhabitants.

We were led in our formation down several small roads which were bigger than paths but not as wide as the streets of the city. Helaman gave us the rest of the afternoon and evening to set up our camps and get situated. After I had set up my tent next to the one Lib and Ethanim shared, I told them I was going to find my youngest brother, Darius, who I hadn't seen at all on the march. He was easy to locate when I took a short walk down the road because we were camped next to Eli's hundred.

I found Darius setting up his own tent. Jarom was standing over him giving instructions.

"I think I know how to put up my own tent," I heard Darius say.

"Dare!" I called as I approached.

They both smiled when they looked up and saw me.

"Lash the poles in first," I told him. "That's what works

for me."

He sat back on his heels and regarded his spread-out tent. "Yeah, that would probably work."

Jarom and I turned to look at each other.

"What? I can take advice," he said defensively. "When it's good," he added with a pointed look at his best friend.

Jarom and I watched him in silence. "Game was hard to come by on the march," I said after a moment.

Darius glanced at Jarom but turned back to his tent and began setting the poles.

Jarom said, "Samuel, one of the boys in our unit, cooked wheat cereal with honey for us each day. He said it's the only thing he can cook. His mother taught him before he left."

I looked up and down the roads. Sure, any boy could cook wild game over a fire, but I wondered how many other mothers had felt inspired to teach their sons to prepare a wholesome meal. And I wondered if Samuel had known where the wheat came from.

"Do you know where we go to get wood for our fires?" asked Darius. He blew a stray lock of dark hair away from his face. Still kneeling on top of his flat tent, he looked around.

I pointed in the general direction of the south gates where Seth had said there were stores of it, already cured. "Near the gates. We're to go out in details later on to cut our own. For now, the soldiers here have enough for our needs."

"When do you suppose the supply teams will arrive?" Darius asked.

I shrugged. "They were supposed to stay close to our column in case they needed protection. Seth says they will be camping over there." I indicated the east end of the clearing, the end nearest the city.

Darius frowned slightly.

"Move over, I'll show you how to construct that tent."

Surprisingly, he let me show him. He had been much too

excited to listen at home when Mother had given us the tents and shown us how to put them up. We had never had much use for tents before, mostly preferring to sleep under the stars, and anyway, these were different from the ones we knew—both lighter and more durable.

After I showed them both how to put it up, I showed them how to take it down. It wasn't complicated and they both caught on immediately.

There was a commotion at the south gates. Someone called out. Another person responded, and I wasn't entirely sure I recognized the language that either man spoke. The huge gates were heaved open by eight guards.

By now, all the Ammonite boys had turned to see what was happening. And when they did, I thought their stomachs must have fallen as mine did.

Troops of men came through the gates in ranks, proud but haggard. Their skin was bruised where it was not cut. Dirty and bloody, some men carried others on stretchers and over shoulders that were huge from much use. Black swords, wood soaked with the blood of battle, were clutched in warrior hands. Torn clothing and hair matted with dirt, sweat, and blood told of their recent battle.

Here were the soldiers who occupied the tents beyond ours. Here were the men who fought so valiantly for our country, our freedom, and our religion while we sat safe in the Land of Melek.

Scores and scores of them kept coming through the gates, but when they saw us they looked as confused as the people in the city had. They eyed us, hardly believing what they saw. Would they hate us? It was the Chief Judge who had allowed us refuge in their country, not these men. I looked at Darius and Jarom, and I thought that these battle-torn warriors might start to laugh in our faces.

"Reinforcements!" someone shouted and a loud cheer

went up among them. They each went to one knee, even those who carried the wounded on their backs, and they saluted us in the way of our people. It was a sign of great honor.

But it was we who should be honoring them. Instantly, I went to my knees. I bowed my head and heard the movements of the other boys around me doing it too.

When I looked up again I knew Helaman had not met Antipus at the west gate when we came in. The man who now strode through the Nephite warriors was clearly Chief Captain and Commander here. I didn't know how I knew, but I did. Perhaps Helaman had met the head guard or even the governor of Judea, but this man, straight-backed and confident, was Antipus, Chief Captain at Judea.

He strode down the path between our tents, glancing now and then at the boys who watched him with awe. Like me, they all knew who he was. We had all heard of his victories. We had all heard of his struggles. The Nephites had fallen back in this quarter of the land, and Antipus had been trying to regain the cities we had lost.

The more boys he passed, the more bemused he looked. As he passed me, I thought there was a hitch in his step. Yes, I was a girl. Was that so terrible? Was it so different from the twelve year old boys I stood next to? They didn't exactly have huge muscles either. I lifted my chin a little higher and watched him walk on.

When he reached my unit's cook fire a few campsites away, Helaman met him from the other direction. I wished I was standing there instead of with Darius and Jarom. How I wanted to hear what they talked of!

"Ket, Dare! Mother's on her way in!"

Darius, Jarom, and I turned to see Kenai jogging in our direction with a huge grin on his face. We followed him down the road toward the east end of the field where I could see that our support teams were indeed arriving. I strained to see but couldn't find Mother.

"Where is she?" I asked.

"Keep looking. She's here somewhere."

All four of us looked, sifting through the confusion. We stood at the edge of our camp, searching the crowd of people that was situating itself between us and the city.

I felt hands at my waist and jumped, turning to face a grinning Zeke. "We saw you run by. Are you looking for Leah?"

I nodded. I saw that Micah was standing near Kenai, their heads bent together as they talked.

If I hadn't been there, would Zeke be doing the same with Jarom? I looked from my brothers back to Zeke. "Aren't you even going to say hello to your brother?" I asked him.

He rolled his eyes and said, "Hey," while reaching out to ruffle Jarom's hair, which was so like his own.

Jarom ducked out of his way and then jumped onto Zeke's back to reach up and return the greeting.

Not exactly the encouragement I had envisioned, but it obviously worked for them. "You two, stop!" I laughed, but I pulled off Jarom's sandal and tickled his foot. Then Darius jumped on, and Kenai decided to make it a dog pile. Micah laughed, but he stood by with me and didn't join in.

They made such a commotion that Mother found us. When I saw her walking toward us with Kalem on her heels, I left the boys wrestling in the dirt and ran toward her. She held out her arms, and I went into them. Closing my eyes, I hugged her tight. When I opened my eyes, Kalem was watching us indulgently. I felt Micah's arm around both of us and heard him kiss Mother's cheek. While my other brothers greeted her, I stepped to Kalem, threw my arms around his neck and surprised him with a hug.

"Thank you for watching over her," I said.

He stood still for a moment. I could tell I had made him feel awkward. Then his arms came around me and he held me close for just a moment, but it was long enough for him to say softly into my ear, "It is my pleasure to do so."

I worried about Kalem when it came to my mother. He had once been a great Lamanite warrior, but he had taken the oath and promised God he would never lift a weapon to kill another man again. I wasn't so sure he wouldn't break it for Mother. If he hadn't loved her from the first instant he saw her, he had definitely fallen in love with her sometime in the last twelve years. I told myself that maybe he wouldn't kill but would just injure if the necessity ever arose. Surely he knew how to subdue a man without killing him. Perhaps he would fight with his bare hands. Would that be breaking his oath? But even though it worried me for his soul, it made me feel better about Mother's safety.

I turned, stepping away from him, and saw my mother greeting her best friend's sons. She kissed Zeke and Jarom on their cheeks, embarrassing them both, and spent an extra moment looking into Zeke's eyes. She held them as lovingly as she did her own sons.

She was telling the boys she would see them later, maybe tomorrow.

"Why? Where are you going?" I asked.

"They've just brought in wounded from the battlefield. I was on my way there when I saw that familiar dog pile."

"Oh!" I said. "You're starting so soon?"

She looked at us all soberly. "Yes, Kanina, the need is immediate. And you will all be starting your work soon as well."

After Mother and Kalem hurried off, we all turned to each other, our happy reunion tempered by Mother's reminder of where we were and why we had come.

"Don't forget the council meeting tonight after the bonfire," Micah said to Zeke. Then he turned to Kenai.

"I know," said Kenai. "And don't forget the captains' meeting in the morning before devotional. Got it."

Micah slung an arm around Kenai's neck and I thought there might be another dog pile, but Kenai rolled out of it and said he was going to go oversee his men. "Come on," he said to Darius and Jarom. "That's an order."

"Very funny," Darius said, but they both followed him eagerly.

Mother had been right. We did start our work right away. But we didn't go to the battlefield—we began fortifying the city.

Chapter 5

On the first morning we awoke in Judea, the horn sounded as it had each day of the march. After the morning meal and a devotional of scripture reading and prayer, we ran once around the city.

"Twice would be better," Seth said. "But since we just got off a long march, one will do for today."

Two times around the city wouldn't have bothered any of us because we were no longer weighed down with all our gear.

After running and other exercises, we moved to the Nephite training ground located to the north of our camp. We practiced our main weapon, slings for me and everyone else Seth commanded, then we began a rotation through all the other weapons so we would be proficient with whatever was at hand when needed.

It was only midday by the time all that was accomplished, so after our meal-time had passed we received instruction on how our unit was to help with the fortification of the city.

When the war had begun, all the people from the surrounding areas and villages had come inside the walls of the city for protection. The Judeans only left the walls with a military guard, and that was for the necessary work of survival—hunting, fishing, harvesting. A lot of the work had been left up to the army, but since they had also been fighting a great deal lately, they were ragged and tired and many of the fortifications had not been adequately maintained.

So some of the units of Ammonites ventured out past the walls to chop wood, hunt, and gather edible plants from the surrounding forest. Soon the fields would be ready for the first harvest, which would relieve the strain on the wild resources but would require heavy guarding and swift labor.

Other units assisted by milking the army's goats and cows, dressing the game the hunters brought in, or starting maintenance on the buildings in the city. Some worked in our camp constructing fire-pits or hauling logs for chairs and tables. Kalem taught the stripling soldiers how to fix and maintain the weapons of Antipus's men while they rested and recovered from their wounds.

Mother and the other healers treated the wounded. I wanted to help her—I had some skill and had seen much working alongside her in the past—but she asked me to stay away from the infirmary until she knew better how to treat and deal with what was there. I suspected she wanted to protect me from it. It must have been bad.

Kenai and his unit had already gone to learn from and replace the Nephite spies near the city of Antiparah to the southwest.

Helaman assigned my unit to dig the trenches.

Captain Moroni, the Chief Captain of all the Nephite forces, had ordered the men to build up large embankments around all of the Nephite cities. These were preceded, as one approached the city's walls from the outside, by a great and deep trench from which the earth for the embankment was acquired.

If I had known a full moon before that digging trenches was the way to build muscles, I would have trenched the entire perimeter of my training meadow near the falls back home.

I rotated through the different jobs with the other boys of my unit who had already started to bicker with one another under the pressure of the hard and boring work.

"Hurry with that bucket," Corban called to Cyrus.

"Hurry with that bucket," his cousin mimicked.

The way they interacted reminded me of my brothers, and despite the rising contention, I smiled to myself. And luckily, they were so busy being irritated with each other, they forgot to be irritated with me.

We were in two lines straight up the embankment. Some of the units stood on ladders, but we didn't have one because there weren't enough of them to go around. Corban and Mathoni were in the bottom of the trench turning the soil with spades and filling the buckets which Noah and Reb took when they were full and passed to Lib and Ethanim, who then passed them above their heads to Josh and Zach who were perched precariously in the middle of the embankment. Josh and Zach in turn passed the buckets above their heads to Gideon and me. We dumped the dirt at the top of the embankment and tossed the empty buckets back to the bottom of the trench where Cyrus caught them and returned them to Noah and Reb.

It was boring and each of the jobs taxed the muscles so there was little to do but get on each other's nerves.

I had begun the afternoon down on the embankment where Lib was, and we had rotated positions twice. When I had been at the top of the embankment long enough to get tired of it, a Nephite soldier came by to check up on our progress.

He looked at me curiously and said something to us both. I knew that he complimented our work, but he had a heavy accent that made him difficult to understand, so I stepped back and he directed the rest of his comments to Gideon. Somehow I wasn't surprised that Gideon conversed easily with him, altering his own accent so the man could understand him.

"Is there a different accent in each Nephite city?" I asked Gideon after the soldier had gone.

He shrugged. "Maybe even a different dialect," he said. "Just because a city is friendly to the Nephite nation, does not mean they have the exact same language, culture, or even religion as each other. There are differences in the way people act even in the distance from your home near the center of Melek to mine in the outer borders."

"Really? Like what?"

"Well, where I'm from, the girls don't want to join the army," he teased.

He effortlessly pulled a bucket up out of Zach's hands. I struggled a little more with Joshua's.

"Easy!" Josh called up, annoyed, when I accidentally dumped some of the contents of the bucket on his head. He shook his head and swatted out the dirt with his hands.

Joshua was the best-looking boy in the unit, at least, I knew he was the one Cana and Leda would giggle about behind their hands back home. His good looks were right up there with Eli's, someone I actually had heard Cana and Leda giggle about. Josh had a lighter complexion than Eli, but he was just as handsome in his own way. A little dirt wouldn't hurt him.

I amused myself with that, but still I felt bad.

"Sorry," I called down.

"You're getting tired," said Gideon.

"Yeah, well so is everyone," I said defensively. "Isn't this sort of unnecessary anyway? Aren't the walls high enough?"

Gideon straightened his back to stretch and sighed. He looked around at all the crews working on the walls—all of them Ammonite boys.

"No. The walls have fallen in many places and Antipus's men have not had the resources to fix them. It is hard work, and since they spend half their time fighting Ammoron's armies, they haven't got a lot of energy left for digging trenches."

"If it's so important, they should make it a priority."

"They've done their best," was all he said.

I hefted another bucket up, managing to avoid spilling it on Josh, but only because I spilled it on my own sandals. I glanced down the steep embankment and caught Lib making eye contact with Gideon.

"Switch positions!" Lib hollered.

"No! I'm fine!" I complained to Gideon. It was clear now that he was watching me for fatigue and reporting it to the unit leader.

"The rotation is for everyone," Gideon said evenly and held out his hand to help me down the embankment into the deep trench.

Cyrus, who had been catching buckets, caught me as I tumbled down the last of the hill, loose dirt tumbling with me. He smelled of sweat and soil. His arms were slick with it, and he had been taking his turn at the easiest job. Cyrus was tall and lanky like his cousins, Corban and Mathoni, but he was steady and when he felt satisfied that I was safely down, he set me away from him quickly. Not sparing me another glance, he picked up one of the spades and began turning the earth. Gideon slid down the embankment on his feet, making it look easy, and snatched up the other spade before I could get a hand on it.

"You're catching," he said without looking at me. "You can catch, right?" Was he flirting with me in front of the others?

I rolled my eyes.

"So...no?"

"Yes! Of course I can catch!"

He glanced up at Zach and Josh.

"They do not have to go easy on me!"

Gideon stopped digging and turned, leaning on his spade, to look at me. "Keturah, I did not tell them to go easy on you. I am not Kenai—I do not have the gift of speaking with my eyes."

"But you do have the gift of tongues."

He turned and started to spade the earth again.

"Well?"

"I suppose I understand more than other people do," he admitted.

"And you changed your accent to speak to that Nephite captain," I said.

He gave me a confused glance. "No I didn't," he said.

"Yes you did." Then I called up to Josh and Zach. "Didn't he?"

"Yes," they both called down.

I raised my brows at Gideon.

He threw his water skin at me. "You need a drink," he said. "The sun is getting to you."

That night my arm muscles ached beyond anything I had ever known. My shoulders and my back didn't feel much better, so after a trip to the quiet pool in the river where I liked to bathe and before I settled into camp, I went to find my mother. Ethanim trailed me, but left when he saw I was safe with Mother and Kalem.

I sat with Kalem while she made me a hot tea that she said would ease the pain so I could sleep. I was very sore, but I believed she could make me feel better. She always had in the past.

"How are the weapons coming?" I asked Kalem.

He took a deep breath and let it out. "Good," he said after thinking on it for a moment. "But there are many left to repair. Between their skirmishes during the day and renewing their fortifications at night when they should have been sleeping, between their wounds and the time spent caring for others' wounds, the soldiers haven't given much to their weapons."

"Same with the embankment," I said. "It has fallen down everywhere. The rainy season was very rough on it."

He nodded.

"I'm glad we've come," I said after a few moments of silence.

Mother brought out the tea. "Drink this slowly," she said, "or it will make your head ache before it makes anything else feel better."

When I was ready to leave, she passed me a container of opaque cream. "Rub this anywhere that hurts. You'll feel good as new in the morning."

I kissed them each goodbye, surprising them both with my affection toward Kalem, a man I had resented very much for most of my life. Then I started back toward the privacy of my tent.

"Keturah!"

I turned and saw Zeke jogging toward me, so I stood stiffly, my shoulders aching, and waited for him to catch up.

"Hi," I said, glad to see him but too tired to offer him further conversation.

"Can I walk you back?" he asked.

"Sure," I agreed, not dwelling on what it would mean to him.

About thirty units were situated between Zeke's camp and mine which made about thirty camp fires and three hundred boys who were in camp cooking their evening meals and who stared at us as we walked past.

Zeke ambled along beside me for a while before he asked, "What did you do today?"

"Dug trenches to build the embankments."

"Sounds tough."

"It was. What did you do?"

"All of the bowmen went hunting."

"That sounds fun," I complained.

He shrugged. "Everyone will get their turn."

I sighed. It had been a long day. I just wanted to go back to my tent and rub Mother's cream on my sore muscles.

I felt Zeke looking at me.

"You got some sun on your cheeks," he said.

"I don't know how, since they were covered in dirt."

"Messy job, huh?"

I just nodded and blinked back the tears that pricked at my tired eyes.

He took the little ceramic jar of Mother's salve from my hand, held it to his nose and sniffed. He made a face.

"Mother gave it to me to rub into my muscles."

"How did the other boys get along?"

"Fine. It was..." I heaved a deep, frustrated breath, grateful when it didn't catch. "It was not as difficult for the boys. They all got along fine—except for Joshua."

"And why is that?" He waved to a friend in another camp, a boy I didn't know who was stirring something in a pot over the fire. "Did he have trouble or something?"

I twisted my lips and looked away. I tried to keep the hurt and disappointment from my words, but I was so tired I couldn't control my voice. "I kept spilling dirt on his head until Lib told everyone not to fill the buckets so full. Everyone knew why. He did it to humiliate me."

Zeke actually chuckled. "I doubt that." But when he saw my frown, he said, "Ah, don't be so hard on yourself, Ket. He probably noticed the other boys getting tired too. He's been instructed to do what is best for the group as a whole."

I might have let that ease my mind except for the smile he couldn't wipe from his face. So I just sighed again and pointedly took back my jar of salve. I hated showing weakness, but Zeke didn't view me as strong anyway. There was no point in hiding my discomfort from him. He knew me so well he could probably see it just by the way I held my shoulders.

That was how well Zeke knew me. But I knew him just as well. I knew that he had a deliberate reason for walking me back to camp, and it wasn't merely for the pleasure of my company.

He wanted the men in my unit—one in particular—to see him often and know what I was to him.

My entire unit was sitting around our fire pit when Zeke and I walked into camp. Some of the men were preparing to roast a good-sized bird over the fire, removing its feathers and building a spit. They all fell suddenly silent when I walked up.

They had clearly been talking about me.

As if to prove this, Lib jumped to his feet when he saw me.

"Keturah," he said awkwardly, rubbing the side of his nose, glancing at Zeke. "We were hoping you would make some corn cakes."

I peered around Lib to see that the other boys looked expectant. They had worked hard too, and they were starving now. I suppressed a sigh and said I would.

"You don't have to," Zeke said as he carried our sack of grain to the fire for me.

"I'll do it," I said but sighed again when I saw the whole grains in the sack. I looked wearily around. "Lib, did they give us a grinding stone?"

He looked to the others, and they all shrugged.

After Zeke had gone into the forested area south of our camp and hauled a large flat stone back, I made him leave.

"My unit will help me."

He hesitated for a moment. "Alright," he said and reluctantly left.

I knelt near the fire and turned cake after cake on the hot stones. I mashed some beans I had warmed and smeared them on top of the cakes. It was hot near the fire, but the air had cooled considerably in the mountains so I was grateful for the excuse to stay huddled near the warm coals. I thought I would also be grateful for the tent tonight.

Gideon was the last to approach the fire for cakes, though I noticed he had eaten heartily of the birds when they had come off the spit. He sat quietly beside me finishing up the remaining food after most of the other boys had sought their bedrolls on the other side of the fire, sitting together to craft weapons, balls, beads, and other adornments. Lib and Ethanim sat on their bedrolls near the entrance to my tent. They both eyed Gideon curiously, and Lib frowned at him.

Gideon would have reached for the last cakes, but I hadn't eaten yet, so I snatched them up and filled them with the last of the beans. But when I looked at them, I felt too tired to eat, so I passed one to him.

"You sure?" he asked.

I nodded. "I'm tired," I said. "We don't have any herbs to season the beans with. I hope they taste alright." I took a tentative taste. They were bland, but when the first bite hit my stomach, I realized I was hungry. The only thing I had on my stomach was the tea Mother had given me.

Gideon gave me a strange look. "I think they're good," he said. "I knew our unit would eat better than any other."

"Just because I'm a girl?"

"No. Because you're a good cook."

"Thanks," I said, deciding just to take his compliment for what it was, too tired to argue. We ate the corn cakes in silence, and I tried not to stuff mine into my mouth too quickly. I wanted the one I had given to him, and I must have been staring hungrily at it because he passed back what was left.

"Zeke sure has a point to make," he said quietly while I ate the remainder of the cake. He reached for a long stick and moved the logs in the fire so it would burn down for the night. It was only dusk, but none of the boys looked like they had much energy for staying up late.

"What he feels for me is duty," I said, trying out the idea. He snorted.

"What is that supposed to mean?"

"What he does for you is duty. What he feels for you..."

54

He let his voice trail off and gave an infuriating shrug.

I rubbed my eyes. I was too tired for this conversation. "I'm going to bed," I said abruptly, and I stood to go to my tent.

But I cried out in pain the moment I put weight on my legs. Gideon shot to his feet and caught me as I stumbled.

Chapter 6

I tried to laugh. "I've been kneeling too long."

"Yeah," he huffed out. "You're a real martyr."

He sounded so irritated that I was surprised when he lifted me into his arms and carried me toward my tent.

"Put me down!" I hissed. My legs felt heavy and as he walked, jarring me up and down, they tingled to a point of pain that made me suck in my breath through my teeth.

But he didn't put me down.

"What are you doing?"

"I'm carrying you to your bed."

"Put me down! I can walk!" I could hear the other boys laughing, but I wouldn't look at them.

He paused as if to set me down, but instead, he bounced me in his arms, jarring me again. I fought down a whimper. Gideon smirked, hefted me higher in his arms and carried me the rest of the way.

Lib and Ethanim shifted to the side so Gideon could kneel and place me into my tent. I bit back a cry when my heels hit the ground and pain shot up through my legs again.

Gideon crawled into my tent after me.

"Shove over," he commanded.

Through the open flap I caught the amused look that passed between Lib and Ethanim.

"Some guards you are," I called out to them.

"We're not guards," Ethanim said dryly, but I ignored him. What were they doing if they were not guarding me?

My tent was the same size as my brothers' tents—more than sufficiently sized for me, but it felt particularly small with a stripling warrior in it.

"You care for others all night but take no care for yourself," Gideon charged.

I was surprised by the level of anger in his voice. "What are you talking about?"

"You try too hard to make them like you."

"That's not true! It's not even possible. They want me to leave, to go home. I know they all hate me."

"Hate you? They are all in love with you now."

"Ha!" That was so far from the truth. I had eyes. I could see they didn't love me. "And that would bother you?"

His lips tightened over clenched teeth, and a flush of anger swept over his cheeks.

"What is with you? I want them—Reb, Noah, Corban, all of them—to trust me, not love me."

"Then stop cooking for them. They all look at you with moon eyes."

I glanced out the still open flap. My wardens were getting an earful.

"They were hungry."

"We had birds."

"That's not a meal."

"Not now that you spoil them with corn cakes all the time."

"What are those boys supposed to do with whole kernels of dried corn?"

"Let the girl pack it up the mountain for them? Let her cook it for them with barely any thanks?"

"I told you I didn't carry it up the mountain. I thought if anyone believed me, you would. Besides, that corn," I gestured out toward the campfire, "came from the ration tents anyway."

"I know."

We were each sitting on an end of my unrolled mat. I sat facing him with my legs outstretched, and I rubbed them, working the painful tingles out. He sat near the door, facing the side wall with his legs bent, his forearms resting on his knees, and his hands falling listlessly in front of him.

Were we really arguing about corn? I stopped rubbing my legs and took a closer look at Gideon. Something was bothering him. He was staring hard at his hands, and I wondered if he had brought me here to tell me something important.

But he was irritating me, so I hurled my satchel at him. It hit him in the shoulder, but he caught it.

"Look for yourself. There is no corn in there."

He just gave me a dismissing look.

I pushed my travel pack toward him, but even as it scraped across the ground, he held up a hand.

"I believe you," he said.

"No, you don't. Look!" I reached over and opened the flap of the satchel, letting it fall open before him.

Uneasily, he began sifting through the items in my bag. They were all small, clearly no bags of corn or beans, no large and fleshy fruit. He pulled out the small codex-type book my mother had given me.

When she took me on her forages through the woods, she told me what she knew about each of the plants we collected, and Darius, with his careful script, helped me record her words for reference later because I couldn't keep it all in my head like she could.

The book caught Gideon's interest. He set the satchel

aside and began fingering through the folded pages. "This is a clever resource," he said.

"It's useful at times," I allowed as casually as I could. I knew what he would find in just a moment, and I wanted to snatch the book back and hold it tight against my chest to prevent it. But I didn't. I let him find it.

When he found the moonflower he had given me pressed carefully between the folds, he was quiet, fingering it and thinking about what it might mean. The book also contained several other specimens I had shown to my mother, but the flower wasn't like those, and I was sure he would know it.

Finally, he broke the silence. "I've been thinking." He looked up at me but then back down at the flower. "About you."

Heart pounding, I waited for him to go on.

"It's not that I love you," he burst out in a harsh whisper.

I could only stare at him as he stared at the moonflower with a flush creeping up his neck, and I could see now that it was not anger but embarrassment.

"It's just, you know I grew up out on the farm with all brothers."

"You told me."

"And I've never had a friend like you before."

"A girl?"

He nodded. "And someone who isn't kin." He glanced at me again, clearly reluctant to keep talking.

But I needed him to. Gideon was my only friend here. It was a different and uncomfortable position to be in, and it worried me how suddenly desperate I was for the Gideon I had known in the meadow, for his friendship and his quiet guidance.

"It seems like you're mad at me, Gideon."

He almost smiled. "I'm mad at myself. I was prepared to go to the army even without the striplings. I found myself wishing all the time that I had joined Teancum's ranks with Jashon."

60

"Why didn't you?"

"My parents. We decided one of us must stay."

"I'm sure they appreciated that."

"I was only going to look into the stripling army. I wanted to go to real battles with real, trained warriors." He gestured to the door of the tent and gave his head a shake. He didn't want to build embattlements with boys. "I want to become a chief captain. My life, it will be traveling, it will be dangerous." He heaved a sigh and looked me firmly in the eye. "A wife and family are not in my plans," he said.

I sucked in a breath. "I haven't asked you to make me your wife."

"I know." A corner of his mouth turned up in a small smile. "But before you marched onto the training ground and demanded entrance into the militia, it was, you know, just me and you—out in the meadow, training, doing what we both love. And I hate sharing you with all these boys." He ran a hand through his hair. "You should hear the things they say about you when you're not around."

"They talk about me?"

"Constantly," he said. "It makes me want to punch them all in the face. I feel like—" He took a breath. "I didn't plan to care about you."

I knew exactly how he felt. I didn't plan on it, either. Didn't want it. And yet, I didn't want to be without it—whatever this was between us, new and sweet and growing.

I wondered if anyone else had ever seen this side of Gideon. Thinking of the pairs of ears outside the tent, I moved closer to him so our conversation could be continued in much lower tones.

"I miss those days in the meadow with you, too." I bit my lip. I shouldn't admit these things. "No one else believed in me."

He scoffed softly. "I taught you to fight."

"You know it was more than that. For me," my voice was

barely above a whisper, "it was more than that."

He turned his eyes to me, dark and searching eyes, and he really looked at me then. I blushed in the silence. Then he closed my book and slipped it back into my satchel, moving the other things inside to make room for it.

He pulled out the jar of ointment Mother had given me. Flipping back the cloth cover, he held it up to his nose and sent me a knowing look over the top of it.

I frowned and held out my hand for it, but instead of giving it to me he reached over to give my shoulder a slight squeeze. I flinched and immediately bit my lip to hold back the sharp intake of breath. But he knew, and his eyes filled with concern. Without a word, he dipped his fingers into the jar, and after a slight hesitation, he touched them to the side of my neck.

"You will get stronger," he said quietly as he rubbed the ointment into my skin in slow circles with his rough thumb.

His fingers stilled as if he suddenly thought better of what he was doing. But with the slight pressure of his warm hand on my neck, he pulled me closer to him, and moving ever so slowly forward, nudging my cheek with his nose the way Kin or Kay would nudge my hand for food, he found my lips in a heart-stopping touch. I dropped my eyelids, and I let him.

"Now I know why you want to punch them all in the face," I whispered through my tightened throat.

I felt him smile.

Lib cleared his throat. "Too quiet in there, Ethanim. What do you think?"

"Much too quiet."

"You two fall asleep or something?"

"Yes," Gideon and I both called in unison.

"Goodnight, Kanina," Gideon whispered in my ear.

He crawled out of my tent and ignored both Lib and Ethanim as he stalked off toward the dying fire.

I watched for a moment as he settled there, and then I

carefully tied the flap of my tent closed. My fingers went to my lips, to the place he had kissed me. He had kissed me! What did he mean by it? Because he certainly didn't mean to marry me.

I slipped my sarong off my shoulders so I could rub in Mother's cream. The relief wasn't immediate, but I could tell that it would help. When I was done I lay down on my pallet and closed my eyes, and I tried not to think of Gideon's fingers or his soft breath or his lips.

The horn woke me in the morning.

A week of days just like this went by, digging the trenches with the men. Mother had been wrong. I didn't feel as good as new in the mornings, but after a few days, I didn't need as much ointment at night. Each morning, I groaned in agony, prayed for strength, and rolled from my pallet ready to go. I didn't tell the boys in my unit how physically exhausted I was, though of course they had to know.

I was glad when our week building the embankment was done. Over the weeks and months that followed, we took our turn tending the herds, refurbishing the weapons, and chopping down trees to build guard towers, fences, and fires.

I liked tending the flocks because it reminded me of home, of being with Micah up on the bluff and hearing him read the words of the prophets aloud while the sheep grazed. But I spent a great deal of that week alone gathering herbs and plants for Mother. In the evenings I took them to her and stayed to eat with her and sometimes Kalem or some of the other women.

"Kanina, you need to eat with your unit," she gently reprimanded me after the fourth day of this.

I bit my lip. "I thought you wanted me to accompany you on this journey."

She studied me quietly for a moment. "That was before you joined yourself with the militia." When I didn't say anything, she placed her strong hand on my arm. "How are things going with your unit?"

She knew I wasn't on the best of terms with any of them, but I had spared her the details of how it really was, how the boys alternated between cruel pranks and outright shunning. I hadn't told her they had given me the permanent assignment of laundering their tunics. I hadn't told her how Reb had accidentally bumped me into the latrine when we were burying the old one and how close I had come to falling in.

I could have savored the idea that Zach had grabbed me before I'd fallen, but it had only been out of common decency. I had thanked him simply and that had been the end of it.

My favorite duty was building the towers. I loved watching the way the boys worked together. They joked and they laughed, and I could pretend I was part of it. I particularly liked watching Lib at work. Apparently, he really knew what he was doing. He took the plans and made them better, and all the boys were eager to do what he asked them.

"Keturah," he said when he caught me watching him.

I stood up straighter, waiting for a new assignment, one that was easy and boring and no one else wanted.

"Do you want to pitch the wood?"

I glanced at the others who were cutting and notching the hewn wood together. "I'm glad to apply the pitch," I said.

He took me aside and showed me how to apply resin to the wood with a soft-bristled brush. After watching me for a moment, he said, "You've got it." He half turned to leave me alone, again, but watched me a moment more. "This is important, Keturah."

I sighed. "You gave the important jobs to the others." I couldn't hide my melancholy or the fact that I didn't want to apply this sticky stuff to the wood when all the others got to build.

"Do you know what the pitch does?" he asked, going to his heels next to me.

I didn't want to admit that I didn't, not really. He was so

64

smart, and I wasn't sure I knew anything anymore.

He took the brush from my hand and did a few slow strokes of his own, showing me how to get it into all the crevices and knots of the wood. "This oil is a preservative. It makes the wood resistant to bugs and decay, and it protects it from the sun and rain and snow."

I watched him pick up another piece of wood.

"We could build the watchtower, but we would have to build it over again each year if we didn't apply this to the wood. Look around at the size of this wall."

He gestured, and I followed the wall with my eyes until it curved and I could no longer see where it went.

"On your home, you can replace boards as they rot, but here, there is so much wall to maintain, so many towers, and any weakness in them makes the city vulnerable."

"I see," I said.

He gave me back the brush. "Nothing those boys build can stand up against the elements unless you first apply this preservative to the wood." He paused. "It is like your mother. She taught you the words of Christ because she wants you to be strong against the elements."

I narrowed my eyes, thinking about his comparison.

"That was the wrong example," he said, a note of apology in his voice.

"No." I shook my head. "I'm not ashamed to be a girl." I looked up into his eyes, flecked green like the forest. "Being here, being a soldier, it's not because I don't want to be a woman. But my mother taught me of agency too, like she taught my brothers, and to everyone is given the privilege to fight for what they know to be right. That's all I want to do here." I glanced at the others, caught Noah's eye. *Maybe you could tell that to them*, I wanted to say, but I didn't. "Mothers want to protect their families too."

He was silent for a long moment, then nodded and left me alone.

Chapter 7

It was several months before we received orders to hunt. All our orders came down through a chain of command. The chief captain over our thousand, an older boy named Isaiah, instructed Seth on where we could hunt. This was to keep us out of the areas that had been hunted recently and also, I thought, to keep us out of the areas that were known to have Lamanites. So we set out to the northeast shortly after dawn and passed the West Road well before midmorning.

I was not used to being cooped up inside city walls, and it was a welcome relief to be trekking through the forest again. The mountainous area in which Judea sat was abundant with creeks and trails that wound through abandoned villages whose occupants had all sought the protection of the city walls long ago. It was eerie to walk past their empty houses. The terrain was craggier than at home, but otherwise reminded me of the forests around Melek.

Seth gave Lib our orders. We were to take down any animal that was small enough for us to carry back, and we were to do it within a half day's walk of the city walls. Later on, depending on how long we stayed in Judea, we would have to go farther out to find game, sending men in long hunting parties of perhaps a fortnight, but for now we were to stay relatively close.

The Judeans had flocks and herds, but only what could be maintained within the walls, so the army hunted wild game as a supplement. Typically, if everyone was responsible—meaning we didn't waste any part of the animal and we never killed females or the young—there was game in plenty to supplement the city.

When we had traveled up into the hills beyond the West Road, we split into smaller groups. I went with Lib and Ethanim. Gideon and Josh veered off to the south, and the other groups split off toward the north. My eyes followed Gideon as he walked out of sight through the trees.

"You wanted to go with Gid," Ethanim said.

It wasn't really a question, more of a statement filled with curiosity. And of course I did. Gideon was the only one of them who liked me.

"I'm glad to go with you," I said brightly.

I noticed a look pass between them.

"Can I ask," said Lib, "what is between you and Gid?"

"We're friends," I told them. "You know Gideon taught me to fight."

"I'm going to follow this track," Ethanim said abruptly and slipped away through the trees.

Lib and I walked side by side in silence until I said, "Shouldn't we have gone to help him?"

"Ethanim does not need help tracking."

"But the animal—"

"He will not need help taking it down either." He paused for a moment. "Keturah, as the head of our unit, with you and Gideon... it is one of my duties to...as a captain, to..." He let out a sigh and scrubbed at the back of his head. "Well, the other captains don't have to do this." He frowned at the ground.

"Do what? Lib, just say it."

"Since you are both under my command," his words tumbled out, "I think you should tell me if you're...I don't even know how to say it," he admitted as he tugged at his ear. "Romantically involved?" His voice held a question. "It could become an issue. In battle. If either one of you can't do your duty. The whole unit has to rely on each other."

I considered his words for a moment. Of course I didn't want to be having this conversation with Lib, but he did have a point. Suppose Gideon left one of our unit members in peril in order to save me, or I did the same for him. It could be dangerous in many ways.

"Gideon and I are friends."

"You keep saying that."

"Because it is the truth." But I was afraid it might not be the truth as my fingers lightly touched my lips where he had kissed me. "Gideon would not allow himself more than friendship." It had only been one small kiss.

"And you? Do you want more?"

"That is an impossible question to answer."

He shook his head hard. "No! It is easy. Yes or no," he bit out tightly.

"What I feel for him is not going to jeopardize your safety," I bit back.

"You think that's what I'm worried about? My safety?"

"Did you not just say...? Lib, no," I said, confused and defensive. "Have you had this conversation with Gideon?"

"Not yet," he admitted uncomfortably.

At least he intended to, I thought, but then I imagined the conversation between the two, and I grimaced.

"What do your brothers think of it?" he asked.

"What do you mean?"

"I thought you were promised to Zeke."

"Kind of," I admitted. "Not formally."

His manner eased a little. "You would go against it?"

"Lib," I said, laughing. "I fought my way into an army of men. What do you think I will do?"

"I think you will do exactly as your family wishes," he said quietly.

My laughter faded into silence. As we continued through the trees, I glanced at the sun. It was time to start hunting in earnest or we would be going back empty-handed.

"Does having honor make me a bad person?" I asked as I trailed my fingers along the tall foliage.

"No, but it makes me wonder what you are doing with Gid."

"I'm not doing anything with Gideon."

"You say that, but we all see how you flirt with him—"

"I do not!"

"And make him think you feel more than you do."

"I do not!"

"If Zeke is your intended, you have nothing you can offer to Gid."

"Are we done?" I said flatly. "Because I see Ethanim waiting for us at the top of that rise."

He looked to Ethanim but said, "Listen, Keturah, I'm sorry."

I shrugged. "You were right to bring it up. I don't intend to demean Gideon's credibility with the men by—"

"You could never do that," he cut me off. "That's not what I meant."

What did he mean? What was he so sorry about?

"We should go up there," I said and started to climb the rise, not waiting for an answer. He seemed to think I needed his permission to go anywhere, but I definitely did not need it.

His hand shot out and he grabbed my arm as if he might stop me, but I turned angry eyes on him and yanked my arm out of his grasp. He took a deep breath. "Yeah," he said and gestured me forward. "We should go."

When I reached Ethanim, he wasn't alone. I glanced back at Lib, who wouldn't meet my eyes.

Reb, Noah, and Zachariah stood with Ethanim. They were waiting. Reb snickered when he saw me, and Noah ineffectually hid a smile by rubbing the side of his nose. When that didn't work, he actually tried to wipe it off with his hand. Ethanim scratched the back of his head. Zach stood off a distance with his arms folded and a hip hitched, glaring at the others. He didn't look at me, but I met the eyes of each of the other boys.

I let them stop at Ethanim. "You get that stag?"

He slowly shook his head.

"The tracks are there," Reb said pointing to the ground. "We waited for you," he went on in a sickly sweet, mocking tone. "Do the honors."

The rest of the boys stepped back, staying silent.

"Well, I guess I'll do the honors," I said as I stepped forward.

Clearly, they thought I would be unable to track the animal, and they weren't being very helpful with all the noise they were making behind me. The animal would hear us long before we ever saw it. I wanted to go faster to get away from them, but I didn't want to miss any of the tracks because of haste. I took a calming breath and said a quick prayer that I would be able to find the beast and that I could win the trust of the boys behind me.

I found the beautiful buck clipping grass in a small meadow and sent up a silent thank you to the heavens. I held up my hand to get the boys' attention and breathed a sigh of relief when they finally stopped joking and laughing. I had a perfect shot. All I had to do was take it. I notched an arrow into my bow, let out a breath, and at the very second I let it fly, something tickled my face.

I nicked the buck, and he darted away.

I whirled to see a long, slender leaf in Reb's hand and his

stupid, grinning face.

"You made me hurt him!" I burst out.

His grin faded, and I could see that hurting the buck had not been his intention. Nevertheless, that had been the outcome of his stupid, childish prank.

This wasn't the first prank they had pulled. They also heaped extra work on me and gave me all the menial tasks in camp. I tried to bear it all without complaint, but this, this was the last time.

"I could have maimed that poor animal! And now we will have to go back empty-handed with nothing but your childishness to show for a day's work." I glared at them all.

Nobody said anything. Reb and Noah glared back at me. The others wouldn't look at me at all. Zach, jaw clenched tight, looked off into the distance and swallowed hard. Ethanim studied his hands, and Lib looked down at the ground as he scuffed a foot over the forest floor. Bullies and cowards.

I strapped my bow back over my shoulder. "I'm going to find game." I jabbed my finger into Ethanim's collarbone as I walked past him. "And don't follow me. I don't need your help, and I definitely don't need your feigned friendship." I looked to Lib and sneered, "You either, you gutless excuse for a captain."

I didn't hear anyone try to follow me, and as soon as I was out of sight, I began running. I wanted to feel free and wild as I had in the forests at home, but to my shame, I began to cry. I was mad at myself more than any of them. When was the last time I had let something like a tickle on my cheek distract me? Gideon had incorporated all kinds of distractions into my training. The disappointment in myself and in that group of immature, jealous boys made the tears come harder, and finally, I had to stop and let the heaving sobs take over for a moment.

How could this be done? I wasn't going to win them over. Couldn't they see I wanted the same things they wanted? I only wanted to help our parents keep their promises and to guard our lands against attack. They thought I was a spoiled little girl who always got her way. They thought I was the weakest member of our unit.

But they were wrong.

Slowly, I became aware of a presence to my left. Wiping my eyes with the heels of both hands, I looked up to see a large mountain lion, lithe and golden, watching me silently. I went still and stared into his eyes, knowing I shouldn't but unable to look away. It was the middle of the day. He shouldn't have been there. I shouldn't have been there. After a long moment, he moved on, leaving me to cry in peace. But I was done crying. I let my eyes track him until he was almost out of sight, and then I followed him. As pretty as he was, his meat would do just as well as the lost buck's.

He must have smelled them, because he led me directly back to the boys. They were fighting amongst themselves—the idiots—and failed to notice the presence of the cat which was now low in the undergrowth watching them. By habit, I let out the shrill call of the margay, a much smaller cat that roamed the forests at home. It was the call my brothers used in the forest when there was danger, but none of these boys recognized it as a warning.

Standing tall, I notched another arrow into my bow, and I waited for my shot.

When the large lion jumped, I let my arrow fly. The cat jerked in the air, and his lifeless body landed on Reb. I couldn't help a private smirk.

The others had jumped back in surprise, but leaned in carefully to inspect the dead animal that still had their friend pinned to the ground. Lib touched the arrow in the cat's side.

"Who shot it?" His voice carried to me on the breeze, the same breeze that had brought their scent to the lion.

The others glanced around at each other, and when no one owned up to the shot, Lib finally put two and two together and began searching the forest. I made the call of the margay again, and his eyes came straight to mine.

As I walked toward them, the boys pulled the cat's body off of Reb, who rolled over and threw up in the brush.

Kneeling, I pulled my father's obsidian blade from my armband. I slit the cat's throat to let it bleed out, getting the spray on my hands and neck and clothing. I looked up to meet the eyes of every boy there. Then I took out my axe, found a slender tree, and cut it to make a pole to tie the cat to. I pulled bindings from my satchel and tied its legs to the pole. I slapped Lib's hands away when he tried to help.

When I was done, I turned to Lib and said, "I'm scouting ahead." What I meant was that I wasn't walking with them. Nothing could make me.

I didn't miss his glance at Ethanim, but he gave me a nod and gestured for me to head southwest.

"Wait!" Reb called from behind me, but I did not turn to acknowledge him.

"Reb," Lib said. "Enough."

"What? It's just a basket so she can carry our wash to the stream." Is that what he had been doing back in the brush? Weaving a basket to taunt me with?

"I said that's enough."

"Are you sweet on her now too?"

"Go bury your puke."

Gideon was leaning against a tree and Joshua was on his heels next to a dead deer when I came across them.

"Been here long?" I asked them.

They both glanced at the position of the sun, but Gideon didn't say anything. It was Joshua who said, "A while. Gid got the buck right off."

That didn't surprise me. Gideon could track anything, and he had excellent aim.

Gideon glanced over my shoulder, and Joshua asked,

"Where are the others?"

"I'm scouting ahead."

Neither one responded to that. We had already been over the terrain. It didn't need to be scouted. It was no wonder they all thought I didn't know anything.

We waited quietly for the others to join up with us. Gideon went over to inspect the cat when Ethanim and Lib laid it on the ground, but I thought he was taking note of much more than that. He knew something was wrong amongst us. He seemed to be looking over the lion, but his eyes kept flicking to me with clear questions he would not ask. I tried not to notice, because what if those things Lib had said were true?

The cousins, Corban, Cyrus, and Mathoni trailed in from the north, and they each carried a string of fish. I could see they were not in the contingent of boys who wanted to humiliate me because Corban came up to me and held the string of fish in my face. I dodged away, nearly breaking my icy silence to laugh, and jabbed him in the ribs. He was proud of his fish. He wanted to share his accomplishment with me. I wanted to hug him.

Instead, I said, "I am scouting ahead again," and I turned and left, leaving no time for a response from Lib. I didn't care what he thought. He could tail me if he wanted, but he would have to keep up.

There was silence behind me, and I thought they were out of earshot, my ultimate goal. I thought I had finally gotten far enough away that I didn't have to hear Gideon not sticking up for me. They would ostracize him too if he did. I knew that. But Gideon was the only one who had ever believed in me, and his silence made me doubt he truly did. Maybe he had other motives.

"This whole thing is a sham." *Noah.* "They are never going to let us fight, not with her in our unit. We'll be hunting and digging trenches until we get bored and go home."

"That's not true, and Lib's right. I've heard enough."

Was that Joshua?

"Zachariah agrees with us. Right Zach?"

I didn't hear Zach's reply. I assumed he didn't give one.

"Reb, why are you so hard on her? It's not like you."

Why could I not get away from them? But it was true. Reb loved to laugh and to make others laugh, and usually his jokes were harmless. He was not a mean person.

"Only as hard as I have to be. Someone has to show her she doesn't belong here with us. You should be glad I'm taking a stand. No one else is."

"She saved your life!"

I began to run, to put more distance between us. I *did* belong there. Everything in my heart told me I did. I wouldn't have been able to live with myself in Melek if I hadn't chosen to come. I would have followed the army on my own.

When I deemed I was far enough ahead of the boys that I wouldn't have to hear their conversations about me, discussing whether or not I had any worth, I slowed. Eventually, the forest opened onto the bluff that rose above the West Road, and before I entered the clearing, I crept near the edge of the trees and cast about for potential dangers. I heard noise, possibly travelers on the road below, so I got low and eased toward the edge to look down. I saw a band of men, maybe fifty, far below me on the West Road.

I watched them for a time trying to determine who they were and whether or not they were my enemies. It irritated me that I couldn't tell. Finally, I decided to go give Lib the news. I was angry with him at the moment, but he was still my captain. I backed up carefully, turned, and trotted back toward my unit.

"What do you think?" I asked Lib and Gideon when they were lying at the edge of the bluff with me.

"Not Lamanites," Gideon said in a low voice.

"They're carrying supplies. Do you think they're headed to Antiparah?" Lib asked.

Gideon shook his head. "They would have taken the Sea

Road back at Antionah. They're heading to Judea."

"Nephite supplies?" I wondered aloud. "For us?"

"Yes, but look there."

"I see it," said Lib almost under his breath.

A distance to the north around turns and hills, we had a view of another band of men—smaller, but, from their dress, almost certainly Lamanite.

"Are they a war party?" I asked.

"No," said Lib.

"An embassy probably, maybe spies." Gideon returned his eyes to the first band of travelers and reached coolly across my back, skimming the skin of my shoulder with his fingertips, to slide my obsidian blade from my armband. I watched as he positioned it and sent a flashing signal down to the men below. We waited a minute in silence.

There. A return signal.

Gideon stood up.

"Gideon!" I protested in a harsh whisper.

He looked down at me. "They're Ammonites. That was my father's signal."

Chapter 8

I looked back down at the West Road to where the men had now halted and some were pointing up toward us.

"Here," Gideon said and gave me his hand to help me to my feet. "You have a good instinct."

That was quite a compliment coming from Gideon, but I said a little sullenly, "I didn't know they were friendly."

"From one look? You did the right thing. Caution is always better."

"Ammonites. Carrying supplies," Lib was telling the others who were still at the tree-line behind us. "And a small band of Lamanites half an hour to the north."

We hurried down out of the hills. Knowing the group was Ammonite, men who would not fight for their lives, and having seen the enemy in the area, even few in number, gave our steps an urgency that no one mentioned. We neared the supply group, who rested while they waited for us.

A man walked out to greet us. Gideon set down his end of the pole he carried and went to meet him. I assumed the man was his father, with the same hair and eyes as Gideon, and I watched them with interest. They hugged there in front of everyone, and his father looked both proud of his son and relieved to see him whole and well.

The rest of us stayed back a little while Gideon spoke to his father and some of the other men, gesturing toward Judea and then back the way we had come. It was getting late in the afternoon now, but we had made good time and would be back within the walls of Judea about the time rations were distributed for the evening meal. We would have these men safely inside the walls of Judea before the Lamanites from the north caught up to us.

I waited a short but noticeable distance away from the rest of my unit. I wanted to leave immediately, to see my mother or to be alone in my tent. I felt odd and different and unwanted. As I stretched my arms and rolled my shoulders I noticed another man break away from the group and begin walking briskly toward us. There was an excited hop in his step, and when I looked closer, I saw that it was Hemni.

I broke away too and ran toward him. Zeke's father swept me up in his powerful arms and swung me around. If any of the men hadn't noticed I was a girl before, they would notice now. But I didn't care anymore. I knew I was a soldier, a good one, and it didn't matter what these men thought about me. I knew who I was and what I was doing here. In that brief moment twirling in Hemni's arms, my perspective changed and I knew that whether I ever slew any Lamanites in battle or not, I had done what I felt was right by joining the militia and being willing to do what was necessary.

"How are you? Have you seen my sons? Is your mother here? Is she well?"

I laughed and tried to answer all of his questions.

"I am well and so are Zeke and Jarom. My mother and brothers are also well. We have been fortifying the city Judea for these months and have yet to see any battle."

He closed his eyes, placed a hand over his chest and

sighed. "That is good to hear," he said. "Very good to hear." Then he gestured to my unit, a question in his eyes.

I looked back at them. They were biting off bits of venison jerky and stretching their muscles while they waited. Some of them watched me curiously as they drank from their water skins.

"My unit and I, we have been hunting today."

"It looks like you got quite a haul." Then he chuckled. "The kind of haul I get when I take Jarom with me."

I nodded and smiled. Jarom had an innate ability to find game and had honed his skill as a hunter. He had supplied his father's business with game for several years before we left Melek. Hemni could hunt, but with Jarom gone, he was missing a large asset to his business.

Hemni stared at me for a moment, smiling. Then he laughed. "Truly the Lord magnifies us when we do his work," he said.

His words bore humor, testimony, truth, and love all at the same time. That was Hemni.

"He truly does," I agreed.

Hemni pulled me into a sideways hug. "The girls sent some things for you. I'll get them to you before I leave."

"How long will you be here? How are the girls? How is Cana? How is Mui?" I wanted to know about the goat, but I didn't want to ask about Kin and Kay, my deer, for they had likely become dinner by then.

"Everyone is fine. Sarai has been taking good care of Mui. She's a better hand with the goats than Isabel," he mused, clearly thinking of some humorous story. "Leda has become betrothed. And a young man has been coming by to see Cana lately."

"That's wonderful!" I said. And it was—for Leda. Her parents had been killed in a Lamanite raid on the village and she had been left alone with no family to care for or protect her. Hemni and Dinah had taken her in. A betrothal was a blessing for her in every way. But Cana was in love with Kenai. Another man courting her would only be a bother.

Hemni took me by the elbow and led me to where Gideon and Lib talked with several of the men from the supply group.

"Judea is not far," Gideon was saying. "You will see it in the distance when we pass this hill." He glanced at Lib. "And we need to get moving right away."

No one questioned his words.

"Well, lead on, Gid," said an older man with dark hair that was graying around his temples. "We want to be there before dark." He clapped Gideon on the shoulder.

Gideon conferred with Lib who ordered the unit to load up and move out behind the supply group, very deliberately putting us between our fathers and the band of Lamanites. Gideon positioned himself beside me, glaring at Lib when he tried to do the same. Zachariah and Joshua, who weren't carrying any of the game, fell back to guard at the rear.

"Who was that man?" Gideon asked me after a while.

"Mmm? Oh, Hemni?"

"Is that Hemni then?"

"Yes. Zeke's father."

"You looked like you're close."

"Of course," I said. "He is like a father to me."

"My father did not twirl me around," Gideon said.

That was an absurd thought that made me laugh. "I told you we were close. Does that bother you?"

"No. Why should it?"

"It shouldn't, but you look mad."

"I'm tired."

"The indefatigable Gideon is tired?"

"Aren't you?"

"Maybe a teensy bit," I allowed. I thought about the exhausting conversation with Lib. I thought about the long run and the hard cry. I thought about the lion, tracking him back through the forest and slitting his throat. I looked down and saw the blood on my hands and clothing.

"Do I smell?" I asked Gideon quietly.

He shot me a sideways glance and a half a smile. "Maybe a teensy bit."

"You've got blood on your tunic too. You don't smell much better," I pointed out. And then, with another quick glance at him, I offered, "I can clean the blood from it for you."

"We all smell pretty ripe," he agreed, avoiding the topic of laundering the tunics. "We'll go down to the river and take baths before the evening meal."

The thought of being clean compelled me onward toward the city.

Lib ran ahead to meet the front of the Ammonite supply group at the gates of the city. I watched the guard smile, clap his hands together, and wave us all through.

It turned out that Gideon and I weren't the only ones who wanted a bath. After taking the game to the designated area, where it would be prepared and then distributed, my entire unit found the energy to run to the river. The boys barely stopped long enough to strip down to their breechcloths—tossing their tunics aside, kicking off their sandals, and dropping their satchels—before they splashed into the pool, an area of the river that the army had dammed off for bathing.

I kept walking, making my way to the calmer pool where I could be alone.

When I got there, I waded in fully clothed as had become my general habit since Lib insisted on sending someone with me. The water came to my waist. It was so warm in the hot evening sun that my sarong would dry as I walked back to the camp.

I plunged down to the bottom of the pool and let myself float back up to the surface. Despite my mood, I smiled to myself as I ran Mother's soap through my hair. After I rinsed, I stretched out on my back and floated for a few minutes more, letting my mind wander as I relaxed.

Hemni was here. He had come with our harvest, just as he said he would. I thought of Gideon, so surprised that my family would trust Hemni with the harvest. Why wouldn't we? And it wasn't as if we had a lot of choice in the matter anyway. There was no choice but to trust him.

Hemni really was like a father to me, to all of us. He didn't live with us, but he treated us all as devotedly as he treated his own children. His hands were large like Zeke's and warm. His arms were strong, protective, and comforting. His heart was filled with love and faith.

Gideon didn't know any of this. Hemni was just a name to him.

Surely his own father was as kind and loving as Hemni was. I remembered how his father had thrown loving arms around him this afternoon on the West Road. Gideon had not resisted, and yet he had seemed hesitant and stiff, even jerky in the way he had lightly pounded his father's back with his fisted hand.

My father's signal, he had said, and dark shadows had crossed his eyes, a storminess I didn't understand.

I had seen that hardness in his eyes on many occasions, but I thought of the soft look in his eyes when he had fingered the moonflower in my book, when he had kissed me all those nights ago.

I thought I heard a noise in the bushes on the bank. I lifted my head from the water and scanned both sides of the river, but I saw no movement. I wondered which of the boys it was. Sighing, I let my feet fall down to the muddy bottom of the pool, and I dragged my tired legs through the water until I reached the bank, my clothes cascading water as I climbed out. I picked up my satchel and carried my sandals.

Gideon and Zachariah caught up with me on the trail back to camp. Their hair was damp and had dripped onto their dirty tunics, which they had put back on because Seth did not allow them to be bare-chested around me. We didn't talk and when we got to our camp, they each gave me a slight nod but wouldn't look me in the eye. Guarding me while I bathed was a duty I suspected every member of my unit liked doing, but it embarrassed them all. We dealt with it the best we could.

After changing into a clean sarong, I combed through my still damp hair before I left my tent. I had learned that if I combed my hair out by the fire, the boys stared at me.

Zachariah sat near the fire preparing a spit for the meat we had brought back.

"Do you know how to cook that?" I asked him.

"Mm-hmm." He nodded confidently.

"Need help with anything?"

"No."

"Okay," I said slowly, wishing there was something for me to help with.

He glanced up at me while he worked, and when he smiled, my eyebrows rose in surprise.

The boys laughed a lot—Reb was constantly telling jokes—but none of them smiled at me. I had won over Corban when I had healed his ankle, and his cousins generally went along with him. Gideon was one of my greatest friends in private, but among the others, and much to my confusion, he still stood back and let me suffer things on my own. Lib and Ethanim continued their feigned friendship, though sometimes it felt so real I nearly let myself think it was. But despite all that, nobody bothered to be particularly kind to me.

And Zach. That afternoon had been pretty typical for him. He never participated when the others gave me a hard time, but like Gideon, he never put a stop to it either. There was something in the way he looked at me—I thought perhaps he had many sisters or even a betrothed that he loved back home. As I watched Zach work, I realized I didn't know much about him other than what I could see. I sat down on a bench that had been constructed near the fire. "Did you know any of the other boys before coming here?"

Another glance. "Sure," he replied. "All of them. Well, except for Gid. But I knew of him."

"What does that mean?"

"Gid lives on a farm to the south of my village—maybe an hour's walk. Gid is Jashon's brother."

"Yes, he told me of Jashon."

"He did?" Zach looked suddenly more interested.

"Well, just that he fights in Teancum's ranks."

He relaxed. "Everyone knows that. I thought he might have told you about when they were younger, when they hunted the Lamanite that attacked their farm."

I didn't miss his hesitation, and I knew what he referred to, so I nodded slightly.

"He told me why he would want to hunt the Lamanite," I offered.

That seemed to surprise him. He leaned forward and spoke in a hushed tone. "From what I heard, when Jashon and Gid got home from town and saw what had happened, they tracked the raiding party. Nobody really knows what happened while they were gone, but it is said they brought the man's scalp back to their mother."

I was intrigued but doubtful. I knew what Gideon thought of taking scalps. But traditions and superstitions like this were deeply entrenched in our culture, especially among the older generations, vestiges of their life in the Land of Nephi.

Zach sat up straighter and continued in more regular tones. "Did Gid tell you Jashon was with Teancum when he killed Amalickiah?"

I shook my head.

He nodded. "The king of the Lamanites. Jashon is one of Teancum's most trusted guards. He was placed there for his viciousness and tenacity and remains there for his absolute loyalty."

"Or his obstinate refusal to leave Teancum's side," Gideon said from behind us.

Zach and I glanced guiltily at each other. How much had he heard?

"Are you saying obstinacy is not the same as loyalty?" I asked, noticing his hair had dried and he had changed into a clean tunic.

"They can be similar," he allowed, "if one's obstinacy is applied to a good cause."

"And one can't be loyal to an evil cause?"

"Many are loyal to evil causes, or you and I wouldn't be here. I just meant my brother is the most stubborn person on earth, and if he is still at Teancum's side, it is because of that, not because of loyalty. I come from a long line of stubborn people."

"I wouldn't know anything about being stubborn," I said airily, and they both laughed, which made my heart a little lighter.

"Have you got the dinner preparations under control?" Gideon asked Zach, who glanced between us and nodded. "We'll be back later, then," Gideon told him, and he held out his hand to help me up.

"Did you know Zach when you were growing up?" I asked when we had reached the edge of the soldiers' camps without saying anything. He had taken a course that led toward the main part of the city where all the civilians lived. With both of us in freshly changed clothing and freshly washed hair, we probably looked like a couple out for a stroll.

I looked more closely at Gideon. Were we?

But he didn't appear to be out courting or anything. He hadn't asked my family if he could walk with me, he hadn't brought me a gift, and he wasn't holding my hand. He wasn't even smiling at me. Gideon was a soldier first and foremost. I had always known that.

He had kissed me several moons ago after our first day on the embankment, but when he hadn't repeated it, hadn't even tried to repeat it, I had reluctantly decided it was something he regretted doing.

"Zach lived in Orihah, the town near my farm. They all did," Gideon said.

I wondered, and not for the first time, why I had been placed in a unit of boys from his town instead of a unit of boys from my village like Darius and Jarom had. They were with boys from our village and the nearby villages of Ezra and Antum. Same with Zeke and Micah and Kenai.

"Keturah," Gideon said. "Tell me about the cat. The boys said you shot him."

"I did."

"Ethanim said you stalked him through the forest and got your arrow in him when he attacked Reb."

"That's about the right of it."

"How was it you came to be separated from all the other boys?"

Oh. How much should I tell him? I didn't want to tell him any of it.

"Ket, why were you alone?"

"I got mad and stormed away." I looked up at him. I could see he intended to question me until he got the whole story. I sighed, resigned, and saved him the trouble of having to pry it out of me. I told him the whole of it, even the embarrassing talk with Lib. I couldn't bring myself to be deceitful.

He stayed silent when I was done. I felt pathetic, and I was embarrassed that I had let the boys rile me, that I had hurt the buck, that I couldn't stop what was happening.

"You could stand up for me sometime," I said, hurt and confused, when he didn't reply.

"Keturah, if I help you, you will only look weak in their eyes. You will lose the respect you've already earned." He shook his head. "I won't do that to you."

His words created a warmth in my chest that spread as I thought about what he meant. He wasn't trying to protect his own ability to lead his fifty men. He wasn't worried about their opinion of him. He wasn't ignoring my plight. I wondered at how difficult it must be for him to watch the others bully me, to keep himself from putting a stop to it.

And I confess, the thought of him wanting to punch them all in the face for it brought warmth to my cheeks, too.

And I wondered if he had a purpose for walking me through the city in the early twilight. On days we sat and made arrows, walking was a welcome respite, but today we had trekked through the mountains. I didn't know what Gideon's intentions were. He never offered much information unless it was asked for, and even then he carefully guarded his feelings. But he was a straightforward person, and I knew him to be honest. I felt nearly certain that if Gideon had anything other than friendship in mind, he would have told me.

But Zeke's jealousy had poisoned me to Gideon's motivations. I knew Zeke. I trusted him, and his blatant wariness of Gideon made me question my own judgment.

We halted for a moment when two little boys ran past us nearly tromping on our toes. They were laughing and running from their mother who caught them up in a huge hug.

"Was your brother really with Teancum when he slew Amalickiah?" I asked Gideon. The news of Amalickiah's death had been proclaimed triumphantly throughout the Nephite cities and villages not long before we left the Land of Melek.

"That's what his letter claimed. And even if the messenger hadn't confirmed it, it is unlike Jashon to lie, even to embellish the truth." He watched as the mother herded the little boys into their home so she could get them ready for their beds. "Besides, it sounds like something Jashon would do."

"Something daring?"

"Something necessary and for the greater good. He doesn't delight in the taking of life as you do." He said this with a smile in his eyes so I knew he was teasing me.

"I do not delight in bloodshed!"

"Your bow, your knife, and your broadsword speak otherwise."

"Is that a compliment?" I laughed.

"I'm sure it is to you."

I jabbed him in the ribs. "Now, I know that's an insult."

"No, never that," he said, dodging away from the jab.

I saw a unit or two of stripling warriors straggling in through the east gates, filthy with dirt and the sweat of a long day in the trenches. Trenchers, as we had come to call them, were clearly recognizable. I noticed one particular warrior stopped in the middle of the road with his hands on his hips.

I would never hear the end of this.

Chapter 9

Micah gaped at me and Gideon, but only for a moment before he closed his mouth and sauntered toward us. These two men, two of the most important people in my life, knew of each other but to my knowledge had never met.

In the custom of our people Micah held out his arm, dirty as it was, first to Gideon. Gideon clasped it firmly.

"We've not yet been introduced. I'm Micah, Keturah's eldest brother."

"I know who you are," Gideon said. An awkward pause followed, and Gideon said more politely, "I see the resemblance."

I felt my ears get hot and knew I was blushing. Micah looked at me curiously, tilting his head a little, the words he was about to say halting on his lips. Then he considered my companion.

"You are Gideon," Micah said.

"I am." Gideon glanced at me. "But it's just Gid," he told Micah. "Everyone calls me Gid."

Micah nodded and folded his arms. Gideon stood up straighter. I wanted to say something to ease the awkward silence, but Micah hadn't addressed me yet.

And because of that, I should have waited to speak, but I didn't. "Gideon lives on the borders of Melek, near the wilderness. He's been fighting Lamanite raids his whole life."

Gideon sent me a look that said to be quiet. But he was too modest.

"Yes," I insisted, placing my hand on his arm. "He is the only protection his parents have had since his brother left for the war."

Micah's eyebrows rose. "You have a brother already fighting?"

Gideon gave me another disparaging look but turned back to Micah and squared his shoulders. "Yes. Jashon fights with Teancum in the north."

"And you protected your home together? Before he left?"

Gideon nodded. He took a half step away from me so my hand slipped from his arm and fell limply down to my side.

Micah eyed Gideon for a few moments. He seemed to be thinking something over. Finally he said, "There is a council of war tonight at the main bonfire. It is for captains of one hundred and members of the council. It will follow the regular captains' meeting. Stay for it."

Gideon was silent for a moment. "Are you authorized to make that invitation?"

Micah gave a slow, pleased smile and a quick, hard nod. This was news to me.

"Thank you. I will," Gideon accepted.

"Good. Well then, I've got to get to my evening meal."

"Us too," I said.

"You eat together?"

"Yes. Why wouldn't we?"

"I didn't realize you were..." he trailed off.

I glanced at Gideon. "Were what? Gideon is in my unit. Doesn't your unit eat together?"

"Yes, of course they do." He spoke genially, but he looked strangely at us. He was seeing too much, things none of us were ready to see.

"You're filthy from head to toe," I said. Best to change the subject.

He looked down at himself. "Yeah. I guess I am. Want a hug?"

I dodged away from his sweat-soaked arm as he tried to wrap it around me.

"I'm off to the river then," he said, and he nodded to us and walked away.

Gideon and I watched him for a moment. "I'm sorry," I said, my eyes still on Micah. "That was weird."

"It's alright. He was just getting the lay of the land. Come on."

"What do you mean?"

"He wants to know what is between us."

And what is between us? The question hung in the air, but I didn't ask it, and he didn't answer it.

I looked up at him, studying him again. Squinting into the distance like he was, swallowing hard, adjusting the strap of his satchel, I wondered if he was the one who wanted to ask it.

How could I possibly answer him? My mind raced and my heart beat faster, but we both remained silent.

He led me away from the more populated areas toward the walls of the city. We passed under a new guard tower as we followed a path that wound into the forested area. I looked closely at the small window, but I couldn't make out who was on duty inside it.

Gideon followed my gaze but didn't comment. Instead, he said, "I thought you might be missing your trees."

I looked around as we came into the pines. I took a deep breath and smiled up at him. "I do. I am not accustomed to being gated in."

"I know," he said simply and added, "I hate to see it."

I took another deep breath and placed the palm of my hand on the trunk of an aspen. I shook my head. "No, being home in Melek, laundering some man's tunics every day would be the prison for me. Here in Judea, even with all our rules, I am free."

Gideon stepped up to me, and his hand covered mine on the tree. "You launder the tunics here," he said quietly.

It was true. "But it is my choice to be here," I said. "That is freedom." I turned my face to look up into his.

His eyes were dark and intent on mine. They dropped to my lips. He even dipped his head, but he did not allow himself to kiss me. After a time, he pulled my hand from the tree, and keeping it in his, turned back toward the city.

We were quiet as we walked, but I felt closer to him than I ever had. When we left the trees, he squeezed my hand and let it go. He wanted Micah to know what was between us—I even wondered if he had planned to meet Micah in the city—but he would not flaunt it in front of the others.

"You have to tell me everything that happens at the council," I said when we neared camp.

He shook his head. "No. I don't."

I sighed dramatically, but as it turned out, I got my own invitation to the council of war.

Helaman was in our unit's camp when we returned from the city. Gideon and I stopped in our tracks at the sight of Helaman sitting near our fire turning our spit and talking recipes with Zach.

When he spotted us, he sent us a smile but did not get up from his log nor stop his conversation with Zach. Cyrus and Corban sat on mats on the ground giving their full attention to our Chief Captain.

Gideon and I moved closer. I shifted from foot to foot as I listened to Helaman tell us about a turkey he had eaten once that had been dressed with a tart berry sauce on it. Gideon set his feet and remained still with his hands clasped together behind his back.

At last Helaman rose and regarded me from across the cook fire.

"Keturah, I thought I might have a word with you." He gestured for me to follow him, and he walked a short distance away.

I glanced at Gideon who raised his scarred eyebrow but said nothing.

I followed Helaman, not even allowing myself to speculate on what he wanted. I wasn't aware that he even remembered my name. But then again, the one girl's name out of two thousand boys' names probably wasn't difficult to remember.

When I reached him, he smiled gently and said, "Don't look so worried. There is a council of war tonight. I want you to come."

"Me? But why?"

He chuckled, his relaxed demeanor at odds with the seriousness of what he spoke of. "There are a great many things to discuss and one major issue we want to resolve. I feel we need..." he paused to think for a moment. "I feel we need many different viewpoints in order to circle this issue and come to an acceptable conclusion. We need the opinions of many, especially those who have experience fighting Lamanites." He looked at me pointedly. "As I have heard you possess."

I looked him in the eye. "I do," I said quietly.

He nodded. "Good. Come with your chief captain..."

"Seth," I filled in.

"Ah, yes. Seth. Good boy."

I bit my lip. *A council of war!*

After Helaman left, I went directly to Seth's tent and found him standing behind it with Gideon. They were talking about the council.

"Helaman wants me to come with you to the council of war," I informed them.

When they turned to me, I met Gideon's dark stare and Seth's tattooed gaze. After a moment, Seth replied. "We leave after the evening meal."

Seth and Gideon flanked me as we walked together to the main bonfire. It blazed in a large open area that divided the tents of the soldiers from those of the support groups. Many men milled about the area talking to one another. Some were laughing. A small group even played a game of ball while they waited.

We stood at the edge and surveyed the crowd. Seth rested his arm across my shoulders, utterly surprising me. Micah often did this, and it felt very brotherly and protective to me. From the first moment Micah had placed me under his command, Seth had accepted me, never seeming to mind that I was a girl. As I stood within the curve of his arm, it occurred to me that I might talk to him about the way my unit treated me. But I knew I wouldn't.

When I looked up at him he said, "Stay close. I don't want to lose you in there." He nodded toward the men.

Seth shouldered through the crowd with ease. Both Seth and Gideon had been attending meetings of this sort and knew many of the young men we passed. They exchanged greetings but kept walking, and I followed them and kept silent because I didn't know anyone.

But then I saw four men I did know near the fire. Micah, Kenai, and Zeke sat together, and they were talking to Eli, Kenai's chief captain.

Seth pointed. "There's Eli."

Unlike most of us, Seth and Eli were both Zoramites, and they had probably grown up together in a village like mine in the Land of Melek. The Zoramites had found refuge among the people of Ammon years ago, but I knew Eli's family had not converted to the church of God and had disowned him.

The Zoramite boys had one advantage over us—they had been raised by fathers who knew weapons. Their experience and heritage was the reason so many Zoramite youth served as chief captains among us.

Seth caught Eli's eye and lifted his hand in greeting, but we didn't join them. Instead, Seth led us to a place to their right far enough around the fire that we could make eye contact, but not so far that the fire would block our view of them. I wondered if this was a meeting with assigned seating because, before long, all the men moved around and seemed to find specific seats.

I sat between Seth and Gideon, who sat next to the boy I recognized as his cousin, Enos, the boy who had loaned us the spears on that rainy day in the training ground. Enos glanced at Gideon curiously but then looked past him and gave me a friendly smile.

Neither of my brothers nor Zeke had noticed my presence.

One of Helaman's assistants, Shem I thought Micah had called him, started the meeting. Helaman was nowhere to be seen. After a prayer, which we all knelt for, Shem began instructions for the daily routine and gave the captains suggestions for dealing with their soldiers and problems that invariably arose within their units.

I stayed quiet, listening intently while I kept my eyes on Shem and wondering why Helaman thought I might be needed at this particular meeting and wondering also just where Helaman was.

The meeting continued in this direction until Shem finally told the men they could go back to their camps. Seth, however, didn't make a move to leave, so I stayed where I was too.

When most of the men had cleared out, the remainder moved in closer to the fire. And that was when I caught Zeke's eye. He was scanning the men who were still present when he saw me. He had to look twice.

I gave him a smile and a small wave. I thought he might scowl at me, but he smiled and elbowed Kenai in the ribs, pointing me out with a nod of his head in my direction. It was a simple gesture between friends, nudging and pointing, communicating without words, and it reminded me of so many nights around the fire with Zeke and Cana and Kenai and our families.

Helaman entered the firelight with Antipus in his company, and he situated himself at one end of the circle so he could see all those present. Men shifted a little so they could see him, too. Antipus stood with his hands clasped behind him next to Shem at Helaman's side.

Helaman looked with piercing eyes around the circle, but when he spoke, his words were gentle. "My little sons," he said, a term he had taken to calling us. "You have no doubt noticed we have some extra men at our council meeting tonight." He stopped and interrupted himself, turning to Shem to ask, "We've had prayer?"

Shem nodded.

"Good. You'll forgive my absence from the captains' meeting, I hope. I was conferring with Antipus and his captains. He wishes to address you tonight." His eyes got a gleam in them, and I wondered with a smile if he was not so very different from me. "So, let us begin our council of war."

Helaman moved back and stood near Shem as Antipus moved forward and addressed us. He had a deep rumbling voice to match his thick chest and burley features. I had already noticed that Antipus commanded notice wherever he went, so tonight it was no surprise that he had everyone's rapt attention the moment he stepped forward.

"Helaman and I have been in council with my own men this evening. We are trying to develop a strategy to engage the army stationed at Antiparah in combat. It is the largest of Ammoron's forces in this quarter of the land." He folded his arms across his chest, his forearms bulging with muscles from years of practice and use. He let a small smile touch his lips as he said, "They have seen our strength increase, the arrival of supplies and men, and they do not want to venture out of their strongholds." Then a large smile spread across his face for just a moment. "We have scared them."

A ripple of approval went through the young men that sat on their heels or had taken a knee near the fire.

Antipus continued. "Until you arrived, the armies of Ammoron drew my men out to fight so often our strength had begun to dwindle. Their numbers are so large, my men were compelled to fight continually, and we lost many cities."

He stopped for a moment and sighed, perhaps thinking of the courage and fortitude his men exhibited, of the impossible task they had faced to protect and hold this city, of the men who had died in its defense. Or perhaps he was thinking of the reason we had lost the cities in the first place.

"With the help of Helaman's warriors, Judea is fortified, secure, and strong!" Antipus looked around at the men and boys who surrounded him. "I want to take back Antiparah," he said more quietly. "I want Zeezrom and Cumeni. I want vengeance for my fallen soldiers and a home for their widows!"

I watched him pace, hands behind his back, as his voice rose and he drew the council into his vision.

"Now is the time to press our advantage! Our numbers are strong. Our supplies are replenished. Our fortifications are repaired. My men are healed, and you, my young friends, are raring to go. There will not be a better time to weaken Ammoron's armies!" He paused while a cheer echoed up through the night with the smoke from our fire. "But he hides his men in his strongholds," Antipus said at last.

"The coward!" someone called.

"No!" Antipus returned. "He is wise, for we would destroy him if he sallied forth!"

Another cheer echoed up.

Helaman stepped forward again. "So you see our charge, boys," he said. "We must get the Lamanite army out of Antiparah to fight us. The question we put to you is—how?" He looked around for volunteers.

"Have the bowmen send burning arrows into their camps. We'll burn them out," called someone across the fire from me.

I began looking around at all the faces of the soldiers as they spoke, making their suggestions.

Never shy when his voice was needed, Zeke spoke up. "Send Ammoron an epistle. Ask him to meet us on an appointed field. He wants to fight or he wouldn't be waging this war."

"I actually like that idea," said a thoughtful Helaman.

How like Zeke to think things could be so straightforward, so honorable. But war-mongers like the Lamanites did not fight honorably. They took by force what they wanted from their enemy. They stole women and little children to use for their personal pleasure and to sacrifice to their idol and false gods. They studied war. They were weaned on the blood of their enemies and picked the raw game from their teeth with their despicable weapons. No, they were not interested in an honest fight.

I leaned toward Gideon to say as much. He bent to hear me, lowering his ear to my lips. I noticed Zeke watching us. His eyes narrowed, and he frowned.

"We will need to be much sneakier than that," I whispered to Gideon, and he nodded his agreement. He was all too aware of the base nature of our enemy.

Suggestions were called out, many good ones and some that clearly wouldn't work. Someone suggested a siege. Someone actually suggested setting the forest around the city on fire.

"Storm the gates of the city with a battering ram."

"Steal in over the walls by night."

Many of the suggestions were drawn from stories we had heard about Moroni, Lehi, and Teancum, the greatest Chief Captains since our forefathers had come out of Jerusalem. But I could tell from the disappointed look on Antipus's face he had hoped for better suggestions, for new and original ideas from these boys who trained diligently and dreamed about getting their chance to fight.

Finally, Gideon got slowly to his feet. Unlike the others, he spoke quietly, but something about Gideon commanded everyone's attention. "Lamanites are dogs who don't know a fair fight. They seek any advantage, as must we. I suggest a decoy."

Antipus straightened. "Go on," he said to Gideon.

"I propose we send the striplings out as if they were taking supplies westward, toward..." He waved his hand. "Toward Antionah. Only they won't be carrying supplies, but weapons."

I glanced at Zeke. Even he grudgingly gave consideration to Gideon's plan.

"The Lamanites will follow us. We'll be large enough to present a battle, not so large that they can't overpower us."

This thought sank into the now silent young soldiers.

"We'll be irresistible prey," Gideon said softly.

The silence went on until Antipus cleared his throat. "And what purpose would this serve? A sacrifice? For what?"

Gideon jerked his chin to one side as if to shake his head and then shifted his weight. "No. Not a sacrifice. A decoy."

Bait.

Understanding lit in Antipus's eyes. "And I would follow the Lamanites with my troops, overtake them, and cut into their lines at the rear."

"But what if the Lamanites overtake us before Antipus overtakes them?" I recognized Micah's voice.

A rumble of noise broke out as the chief captains and the members of the council discussed the possible ramifications of this plan. It merited more discussion than any other suggestion had all night. I still hadn't contributed anything to the discussion and wondered again at Helaman's invitation to be here. I was obviously of no help.

Kenai stood and raised his hand until quiet fell over the council of war. "My men can keep Helaman apprised of the Lamanite movements and ahead of their forces, given the striplings don't fatigue too easily."

"My men won't fatigue!" called Seth and others.

"We've been jogging around Judea for months in endless circles!"

They were all clearly as eager as I was to be involved in a campaign. We had been sitting in Judea for months, laboring on the fortifications, waiting for something—anything—to happen.

I felt the weight of Zeke's eyes on me. I knew he was thinking of the dangers—not for himself, but for me. He gave no thought to his own life, endeavored only to protect mine. But didn't he know what life would be like for me if he was killed? He would seek better to protect his life. I could protect my own.

Finally I turned my head to look at him. His face was stricken with regret, but when Helaman called for a vote on the plan, he stood to be counted in the unanimous yes.

Chapter 10

Antipus commanded the plan to go forward as soon as the arrangements could be made.

But as the days went on and the men from Zarahemla did not arrive, our leaders determined we would wait. Each day we ran, trained, sparred with one another, and worked, and before the time came to implement our stratagem, I had the pleasure of another turn in the trenches.

On the first day, Lib told the unit not to fill the buckets completely full.

"So we won't tire as quickly," he said.

He had also gotten to the trenches early to secure ladders for our unit, which I found to be helpful as they gave me some leverage. I could step down to retrieve the buckets and up to deliver them to the next boy. A few months ago I might have been embarrassed by Lib's obvious concessions for me, but I looked at him, and I only felt grateful.

The last morning, everyone paired off as usual, but Lib said, "Ket, you're with me."

Ket. It seemed he had taken to calling me Ket a lot lately. Most of the boys had. It was something my brothers and Zeke called me. It was affectionate. It meant we were becoming friends.

Gideon paired up with Joshua, and Ethanim started alone at the bottom of the trench catching buckets. I got settled on the ladder and inspected the embankment as far as I could see. Most of it had been repaired, but here on the northwest corner it was not as tall and the trench was not as deep. It was a weakness, and we, along with several other units of boys, meant to fix it. It wasn't right, I thought as I hefted the first bucket, to leave Judea without completing this embankment.

For a long time, I thought of the women and the little children inside the city, the ones I saw when I went into the market. They reminded me of the ones at home I had come here to fight for—Dinah, Cana, little Chloe, and all the others of the village who I knew and loved. I was so thankful I had heeded the prompting to join the militia and march out with them. Judea surely would have been fortified without my help, but I had received blessings for the work I had done.

"What are you thinking about?"

I was so lost in my thoughts, I nearly didn't register Lib's question. I took a last look at the work we had done and turned my eyes to Lib. "The women and the children this wall protects."

He was quiet for a moment. "You can empathize with them better than we can," he said after he had passed a bucket over his head.

I stepped back down a rung. "What do you mean?"

He gestured to the boys below us. "We've no notion what it's like to send a loved one into battle."

Neither did I, not really.

"You know what it is to be a child," I pointed out.

He let his eyes roam over the embankment and the watch towers we had built while he waited for Noah to pass the next bucket from below. "Not like the children here."

These children, he meant, had been inside the city walls

their entire lives. We had grown up quite sheltered in Melek, but wounds and death and loss were common among the children here. Many of their fathers bore permanent disabilities. Many of their mothers were widows.

"No, not like the children here," I agreed quietly. I hefted another bucket up to Mathoni. "At least their fathers will fight for them."

Lib straightened with a bucket in his hand. His long fingers gripped the rope and his arms were strong and sinewy. He had definitely put on muscle since we had been here, as had all the boys. I had, too, but it didn't show like that. It showed in other ways.

"It is a strong man who keeps his promises, Keturah, and a wise man who keeps his promises to God."

I knew that. I did. But my father was dead because he had kept a promise to God.

I felt a hand on my elbow and looked over into Lib's eyes.

"What's wrong?" he mouthed.

I shook my head.

"I heard your father was Anti-Nephi Lehi." The words came from Mathoni.

I looked up at him but didn't know how to reply. My mother had never admitted to it, even to being of the noble class in the old days in Middoni, but I knew it was true. It was not a secret. How could it be? The people remembered who we were. My father had been the king over our people, and he had lain down and died to avoid a fight. But Lib was right. Father had promised God he would never again take a life, not even in battle, and there was honor in keeping that promise.

"Well, I heard Ket single-handedly fought off a pack of Lamanite dogs," Reb light-heartedly called down from the top. "I heard she threw them a curelom tail."

It was a joke—it was so far-fetched. Most of the boys chuckled, but I glanced down at Gideon who was holding onto a rung and staring up at me. It wasn't that far from the truth.

Reb had cut through the tension on purpose to save me from having to answer, from having to explain, from having to admit that if my grandfather had not accepted the gospel the missionary Aaron taught to him, these boys wouldn't have been considered worthy enough to even look me in the eye as I passed by them in my grand chariot.

But Grandfather had accepted the gospel, and so many in his kingdom, including these boys' parents, had converted and come here to the Nephite lands. We had judges now, like the Nephites. There were no kings. And there were certainly no princesses.

Reb had changed the subject, but I saw the way the others looked at me. It was different. And none of them would look me in the eye.

We finished our final day in the trenches, and I dragged myself toward my hidden pool in the river. I was tired but filled with a sense of accomplishment. Lib and Ethanim went to bathe with the rest of the unit, but I promised Ethanim I would find one of my brothers to come with me and stand guard.

"I don't believe you," he said.

"Are you kidding? I've let you follow me everywhere for the past eight months. Have I ever given you any trouble about it? Have I ever gone anywhere without telling you?"

"No," he admitted, sighed, and trotted off after the other boys. But he called back over his shoulder, "Find your brothers. You promised."

And I actually planned to—if I happened to see one of them on the way.

I hadn't thought I would run into anyone, but when I passed Zeke's camp, I saw that he sat inside his tent, so I walked slowly toward it and called out his name.

He smiled the moment he saw me. "I was just going to go into town to catch the end of the market. Do you want to go?"

Then he got a good look at me. I must have looked bedraggled because he said, "Or we could just stay here and rest."

I looked down at myself. I was dirty, but I could walk to the city with him. "No," I said. "I'll go."

He gave me one last doubtful look, but emerged from the tent and jumped to his feet.

The main square of the city was still filled with people, though fewer than during the height of the market, which was in the early part of the day before it got too hot. The nights had become quite cool, but the days were still as hot as mid-summer.

Zeke walked first to the tanner's shop where he talked about leather and tanning with the owner while I fingered the beautiful pelts and soft skins he had available. Zeke and the tanner, whose name was Paachus, seemed to have developed a camaraderie already. It was obvious they had talked like this on other occasions. That didn't surprise me as Zeke was friendly and a good tradesman for his father's business. Perhaps this friendship would open lines for trade in the future.

Zeke purchased two lengths of buckskin and waited while Paachus tied them into a bundle that he could carry home. With a cheerful goodbye to the man, he turned me by the shoulders and hurried me out of the shop.

"Come on," he said. "I need to purchase soap as well."

"Didn't your mother send soap up with your father?" Dinah and Cana had sent me scented soaps, scents that would keep the mosquitoes, biting flies, and other bugs away.

"Yes," he said. "But I've used it all."

"Zeke!" someone called from behind us—a female someone.

As I whirled around, I caught the grimace on Zeke's face. But he had replaced it with a pleasant smile by the time he turned to face the girl who ran after us.

She was a pretty girl, shorter than me with rosy cheeks and large, bright eyes that shone when she looked up at Zeke.

She barely spared me more than a curious glance.

"Eve," he said. "Is something wrong?"

She shook her head, the soft glow on her face and neck accentuated because her hair was pulled up and braided around the crown of her head.

"No," she breathed. "Father said you purchased some buckskin and were working on a project. I thought you could use this." She held out two rolls of thin rawhide that could be used to sew or tie.

He glanced at me and then pulled out his coins.

"No!" she said. "I mean..." Her eyes dropped to the ground. "It's a gift."

Zeke sent me a pleading look. He was asking me what he should give to her in return. It would be very rude indeed to let her leave without a gift in return. I thought quickly. I didn't want him to give her a gift, but I wouldn't let him suffer the embarrassment of being unable to do so.

I cringed as I let my eyes fall on the cloth he wore to tie his hair back. It was old now, and plain, and though well-used, it was obviously well-loved and in good repair. It was the perfect gift.

It had been perfect when I had given it to him, too.

I had noticed he wore it a lot, but I hadn't understood that he wore it as a talisman until I saw in his expression how much he didn't want to give it to Eve. With an almost imperceptible sigh and a pained look in his eyes he reached back and slipped it from his hair which then fell down over his shoulders.

I watched as he let it fall into Eve's open hand.

After a pleased and blushing Eve left, we quickly went to buy the soap. Neither one of us spoke. I couldn't. The lump in my throat was too big. But as we walked back toward camp, I thought about that ragged piece of cloth. I had let him use that for so long. Had I never given him anything else to hold onto?

I realized he was guiding me toward my tent.

"I've got to bathe," I said, suddenly realizing that I was filthy and smelled terrible, and I had been standing next to that fresh-faced, petite young woman.

"Oh," Zeke said.

"Ethanim made me promise to take one of my brothers. I guess you'll do," I said with the best smile I could muster.

We changed directions and began to walk toward the pool.

"I wish you didn't think of me as a brother," he sighed.

Something about the blush on that girl's—Eve's—cheeks made me admit, "I don't think of you as a brother, Zeke."

He didn't say anything, didn't even smile, but the look in his eyes when he turned to me was so intense I had to look away. But I made myself look back.

"I'm sorry about before, about Eve," he said.

"It was just a bit of cloth."

"No it wasn't." He affirmed what I had only just realized.

We came to the pool. I dropped my satchel and looked up at him, squinting into the early evening sunlight that slanted toward us.

"I'll make you a new one. A better one," I resolved, and I hoped he knew I wasn't talking only about the hair tie.

He looked at me for a long moment, nodded in understanding, for once without disbelief or doubt in his eyes, and then he turned so I could take my bath.

Chapter 11

E arly in the evening before we were to march out as the decoy, I sat in my tent studying my plant book. In case I needed the information on our upcoming march, I told myself, but I turned to the page where I had pressed Gideon's moonflower. It had discolored, turned brown and yellow with time, but I fingered it and smiled, remembering the night he had given it to me.

"Keturah!" Darius's voice startled me. Everyone was away preparing the clearing for tonight or quietly making last minute adornments for their fine dancing clothes. It was quiet in camp, and I had been absorbed in my thoughts.

"I'm here," I called.

"Are you ready to go?" It wasn't my brother's dark head that appeared inside my tent, but Jarom's. When I looked over at him and met his eye, his face was close to mine.

"Hi," he said more softly, and then his eyes dropped to the flower I was twirling by the stem. "That from Zeke?" He frowned deeply.

"No," I said, but it did not ease the frown.

He looked at me for a moment. "It's time for the bonfire."

When I stepped from my tent, there was no one in camp except Ethanim who had undoubtedly been assigned to watch my tent, and was likely sore about not being with the others, wherever they were. It was still light out but the main bonfire had been lit. Other large fires were burning around the camp as well.

"I'm going with my brothers," I said, and Ethanim gave us a wave and went back to lacing bright red feathers into his headband.

I followed Darius and Jarom to a fire pit that lay between our camps. Young men milled around in the nearby camps—wanting to be present when the time was right, but not many approached the fire that already burned extravagantly in the midst of them. Chopping wood had not been one of my chores at home, as it was here, and one thing I had learned in the militia—fire was much more extravagant when you had to chop the wood yourself.

"Where's Kenai?" I asked. Since he was their captain, Kenai was usually with Darius and Jarom for things like this.

Darius gave a loose shrug. "Eli said he's gone."

So, I thought, Kenai had been sent as a pathfinder. He was scouting the terrain in preparation for the march. Knowledge of places to camp and natural embattlements to fight from, if it came down to fighting, would be to our advantage. When Kenai was gone, Eli assumed his duties, and the rest of us just accepted it and prayed for his safety.

I saw Zeke talking to some boys not far off. He gave me a small wave but stayed where he was, giving his attention to his men. Micah must have been around somewhere too, but I didn't see him.

"We're going to Eli's tent to get painted," Jarom said, and they hurried away. Darius was almost hopping in his excitement, but Jarom moved more slowly, glancing back at me over his shoulder.

I watched them go and then wandered closer to Zeke to

wait for him to finish his conversations.

It was too hot yet to be near the fire, though the nights and evenings had been getting cooler. It would be the rainy season before long—they said it even snowed here in the higher elevations. That was why we needed to draw the Lamanites out to battle soon. If we didn't, we would endure the long winter here in Judea with little left to do.

The trench and embankments were completed. The new watch towers were in use and occupied by soldiers at all times. The stores of wood and grains and other supplies were plentiful and the weapons of the city were strong and ready. I let my eyes fall on the embankments, visible above the city walls in all directions. We had built an impenetrable fort.

"The sunset is nice tonight." Zeke's warm voice filtered into my thoughts.

"Mmmm," I agreed as I moved my focus beyond the west towers. I took a deep breath. "Not like those at home, though."

He shook his head. "Do you miss it? Home?"

I took my time considering. I did miss our little house, my beautiful vegetable and herb garden, Mui, Kin and Kay, the meadow and the falls, and the familiar paths through the forest.

"Everyone I love is here with me," I finally concluded.

He was quiet for a moment, looking into the distant sunset. "That must be nice."

"You miss your family," I realized.

But of course he did. He loved his family. He had seen his father for a little while a few months ago, but that was hardly the same as living under the same roof with him. It couldn't compare to praying with his family each day, teasing his sisters, learning his father's trade by his side at the tannery, and eating his mother's cooking.

When he turned to look down at me his brown eyes were bright and thoughtful. "There are people here that I love."

It had been almost a year since we had marched to Judea.

I had turned sixteen and Zeke was nearing eighteen. Almost everyone had celebrated the day of their birth since we had come here. And in all that time, other than the way he looked at me sometimes, Zeke had shown me precious little affection.

"You know, it's not as bad as I thought it would be—having you here."

"You make my heart burn with adoration," I laughed.

He smiled too.

I hadn't realized how much I had missed his affection for me. Though I had made new friendships—Lib and Ethanim and Zach, Corban, and even Reb—no friendship would ever be like what I had shared with Zeke growing up. Not even what was growing between Gideon and me.

"You know what I mean." He took a breath. "But that could change tomorrow."

"I know," I said quietly. He would spend the march worrying about me. If the Lamanites overtook us and he was preoccupied with my safety, it would compromise the safety of his men.

The drum beat began. It was nothing like the incessant thrum we had heard on the march to Judea, but it was insistent in a different way.

I felt the rhythm in my chest like a heartbeat giving life somehow to my surroundings. The boys around me moved toward the fire. There were no stools tonight, no tree stumps or mats, none of the chairs that had been showing up recently at the camp fires. Even tents had been moved, and the area was clear and ready for this night.

I looked up at Zeke. He loved to dance and he was good at it—one of the best. I loved to watch him, and I knew I wasn't the only girl in our village who did. At home when we had bonfires in the clearing, Cana and Leda and I would dance with the other young girls. By the time I returned, they would both be dancing with the married women.

Each dance had a meaning and a purpose. The purpose of the dancing tonight was to prepare the men for battle, to excite them, to build up their courage. The steps and movements depicted combat, and the dance was even performed with an axe in hand.

Dancing was like anything else—not everyone was good at it. Not everyone liked doing it. Not everyone even approved of it. Some said it was too similar to the idol worship and drunken merriment of the Lamanites we had fled from. But some said God rejoiced in music and dance and it was a beautiful form of worship.

I happened to agree that it was a beautiful form of worship.

Satan had a way, I thought, of taking something beautiful and wholesome and twisting it into something sordid.

Darius and Jarom skipped up to us then dressed for the dance and clearly excited to begin. They wore beaded headbands made during long hours between training and work assignments. Streamers in greens and blues adorned their axes. Long yellow feathers had been assembled into fancy bustles for their shoulders and waists. Their sandals had been replaced with soft leather boots similar to the Zoramite style that went nearly to the knee. Besides those additions, they still wore their everyday tunics.

"You two better hurry," Darius said. Neither one of us was dressed in fine dancing clothes.

Before I could reply, Zeke said, "We'll be ready."

The younger boys looked us up and down, shook their heads, and ran off to join their friends.

I hadn't planned on dancing the war dance with the men—they wouldn't want me to, and besides, it just wasn't done. I had not gone to any trouble when dressing except to put on a bright-colored red and orange sarong and the long, soft boots Hemni had brought me from home. Dinah and Cana had done

115

some pretty bead work on both mine and Mother's. I looked down and admired it for a moment.

Zeke was wearing his everyday clothes too.

"Are you going to change?" I asked.

"I was headed to my tent when I saw you."

"I'll wait. Go on," I encouraged.

The sun slipped slowly behind the peaks to the west, leaving the horizon orange and red and the rest of the expansive sky a deep purple. After a few minutes more, the only orange left was that of the flames that shot up in large columns through the darkness.

There was no moon to give off light. I took a deep breath and looked around. I told myself I was looking for the other members of my unit—Lib, Ethanim, Josh, Corban, Reb, all of them—but I knew I was looking for Gideon.

Many of the young men had begun to dance. A few of the Nephite soldiers showed them the slow and simple steps of the war dance. I watched them for a while and committed the steps to memory as I had once done with the movements of the sword from my hiding place on the training ground.

"Here," Zeke said. He had come up behind me, and he wrapped a bright-colored blanket around my shoulders for warmth. I recognized it as the one from his bedroll, as one his mother had made. These were her geometric patterns woven into the thick cloth. Blue, green, orange and yellow patterns interlocked on a red and purple background. Fringe lined two sides. I pulled it close around me. It smelled like Zeke.

"Thank you," I told him.

"I thought the bright colors would be pretty."

I realized he didn't intend for the blanket to keep me warm. He intended for me to use it in the dance.

"Oh, I don't think they will be playing the shawl dance tonight," I protested, but there was wistfulness in my voice and in the silence that followed, I was sure Zeke had recognized it.

"So make your own dance," he said simply. He stood behind me with his hands holding the blanket on my shoulders as we watched the dancers together.

I craned my neck around and stared up at him for a moment. He had painted two red lines under his eye. I laughed lightly as I turned back around. "No one ever does that."

I could hear his smile in his voice when he leaned down to say into my ear, "And when have you done what other people do?"

I grinned because he was right.

That was when I saw Gideon and the rest of my unit approaching the fire. I thought they each looked taller than when I had first met them a year ago, and they were definitely stronger, made so by all the work and training we had done. Like Darius and Jarom, they had dressed for this occasion. Some wore feathers of various sizes and colors. Others wore skins or fringe made from flax or horse hair. Talons, teeth, beaks, claws, and various other special pieces decorated their costumes.

Most of them waved at or nodded to me as they passed and immediately joined the dancers in the large clearing around the fire. Gideon raised a brow at me and nodded to Zeke.

Embers shot up through the air, swirling on wisps of smoke. They were burning something that made me dizzy and I spread my feet a little to keep my balance.

"Are you alright?" Zeke asked.

I nodded. "The smoke," I said. "It's making me dizzy."

"Tuck your face inside the blanket for a few minutes," he suggested. "You'll feel better."

He was right. I did feel better, and soon I noticed we were both bouncing on the balls of our feet in rhythm with the drum.

"You want to dance," I said. "Go ahead. I'll be fine here."

I could feel his hesitation behind me, but he said, "Alright." I missed his warmth at my back when he moved away.

As he walked toward the fire, I caught my breath. Zeke

was not wearing a tunic.

My unit never went without their tunics. It was one of Seth's orders and was one of the inconveniences my unit suffered because of me. I knew most of the boys took their tunics off in the heat when they worked. Zeke's bare chest was bronzed from the sun as well as hardened from work. He wore only buckskin pants, a style that was common in Judea. The style suited him.

The pants were tied down the sides with laces of Eve's rawhide. I briefly thought of the bright-eyed girl from the Judean market, but I couldn't dwell on her because my eyes kept roving over Zeke as he crouched and began the footwork of the dance.

Zeke was traditional in every way. He asked my brother before he took me for a walk. He sought a traditional betrothal, forthrightly stating his intentions between our families. He worshipped as his parents did. He learned everything they said he should learn, including his father's trade, which I knew he didn't like all that much. He obeyed their wishes even when they weren't around. Traditional.

That was why the buckskin pants surprised me. Not because others didn't wear them, but because Zeke, of all people, was wearing them. And he looked fantastic in them.

His back was to me but soon, in the course of the dance, he turned toward me. Half of his face had been painted black and two horizontal red lines under his eye marked the other half. His chest was painted simply with the symbol of the wolf, which was his birth sign. His black hair, without my length of cloth to hold it back, fell loose beneath a simple rawhide headband that held feathers at the back.

He could not have stunned me more if he had tried. I tilted my head as I watched him dance. Perhaps he had tried. Perhaps this dance was for me.

He spun, arced his arms, planted his heel and then his toe on the ground in the intricate steps. He wore his father's soft boot moccasins too, making his steps appear feather-light. But I knew each step was deliberately placed and firmly planted.

Gradually, boys backed away and began watching Zeke. This was a dance where a dancer could show his expression and emotions, and Zeke was getting his across because everyone noticed. He performed with traditional exactness, but he had introduced a new element into it that I couldn't define. As I watched the stunning dance, I held a prayer in my heart for the beautiful things of this earth and a petition that I might be an instrument in destroying the things that were evil.

The music abruptly stopped and Zeke stood instantly motionless. A perfect ending.

When the music resumed, it was the slow beat of the war dance and the older Nephite men began showing the younger boys the steps once again. In the flicker of the firelight, it was an incredible sight to behold. I hoped the Lamanite spies were looking down from the hills on us now, and I hoped we struck fear into their hearts.

Zeke danced the war dance for a while, picking up the unfamiliar steps very quickly, before taking a short break to stand near me. Jarom and Darius danced in their feathers and swung their axes. My unit danced on the opposite side of the fire, even Gideon. Dancing seemed to me like something he might disdain. I had wondered if he would do it, but he was dressed up, and he was good at it.

The beat began to quicken into a beat I recognized, and someone began to sing.

Micah.

I looked around toward the drum and sure enough, Micah sat with three other men who played together in precise synchronization. I caught his eye, and he nodded at me.

It took me several long moments after the beat changed to realize Micah was playing a dance for me. Others could dance to this beat, but this was traditionally a song played for a girls' shawl dance. I stood stunned on the side of the clearing in the darkness beyond the firelight.

Boys began to look around. Antipus's men looked up in confusion when the younger boys began backing off the clearing. The beat thrummed on.

"Go, Keturah," Zeke said into my ear. He nudged me at my elbow and when I didn't move, he pushed me lightly at my shoulders.

I stepped tentatively out into the firelight. A shout went up and the singing got louder as more and more boys began to take it up.

I didn't know why I was so reluctant. The actions of the boys in my unit early on had affected me more than I had realized. I assumed the others wouldn't want me to dance because I was different. But that wasn't true.

I took a deep breath and began.

I spread my arms and let the bright colors of my shawl show. I spun my arms in circles, up and down, in a movement I knew from much experience would make the colors of the shawl impossible to look away from. I moved my feet in the exuberant kicking and pointing motions that created the illusion that I was skipping, that I ran and had no cares.

In my mind I was in the forest running as I had so often at home in Melek. The freedom and the beauty were too much for me, and soon I was dancing with wild abandon. I veered off the path, making the dance my own. I hopped over limbs, bounced off rocks. I was free. I was fast and light. But I saw something that almost made me stop.

My mother was dancing with me.

She held a shawl too, and we twirled around each other in a feverish whirl of color. We each made our own steps but they were one with the beat, and we had become one, and God looked down on us and smiled.

Chapter 12

That night was cold. I huddled alone in my bedroll within my tent, still giddy from the dancing.

After my mother and I had finished our dance, Kalem taught us the war dance, and Mother made us all laugh when she picked up a stick that was meant for the fire and wielded it in the dance as Darius wielded his axe.

Men had wandered in and out of the drum circle, so Micah had a chance to dance too. The only one missing was Kenai.

I thought of Kenai in the wilderness, sleeping out in the open. I wondered if he was cold. I wondered how many men he had with him. Would it be enough to keep a proper guard while they slept?

I drifted in and out of sleep. Finally, cold and tired, I sat up thinking I would make a fire outside and sleep next to it for warmth. But when I nudged back the flap of my tent, I saw that a small fire already glowed in our camp and Gideon sat alone and awake next to it. He was half turned away from me, a thick blanket wrapped around his shoulders. When he heard me, he glanced up.

I reached behind me for my own blanket.

"You should be sleeping," Gideon said as I situated myself next to him.

Ignoring his comment, I looked up at a deep blue sky awash with stars. It was very early morning. I wondered where we would be tomorrow morning and if it would be as cold as this one. I shivered. Hopefully we would be down out of the mountains a little.

"You can't sleep, either?" I asked. "Are you nervous about the campaign?"

He stirred up the embers with a long stick. "I would be foolish if I wasn't nervous, but I have faith that God will deliver us from the hands of the Lamanites. And anyway, that's not why I'm awake."

"Why are you awake, then?" I asked, my eyes still searching the heavens.

He didn't reply, but I felt him looking at me.

I drew in a quick breath and dropped my eyes to him. "Don't tell me you are still taking the third watch!" I exclaimed in a loud whisper. I shivered again and pulled my blanket more tightly around me. "I thought you guys had given that up months ago! I told Lib there was no reason, absolutely no reason, for you to stay awake to guard me here in camp."

The night consisted of four watches. An hour or so before dawn, this was the fourth watch, but since there were only three boys who wanted to guard me, they had divided the night into thirds.

"It was actually Mathoni's watch, but he stayed up so late dancing." Gideon shook his head. "I just let him sleep."

"You've been up since..." I quickly calculated in my head. "You've been up since midnight?" He couldn't have gotten much sleep before that. He had been awake nearly all night.

He shrugged. "I came back from the fire early."

I tried to remember the last time I had seen him at the

bonfire. How late had it been?

"Did you see me d-dance?" My teeth were chattering.

"I did," he said softly. "Come here." He opened his blanket to me. I hesitated for a moment, but slid over and let him wrap me in its warmth.

I settled against him, feeling lulled and natural in his arms. If he had come back after seeing me dance, he had gotten at least a little sleep. But it was the eve of our march past Antiparah, and he needed more rest.

"Did you say this was Mathoni's watch?" I asked suddenly.

"Yes, but just look at him." He gestured to where Mathoni lay snoring lightly on his pallet on the far side of the fire. His mouth hung open and the feathers on the headband he still wore lay askew. He looked like a little kid.

I smiled. "I see your point. But why was it Mathoni's watch? I thought the only ones who took a watch were Lib, Ethanim, and you."

"At first it was. But after a week or two, everyone wanted to take their turn. Sometimes your brothers arrange to come by and take a watch. Zeke too. Nobody ever told you?"

Completely taken by surprise, I just stared at him without saying a word. He was telling me the truth. Finally I turned back to the fire. "And has there ever been one single person or prowling animal approach my tent while I slept?" I asked tightly, trying to control my temper. It set me completely apart from the other men. It inconvenienced all of them.

"No."

"I don't understand," I burst out, still trying to keep my voice low. "There is no reason for this! Why do you keep this guard? And what are you even guarding me from?"

He pulled his blanket tighter around me trying to ease my shivering. He didn't answer right away, and I found that his slow breaths calmed me. When he finally did speak, he said, "Do you remember the stories of the battle at the city of Noah?"

"Of course."

"And what happened when the Lamanite soldiers saw the embattlements there?"

"The Lamanites intended to attack Ammonihah, but when they saw the embattlements, they retreated. They found the same thing at Noah, but they fought anyway and lost."

"And don't you think that if someone intended to do you harm, he might be deterred by a vigilant guard?"

I sighed. "I see what you're saying. Having a guard is not a matter of protection, but of prevention."

"Moroni has kept this nation alive with his preparations. If we do as he does, how can we fail?"

"Of course you're right. I just hate that you all put yourselves out for me. We all work hard. Everyone needs their sleep."

A smile lit his eyes. "All your good cooking makes up for any strength we lose from lack of sleep."

I smiled and tucked my chin into the blanket.

"And I don't know about you," he continued, "but when God commands me to do something, I do it."

I rolled my eyes. "God did not command any of you to guard me, though I do think Ethanim and Lib are under orders to befriend me."

"That is where you're wrong, Kanina." His voice had softened. "The Spirit of the Lord has spoken to each man in this unit. Our situation, with you among us, is unique. The Spirit directs us. How can we ignore it? Maybe you're right and you don't need the protection, but perhaps it is we who need the opportunity to prove our obedience." He pulled me closer against him.

Unable to resist the warmth, I relaxed into him. It surprised me when Gideon showed affection this way, seldom as it was, because he was so often aloof, glowering at others and keeping his opinions to himself even when they would be helpful. He was especially like this with me, but I knew it was because he was fighting his feelings for me. And if I hadn't returned his feelings, it might have been an easier fight for him.

We watched the fire together, burning there before us. We were illumed by its light. We were warmed by its heat.

"Gideon?"

He nuzzled my hair aside, and lightly kissed my neck. "Don't say it, Kanina. You won't be able to take it back, and you'll wish you could."

"Tomorrow," I went on, determined, sure his warm breath on my neck was an invitation. "If we have need to give battle—"

He drew back a little, letting a small chill inside the blankets. "I mean it, Keturah. One day you'll wish you had never said it to me."

I turned and looked deeply into his troubled eyes. How, I thought, could he speak with the Spirit in one moment, and be so anguished in the next? I searched the storms in his eyes for long moments, but of course I saw no answers.

Gideon rested his forehead on mine and murmured, "You can't take back the words."

"I won't say it then," I whispered, which I thought was as good as saying it—admitting the feeling was there. But my heart was bursting with unexplained feelings, feelings Gideon forbade me to give a name.

Why was it so hard *not* to say you loved someone?

"Thank you for teaching me to fight," I said instead.

The crackle of the fire punctuated his reply. "It was my honor."

My throat was tight and my heart was pounding with hard, fast beats that I was sure he could feel.

Then I felt his smile, and he said, "It was my pleasure."

I nearly laughed. "Did you only do it so you could be alone

with me in the meadow?"

He was quiet for so long I wished I hadn't asked it, but after a time he said carefully, "I did it because it was the right thing to do."

"Did you follow the Spirit or follow your heart?"

I was teasing a little, but he was thoughtful again. "They are impossible to separate. The Spirit works through our hearts, Keturah."

We fell silent again, listening to the sounds of the camp— the fire crackling, the chill breeze ruffling the tents, the rustling of blankets and the soft snores and slow breathing of the men around us.

"Even if we never get the chance to fight," I murmured into the blanket, "we at least have honor in being willing to do so."

Gideon put his lips to my hair and nodded. "You are wise, Kanina," he said.

"I'm a brat who always gets her own way," I replied.

"You can say that again," came a third voice.

I jumped and turned to find its owner in the pre-dawn darkness.

"Kenai!" I struggled to stand, wriggling out of Gideon's arms and throwing off blankets. "You're back."

He waved to the three other boys who had been with him as they continued walking past my camp, glancing at me with barely any interest. He stood with his hands on his hips, and I thought he looked a great deal like Micah. "I thought you'd have the corn cakes ready by now." He smiled at me but sent a curious glance at Gideon, who was now stacking wood onto the fire.

"It's not yet dawn," I said.

He nodded toward the east where the sky was fading from deep blue into a silver gray. How had I missed that? Boys in the other camps were starting to rise. My unit was still abed, not one of them stirring yet. My face turned hot when I realized they couldn't possibly have been asleep. My eyes shot to Gideon, something my brother didn't fail to notice. Had Gideon known the others were awake?

"I'll go to the supply station and get the things for breakfast then," I said. "Do you want to walk with me?"

He considered then shook his head. "I've got a blister on my heel I want to look at. I'll just stay here and talk to Gid for a minute."

I rolled up my bedroll and put it next to my tent. I reached inside for my satchel and began to rummage through it.

"I've got some of Mother's salve. It will prevent infection."

"I've got my own," he said flatly. "You go on." He sat near the fire, and he wasn't making any moves to check his feet.

I hesitated for a moment and then left. Something in Kenai's manner had been so weird. Had he seen trouble outside the walls? I turned as if one last look at him might make it clear.

I saw Gideon nudge Mathoni with his foot. I sighed, stopped, and waited for Mathoni to catch up. I had long since gotten used to their practice of sending someone with me everywhere I went. Lucky Mathoni would get to walk me into the forest before we fetched the rations from the supply tent. There was a latrine, but I always chose the forested area inside the walls for privacy. Another long walk that inconvenienced my unit.

If I had understood before I left the campfire why Kenai was acting weird, I wouldn't have gone. But with the busyness of the morning, I had little time to think about Kenai having a man to man talk with Gideon.

"Do you take guard duty a lot?" I asked Mathoni when we were walking away.

He yawned. "When it's my turn. A couple times a week, I guess."

"Why?"

He shrugged, and then he rubbed his palms into his eyes.

"How much of that did you hear—with Gideon?" I dared to ask.

His silence was answer enough.

"He's not the only one, you know," he said after a few moments.

"What do you mean?"

"When we take the watch, it's a duty. It helps to see you as a duty instead of, well, a girl."

"So flattering," I said, but I could see his point.

"I think that's why Gid does it twice as often as the rest of us."

Whether it served as a measure of prevention or perspective, I still didn't think I needed the constant companionship of my unit. But then someone at the rations tent, a large boy with a square face, snickered when he saw me and told the others I wouldn't be able to keep up with the army when we left the city.

"We'll have to stop and wait for her to catch up," he laughed as he eyed me up and down.

Mathoni pushed past him and led me swiftly back to our camp, and I thought maybe the companionship wasn't so bad sometimes.

After the flurry of morning preparations, we stood in our ranks. The Nephite soldiers paused and watched us leave. We traveled light with just our bedrolls on our backs, but every chief captain had been assigned a large pallet on which we carried our weapons and supplies under the large cloth covers.

We marched out through the main street of the city through the east gates, the same gates we had entered when we had first arrived in Judea. Having made friends here, many people came out to see us off. I saw Paachus and Eve and what must have been the rest of their family, a woman and a boy, standing in the main square where the markets were held.

Eve waved the cloth tie Zeke had given her. I thought of

the sword strapped to my back, and my hand went to its hilt over my shoulder. Lib followed the direction of my glower and cast me a questioning glance, which I did not answer.

I was close enough to the front of the column that I heard the heavy gates creek open, and I quickly forgot Eve. We paused before going through them as Helaman conferred briefly with the governor and Antipus. Shem strode quickly along the length of the column speaking briefly to each chief captain.

Finally, we were moving out through the gates. We cut across a meadow and met up with the West Road south of Judea. By midmorning we had reached a turnoff, and we took it. The West Road continued on to Manti, Zeezrom, and Cumeni to the south and east, all of which were controlled by the Lamanites. By taking this new road, we would pass close enough by Antiparah to be seen by the spies.

That thought made my stomach roil. I remembered what Mother had said that morning—and many other times—when she had hugged me tight.

"If you do not doubt God's power, He will protect and preserve you."

I sent up a prayer for courage. But for more than courage—for faith. Notwithstanding all my past bravado, just then my courage was waning.

I would be foolish if I wasn't nervous, but I have faith that God will deliver us from the hands of the Lamanites, Gideon had said.

I caught his eye and he offered me a small, reassuring smile. I offered him one in return, and the simple connection gave me some of the courage I needed. He believed in me, and I trusted his opinion.

I hadn't seen Zeke that morning or Micah or Dare, only Kenai when he had found me wrapped up in the blanket with Gideon. Mother and Kalem had come to say goodbye as I was cooking the last of the corn cakes. Some healers and cooks would follow Antipus and his men, but Mother and Kalem had decided to stay in Judea, a decision I supported because of the possible danger.

Kalem had taken me aside and offered his own words of advice. "If it comes to combat, go in with all your heart, heedless of all around you, mindful only of the man you're fighting. But keep a part of your senses open to other dangers."

I had nodded. Kalem and the other men had trained us on the tactics of the Lamanites. If I was fighting one man, there would be another waiting to cut me through the back. They liked to have two men to every Nephite. Kalem had been a skilled warrior for the other side, and I knew that when he offered this advice, he meant every word with the utmost fervor.

"Take care of Mother," I had said lamely, as if he wouldn't, as if he hadn't been doing so for thirteen years.

By midday the cool air had burned off. We ate our meal quickly and continued on the road. Our column was narrow, just five men wide, and the men on the outside edges could reach out and touch the trees of the forest that flanked the road in a foreboding enclosure.

We made camp early so we wouldn't be too close to Antiparah while we slept. At subsequent council meetings, we had discussed the idea of marching out in the late afternoon a day earlier, but in the end, Kenai recommended we leave at dawn and camp early in the evening. This way, we would have plenty of rest before gaining the attention of the Lamanite spies and having to start our retreat.

These were details not many of the soldiers knew. I had been lucky to gain entrance to the relatively small council that knew them, though I still didn't understand why, as I had no input of worth to offer.

Corban and Mathoni began food preparations when we stopped, so I had some time to wander down by the river. Reb and Cyrus trailed me.

"You guys could walk with me," I invited grumpily. "You don't have to trail behind me."

"We're keeping a distance for our personal safety," said Reb. "You're in a bad mood."

He was right, and I couldn't explain why. I had worked tremendously hard to get myself accepted into the militia, and I had been waiting and working—back breaking work—in Judea for nearly a year. The time had finally come when I might be of some use in forcing the Lamanites from our lands—and I was in a bad mood.

"I won't bite you," I said, annoyed.

"It's not your mouth I'm worried about," Reb said with a laugh, the same laugh that accompanied everything he said. "It's that obsidian blade you carry on your arm."

"I heard she took a man down to the ground with her blade at his throat," Cyrus put in.

"Oh yeah? I heard she can break a man's arm."

"I heard she can fight all day without breaking a sweat."

This had become a kind of game my unit played at my expense. It usually made me laugh, and I knew they were trying to cheer me up.

"I heard," Reb went on, "that she can slit a man's throat while serving a meal."

"Okay, okay," I finally laughed.

But they were both enjoying the game and kept it going.

"I heard that she once scalped a man and used the hair to build a nest for a bird that had fallen from a tree."

The noise of rushing water began to drown out their game as we approached the river. I had walked far from camp because I wanted to be alone to think. I should have realized what a joke that idea was. We had gone beyond the boundary of the stripling camps. We were carrying provisions with us, so no one had even ventured out this far to hunt. Sitting by this beautiful river would have been perfect for sorting through my thoughts if Reb and Cyrus hadn't been here. The sound reminded me of the sound of the falls near my home, my very favorite place to think.

As we emerged from the trees a movement caught my eye. When I turned my head to follow it, I saw three men in dirty loincloths on the opposite bank. One drank at the river. One stood to his knees in the water biting into a still wiggling fish. The third crouched alone on the bank near the packs and weapons they had dropped there, and it was this one who spotted us first.

We locked eyes.

Chapter 13

I had an arrow in my bow in seconds aimed at the man near their weapons. I wanted to shoot the disgusting man with the fish, but logic and training told me I must shoot the one nearest the weapons.

Later I would register that they had set their weapons down and what that meant—they had no idea we were camped nearby. Later I would register the look on the man's face when my arrow hit his chest. Later I would be glad Reb and Cyrus had trailed me into the woods playing their ridiculous game when I wanted to be alone.

But for now, it was kill or be killed.

Seconds after my shot hit its target, I saw the man with the fish grab his thigh. Good, my guards had both slung a rock and one of them had gotten a hit.

I grabbed another arrow as he stumbled onto the riverbank, took my aim, and he went down for good.

The third man had looked up sharply when he noticed the jerky movements of his companions and scrambled instantly into the trees. I could see him crouched there now, determining how to get his bow, which was out in the open, pinned under the first man I had shot.

I thought quickly, ducking into the cover of the forest behind me. The remaining man probably had at least one knife on his person, maybe more, possibly an axe, too. The river was not wide enough to prevent a good throw, and I was betting he had good aim. If we provided a target, he would hit it.

"Get down!" I yelled over the rush of the water, though Reb and Cyrus had already wisely done so. I snake-crawled toward them so we could talk.

"You guys run to find Helaman," I said when our heads were together. "Tell him the spies have seen us. I'll cover you."

We had to leave the last spy—for that's what they were—alive so he could report our presence to his leaders, but if we didn't watch him, we could each find a knife in our back.

They looked at each other, clearly unwilling to leave me alone. Hadn't I just killed two men while they had only managed to wound one between them? What would it take before they took me seriously, before they saw me as a capable warrior?

I could still see the Lamanite lying low on the opposite side of the river just as we were. I wasn't about to take my eyes off of him.

"Fine," I said harshly. "Reb, you go."

Reb was small and fast. He would be out of range before the Lamanite ever got a shot off, especially if he edged around the two thick trees behind us before he stood up.

A quick look passed between them and he was moving behind the trees and then up and running, darting between the trees before anyone could say another word.

A knife sank into the tree above our heads at the same time my arrow hit the dirt near the Lamanite's knee.

Cyrus and I waited out the Lamanite warrior for nearly a quarter of an hour. Other than throwing the knife when Reb left, he hadn't moved.

The man wasn't far away from us, but he couldn't come

at us because of the river. He would never get across it alive. We wanted him alive, but he didn't know that. He didn't know that if he just got up and ran in the other direction, we would let him go. But he wouldn't leave without his weapons, and I didn't blame him. I wouldn't have either.

Even if he got across the river, he knew there were two of us. Lamanites preferred the odds in their favor. That knife in the tree might have been his only one, but I doubted it. He could take both of us out if we weren't careful, and there was no doubt his plans didn't include leaving us alive if he could manage to leave us dead.

But Reb had already gone to report and to bring help, and that was the important part. I didn't know exactly what I expected Reb to do or how I planned to get myself and Cyrus away, but I didn't expect Reb to return with the other members of our unit.

I saw them all slipping quietly through the woods toward us using the trees for cover. Relieved to see them as I was, I sighed inwardly. Did they have a grand plan to get us away and leave the Lamanite alive? More than likely, they were just eager to see some action. I wondered if Reb had even reported the situation to our superiors.

I assessed this all in a glance, as I had my eyes and my weapon trained on the man across the river. After a few more moments, I felt Gideon ease up next to me.

"How many are there? Reb said there was just one," he said, his mouth near my ear. Even then, the rush of the water was so loud it was hard to hear him. Or was it the blood rushing in my ears?

I held up one finger on the hand that held my bowstring taut.

I felt him nod.

"The others have you covered. He can see he's outnumbered," he said a little louder. He placed his hand over mine on the bow. "Ease off," he instructed. "They won't shoot to kill."

At least Reb had described the situation accurately then.

With Gideon's strong hand on mine, I let the bowstring relax, and I let my eyes take a long, slow blink for what felt like the first time since spotting the Lamanite spies on the riverbank.

Unbidden and totally at odds with our dangerous situation, I thought of those days at the falls with Gideon. Back then, he had only touched my hand like this to adjust my aim. But he didn't adjust my aim now, just gently squeezed and said, "Come on. It's over."

Almost like we were running a drill back on the training ground, we took turns covering each other and dodging through the trees and underbrush to get further away. When we judged ourselves to be out of danger, we ran together as one all the way back to the commander's tent.

I could see that Reb had indeed relayed the information about the spies to Helaman because the whole camp was a flurry of motion. Men were packing gear and putting out cook fires.

Would the spy circle around until he had seen the size of our army? How long would it take him to get back to Antiparah? How long would it take to mobilize the troops there? Would they mobilize them? If we left camp now, where would we be when the Lamanites caught up to us?

Because they assuredly would catch up to us. Antipus anticipated that we wouldn't catch the attention of the spies until early tomorrow afternoon when we neared Antiparah, but the spy would be there long before that. He would run through the evening into the night. We had to be past Antiparah before Ammoron sent troops out, and unless Antipus left Judea earlier than planned, he would be unable to overtake the Lamanites in time.

I stood in front of the commander's tent and told Helaman all I had seen and done. Micah trotted up as I was finishing and made me tell it all again. He went pale and clenched his jaw when I told him how I had killed two men on instinct and adrenaline, but he didn't remark on it further. Reb and Cyrus vouched for the accuracy of my story.

"I feel we should move out," Helaman said grimly. "The Spirit is prompting me to march."

"We could go back the way we came," suggested Micah. "They wouldn't catch us."

"And lead them straight into Judea?" I exclaimed.

Helaman shook his head and frowned. "Keturah's right. We should continue as planned, but I can't see the wisdom in it."

"Not yet," said Shem with quiet resolve.

Helaman's hard look softened and he took a deep, renewing breath. "I can't see the wisdom yet," he agreed.

Helaman dismissed us to get our camp ready to move. Reb and Cyrus hurried back to camp but Gideon waited while I talked to Micah.

"It's my fault," I told Micah. "If I hadn't gone into the forest so far—"

"Why *did* you go so far?" he broke in, and he glared at Gideon as if it had been his fault.

"I wanted to think. The sound of the river reminded me of the falls at home. I just...I wanted to think," was all I could say.

Micah let out a long breath. He nodded. He knew how often I had gone to the falls to think and be alone. He had his own private places in the pastures where he went to be alone.

"Go pack," he said. "Quickly." Then he added, almost to himself, "I wonder how long until the whole of the Lamanite army knows there are girls in ours." He shook his head and gave me a hard, quick kiss on the forehead.

"It's not your fault," Gideon said when we were out of Micah's earshot.

"You know it is," I said morosely.

"Then I share the blame for suggesting we decoy them

from their stronghold in the first place."

"No!"

"Keturah, it is no one's fault. You have to stop thinking that way."

"But, if I hadn't gone so far, they wouldn't have spotted us so soon."

"Yes they would have. They were almost on top of us, Keturah. Once they left the river, they would have noted our position almost immediately."

"Not if they went in the other direction!" I protested.

He shook his head. Then he laughed.

I looked at him in confusion and when he didn't stop grinning, I started to get annoyed.

"What?" I finally snapped.

"You really are in a bad mood. You just shot two men through the heart, and a third had only a narrow escape."

Pouncing suddenly, I put him in a headlock. I moved so unexpectedly he didn't have time to defend himself.

"But the really funny part," he said, laughing, from inside the crook of my elbow, "is that you're more concerned about the one who got away."

I brought my foot down hard on his, but I released his neck.

"What do you mean?"

"You're the only one in this army who has ever killed a Lamanite."

Did that mean he hadn't found the Lamanite who raided his family's farm? I wondered, but of course he didn't elaborate on his past.

"And at this moment that spy is doing exactly what we want—running back to Ammoron's army to tell them we're here. This is exactly what we wanted to have happen, and it's even better because we hadn't anticipated being able to pinpoint the exact time the spies knew of our presence."

I stopped walking. "I hadn't thought of it that way."

"I noticed," he said rubbing his neck.

"Sorry," I said.

He waved it off. "I have three brothers."

I resumed walking, increasing my pace, feeling the urgency of our situation as I watched everyone around me hurrying to pack up their camps.

"Who told you I was in a bad mood?" I asked.

"You've been melancholy all day. It's just nerves. You're wound tight—that's all. Everyone is," he said, trying to spare my feelings. I knew all the boys in my unit were talking about it. It spoke for the boredom we had been feeling in Judea when my bad mood was the most interesting topic of discussion. But Gideon was right. Everyone was feeling nervous and edgy.

When we arrived at our camp we only had moments before the drum sounded the lineup. Lib stood there holding my pack, having already secured my belongings to it. I thanked him gratefully and let him strap it onto my back. Then we hustled toward the column.

As soon as we were under way, Reb said, "I heard Keturah was in such a bad mood she killed two men before the evening meal just to whet her appetite."

"The way I heard it," called Corban, "was that Keturah killed two men before you two ever pulled your slings."

"I heard Keturah shot two men in the heart with both hands tied behind her back," called Noah.

"No, no! I heard she did it with her eyes closed!"

"While laundering tunics!"

"With a basket on her head!"

Lib and Ethanim both laughed. They all laughed. I couldn't help it, and I burst out laughing too. My eyes, shining with amusement, caught Gideon's. He shrugged and gave in to laughter too.

By nightfall, word came back through the line that we had

made it beyond Antiparah and we were northwest of the city by an hour's walk. Knowing that potentially, though probably not realistically, the Lamanite army could descend on us before we got our cook fires lit was a daunting prospect. Not that there would be cook fires tonight.

I watched as small groups of boys dismantled the pallets full of food, tents, and extra weapons. They began to distribute the provisions to be carried in individual packs. The pallets couldn't be carried at a fast clip, which I assumed Helaman anticipated for the next day. Besides, we were no longer pretending to carry provisions. We were fleeing.

Once we had settled in and had eaten a cold meal, there was nothing much to do but sleep. Mathoni had already succumbed to the fatigue of the march when Ethanim nudged him awake for a unit prayer, something we had taken to doing at Seth's behest.

One by one the boys in my unit, whom I had begun to regard almost as brothers, fell into even breathing and light snoring. I was tired, but I couldn't sleep.

As was apparently his habit, Lib sat up for the first watch. I was still awake when he woke Reb for the second watch.

I lay curled on my side staring at the moon through the pines. I was still and silent. I assumed that I appeared to be sleeping, but after the few minutes it took Lib to drop into sleep in his bedroll, Reb moved so he was sitting beside me.

My back was to him, but I heard his low voice when he asked, "You okay?"

Was he talking to me? I rolled slightly and looked up at him. He sat with his knees up and his stubby arms clasped around them. He was regarding me with the most serious look I had ever seen on his face. "You want to talk about it?" he asked with an unexpected understanding in his voice.

But of course he understood. He had been there. He had gotten off a shot as quickly as I had, and he too had hit his target—a living, breathing man.

I lay on my back and looked at the stars, so brilliant in the dark sky. The slivered moon was low in the sky and gave off little light to diminish the brilliance of the stars.

"I don't really want to talk about it," I said. I wouldn't have even known where to begin. "But thanks," I added.

I saw his slow nod from the corner of my eye. He waited quietly and didn't push me to talk.

Without realizing I had put words to my thoughts, I asked him, "Do you think we did the right thing?"

He looked down at me. "It was perfect. Flawless."

His comment surprised me because his face looked so pensive, maybe even a little regretful.

"Yes, but did we need to kill them?" This question had been going through my mind over and over.

"Of course," he said immediately. "Do you think they would have let us walk away? Three kids tramping through the forest, miles from anywhere, each carrying weapons of war?"

"I guess not."

"If nothing else, they would have taken us captive. They would have had to."

I nodded, considering this, realizing the truth of his words.

"You got off a nice shot," I said.

He smiled ruefully. "We were close enough I should have hit a more vital part. But to tell you the truth," he leaned toward me and lowered his voice, "it all happened so fast. I had slung my rock before I even realized I'd done it. I don't even remember drawing the rock from my bag."

I hummed my agreement—yes, it had happened very fast.

"I guess you can't really second guess yourself in situations like this. You just have to hope that your training and preparation has been enough to help you do the right thing," he said.

Our conversation died out then. But just before I let my eyes drift closed I said drowsily, "Thanks, Reb, for taking the watch."

I thought I had only closed my eyes for a moment, but when I opened them, Reb was gone and nothing but darkness sat above me. Disoriented, I leaned up on my elbow and saw Zeke sitting quiet and alert a short distance away. I could just make out his features in the dim night. I could see he was looking at me because the starlight glinted from his eyes.

"What's wrong?" he asked quietly.

I looked around. Had I heard something in the brush? Felt something in the earth?

Everything was still. A chill breeze rustled the leaves on the trees. I could hear the murmur of the camp's guards to my left. I couldn't see the moon. Most of the night had passed.

"I heard what happened," Zeke spoke with concern in his voice. After a moment he added, "Did you have a nightmare?"

I rubbed my forehead and sat up. "I don't think so. What are you doing here?"

"I'm on watch."

I accepted this and looked around again, scanning the darkness. Something was wrong. I felt it. I couldn't explain it. But I felt it.

"And anyway," Zeke broke into my thoughts. "It's almost morning."

I nodded, and I moved to sit next to him.

"I..." he paused, tried to form what he wanted to say into words. "I didn't believe it when Micah told me why we were continuing the march, but his manner was so grim I knew he wasn't lying."

I smiled tiredly. Micah would never lie. He was so good.

"I've been keeping the watch. Gid tried to take it, said it was his turn, but I told him to go back to sleep. I just had to see for myself that you were okay."

"I hope you weren't up all night worrying about it," I said. "You'll be tired."

"That sounds like concern."

"I'm not the one taking an extra turn at watch duty."

"I was worried about you, that's all," he admitted. "And anyway, I couldn't sleep."

"Did Gideon go back to sleep?" I glanced over at him in his bedroll, answering my own question. He lay on his stomach with his face turned away from us.

"Not right away. He sat up with me for a while."

I went still. After a minute I said, "Glad I was asleep for that."

Zeke reached out and touched my cheek with the back of two fingers. He stroked slowly for long moments. I kept my eyes averted. He paused, then slid his fingers under my chin and tilted it up until I met his gaze.

"Don't become so hardened that you can't accept gentleness," he said.

I looked down into my lap. "At the river...when I killed those men...I had to do it."

His long fingers went into my hair at my nape and his thumb stroked my face in their place. He dipped his head to catch my eye again, and I acquiesced and looked at him through my lashes.

The sky was beginning to lighten, though dawn was still beneath the horizon.

"I know you did, Keturah. From all accounts, it was the perfect outcome. Killing two of their spies will be enough to incite their anger. They will assuredly leave their stronghold now to march against us."

I looked at him woefully. "We cannot stand against them, Zeke." A note of unfamiliar despair touched my voice.

"Helaman sent messengers. Antipus will come," he replied firmly.

I shook my head, and unable to hold his gaze I said, "No, we've marched past Antiparah too early. He will be too late." I took a deep and shaky breath. "And it is my fault."

A lump had formed in my throat, but I spoke my fears and my guilt to him because we had an ease between us that I didn't have with anyone else, an ease that had been formed over a lifetime of playing and arguing, of living together in the village. Reb and I had briefly shared what we had in common, but that was all. I could talk to Gideon about many things I would never bring up with Zeke, but not this. This was a path through my heart that I could only travel with Zeke, my oldest, dearest, truest friend.

He listened while I spoke. Still his thumb moved over my face, slowly and gently. "Do you not think God guided your steps yesterday? Do you not think he guided your arrows?"

I was a good shot, but under duress? Reb's prank while we were hunting proved I wasn't as good as I thought.

"Keturah, have you asked God for his assurances?"

I didn't trust my voice not to break. Gazing gloomily into my lap, I shook my head. A tear slid from my eye and Zeke swiped it quickly away.

"I worry. This is not a Keturah I have seen before—sulky and afraid." He hesitated. "If you wish it, I will take some of my men and escort you back to Judea."

I looked up sharply. "No!"

He looked at me sternly for a moment. I could see his features clearly now in the gray, pre-dawn twilight. His long hair was tied back with a strip of bandage. The long, handsome lines of his face had firmed over the last year, as had the muscles in his arms, shoulders, and back. His faith, too, had become rock solid.

"Then take your courage in your hands, Daughter of Helaman," he said roughly as he took my small hands and clasped them between his large, strong ones, a contrast that was impossible to miss. "Lean on the faith that has gotten you here, and do not doubt it!"

His words stung me, cut to my soul. I looked at him with wide eyes I knew shimmered with tears that I resolved I would not shed. Neither Lamanite spies, nor Ammoron, nor his vast host of savage, blood-drinking warriors would draw my tears from me.

Zeke glanced at the sky and then stood. He pulled me to my feet and hugged me to him. His words had been full of faith and comfort, but I felt all the fear he had for me in the desperate strength of his embrace.

There was a commotion down the column of sleeping boys. I turned in his arms to look toward it. A torch had been lit at the command tent. Kenai stood there talking earnestly to Helaman, their heads bent together.

I looked up at Zeke.

But he didn't look at me.

Suddenly Gideon was standing beside us.

"Zeke, what is it?" he asked.

Zeke spared him a glance but didn't answer, just stood staring at Helaman's tent, trying to determine what was going on.

I looked between them. We all knew what was going on.

A shout rang out. Then more shouts. A boy I recognized from Kenai's fifty, a nice boy from my village named Jonas, ran down the column calling for us to line up.

Zeke turned back to me. "Get your things. Quickly!" He kissed me hard on the mouth.

A look passed between Zeke and Gideon, but it had nothing to do with the kiss. It was an appeal for Gideon to watch over me while Zeke could not, a transfer of responsibility that, at that moment, I felt comfort in, not resentment. Gideon gave an almost imperceptible nod. Then Zeke was gone, rolling his bedroll up as he ran toward his men.

Chapter 14

We hadn't been told why the march had been called so early, but all two thousand of us had a pretty good idea, and none of us wasted time asking questions. Even if we hadn't been aware of the danger, when Helaman gave a command, we followed it.

Not long after we began to march, the sun rose. We descended down out of the hills, as I had been hoping we would, and around midday we could see the seashore through the trees. After that, our elevation dropped so low we could no longer see the sea.

We did not take any breaks through the morning, and six hours went by before we stopped. Though we spread out a little and sat down on the road to eat, we did not break ranks.

No one had yet informed us of the situation. We knew we fled from the Lamanites. We guessed they were pursuing us and wondered how close they actually were. Had our haste been a necessity or merely a precaution?

Everything we had done up to that point had been precautionary—constructing the embankments, building the watch towers, and refurbishing the weapons. We had always had plenty of time to do what needed to be done. As exciting as it was, acting with this immediacy also made me nervous.

I was sitting on the dirt road between Lib and Ethanim eating my rations when I heard Helaman call for our attention.

"My little sons," he called out. When we quieted, he began speaking to us. "Before dawn our spies came to the command tent with news of Lamanite movement within the city of Antiparah. We had hoped it would take them longer to mobilize, but they were marching out of the gates before the sun arose. This is the cause of our haste this day."

I heard hushed murmurs go through the column of boys, but they didn't last long because everyone wanted to hear what else Helaman would say.

"In a few minutes we will take up our march again. You have well prepared yourselves for this day, but I feel a great urgency that the Lamanite army must not fall upon us. I am waiting for the spies to return. Then I will decide on a further course of action."

This time only somber quiet fell down through the column.

Helaman went on. "Unit leaders, see that each of your men tends to all his needs—eats, drinks, and rests. Then, my little sons, gather with your units for a prayer."

A messenger jogged to the rear of the column to repeat the message in case they hadn't heard it. I turned to watch him go. When I turned back around Lib was waiting to catch my eye.

"I'll walk you into the forest." He got to his feet and then gave me his hand. "Come on."

I nodded and took the hand he offered. His grasp felt firm, certain, and reassuring.

Lib, Ethanim, Reb and Noah all walked me into the forest. We talked and joked, but I could see their eyes roving through the vegetation and though they didn't rush me, we all felt a sense of urgency and a desire to be back with the main company as soon as possible—though even that would not be enough protection if the Lamanites caught up to us.

I wished we were higher in the hills again so it might be possible to get a glimpse of the enemy troops, to judge their distance from us and their numbers. But then again, that might make matters worse. I was having trouble keeping my midday meal down as it was.

I must have looked pale because Lib sat me back in the column and sent Corban, Noah, and Mathoni to fill my water skin for me.

"I can do that," I protested as they walked away.

"I know," Lib said, but he didn't call them back.

Kenai had been out scouting last night, which meant he was probably in the column now. Good. Worrying about Kenai, where he was and how he fared, was wearing on me.

I felt a sudden flash of guilt thinking of all the people who worried about me because of my stubborn insistence on being here—Zeke, for one, and my mother and brothers, Kalem. Even the boys in my unit worried about whether they could keep me safe. I said a quick prayer that God would bless those people with peace concerning me and then I put it from my thoughts, following Kalem's advice to keep my whole mind on fighting the enemy.

I drew my knees up and lay my cheek on them, letting my eyes drift closed to rest as Helaman had advised. I had only intended a brief respite, but I had been up early the past few mornings, not to mention marched a myriad of miles through the hills, and Lib awoke me with a gentle hand when the rest of the unit gathered to pray.

Gideon offered up a prayer when we had all knelt in a circle in the center of the road and bowed our heads before God. It had been nearly a year since I had met Gideon, and I had heard him pray plenty of times. This prayer, however, was filled with so much conviction and faith I did not doubt that Gideon knew

God would protect us.

"We know that Thou art with us," he said, "and will not suffer that we should fall by the hand of our enemy."

When the prayer was done, I looked up, and our eyes met across the circle. It was the wrong time. He was the wrong boy. But I loved to look into his face. I loved the private smiles he gave to only me. But Micah would betroth me to Zeke when we got home, and this all had to stop. I found myself rubbing the ache from my throat.

I turned to Lib. "I want to go talk to Micah."

"I want to see what the hold-up is," said Gideon quickly, and he jumped to his feet.

Gideon led me away toward the middle of the column. Many of the boys we passed were resting as best they could on the road. Many were talking quietly to each other, their nervous faces showing anticipation too.

I was too aware of Gideon walking next to me. I wanted to touch his hand, his arm. I wanted to go into the forest and forget about the boys on the road. I was sure just a moment alone with Gideon would ease the ache in my throat. But it was not only impossible, it was wrong to want it.

We found Micah standing with arms folded listening to Shem. His eyes flashed to me long enough to register my presence, but he kept his attention on what Shem was telling him.

While Gideon and I waited for him to finish, I studied Gideon. He was nineteen now to my sixteen. His shoulders were broad and thick like the Nephite warriors Antipus commanded. His brown hair was cut short and it curled at the ends, a wayward lock, sweat-soaked and windblown, falling across his brow. His forearms were hard as rock, his hands rough and scarred from hard work. The light scar that curved around his eye made him look dangerous.

And he was dangerous. Everything about him was lethal,

but the biggest threat he posed was to me alone.

"Gideon?"

He had noticed me studying him but had stood still and let me do it. He kept his eyes on the trees behind Micah and Shem.

"Hmm?"

"Did you find me on purpose that first day we met? Near the obsidian." The words tumbled out. "I mean, did you follow me or hunt me down or something?"

He frowned. "Have you been wondering about that?"

"Yes." *Very often.*

The broad-shouldered man disappeared and the toe-shuffling kid appeared in his place for just a moment. When he spoke though, he was bold, refusing to be embarrassed, and he spoke slowly as if he were choosing his words carefully as he went. Either he didn't want me to misunderstand—or he did.

"I had been out hunting." He cleared his throat. "I was returning when I saw you in the thicket of trees, twirling that moonflower around absently while you watched the boys on the field."

I looked down, trying to recall the moment.

"And you followed me when I ran into the forest?"

"Not exactly," he hedged. "At first I thought to let you leave unchallenged. I thought you were only taking a moment to watch your brother or maybe a betrothed, but then I remembered the rumors of the girl warrior, Kenai's sister, who could best any man on the battlefield, and I wondered if you might be her. I tracked you more or less out of curiosity."

Curiosity. I rolled the idea around.

"And the first time at the falls? Did you follow me then?"

"I wouldn't mind knowing the answer to that myself." Zeke drew up on us from the flank. "Though I am much too polite, you know, to ask."

I could hear the playfulness in Zeke's voice. I spun

quickly and jabbed him in the ribs. He smiled and batted my hand away.

"Hey, Gid," he said. "You still putting up with this little rabbit?"

I jabbed at his ribs again, and again, he batted me away.

"Keturah is not hard to put up with," said Gideon. "If you think she is, perhaps you should revise your plans for her future."

Zeke's eyes narrowed slightly, but he kept the smile on his face. "I bet you just stay up nights thinking of ways to put up with her," he said.

They glared at each other.

But before I could reprimand either one of them for the complete inappropriateness of their comments, Zeke surprised us both. He broke the eye-contact, looked at the ground and then back up at Gideon.

"Gid, I'm sorry," he said deliberately. "I didn't mean that. Truly." He scratched the back of his head. "I thank the Lord every day that Keturah sleeps within the circle of your protection. I know that if it was necessary, your sword would be swift."

Gideon shifted uncomfortably. Zeke was not speaking of using the sword against the Lamanites. Surely it would be better for me to die a swift death than to be taken captive by our enemy.

"As would your arrow," Gideon said softly.

I looked between their hard faces, and rolled my eyes. Nobody was going to have to kill me swiftly. "The only thing killing me is this conversation," I said.

"See?" A small smile played at Zeke's lips. "No one else could put up with Keturah." I punched him in the arm, but he grabbed my hand and locked my arm behind my back. "Any man would fall in love with her if he were in your place."

Gideon didn't deny it. I wanted him to look at me, but he held Zeke's gaze.

Zeke lowered his voice and stepped closer to Gideon. "I know she trusts you, and I trust you with her safety." He eased the tension on my arm then, and when I looked at him, he said softly, "Forgive my rash speech, Ket. I overreacted."

"No, I spoke out of turn," said Gideon quickly. "I provoked you."

Zeke shook his head. "Either way, I do not wish to go into battle with ill feelings between us."

"Battle?" I broke in. "Have the spies come in then?"

Zeke turned to me and nodded. "I was just at the front talking to Kenai."

"He wasn't out today was he?"

"No. But they all report to him. You know that."

I hadn't known that, but I nodded.

"We have to march out immediately," he said. "The only delay is Helaman." He gestured to the woods at his back. "He's in the forest praying."

This was the exact reason the stripling warriors had asked Helaman and not some other commander to lead them, so no one begrudged him the time he spent now seeking the Spirit's guidance.

Micah finally joined us, eyeing both Zeke and Gideon carefully. He knew something had just happened. He had seen me with Gideon, and he had talked with me about Zeke. He wasn't blind. He knew I cared for both of them. In fact, we all knew it, and that was what made it all so fraught with tension. It was also, I suspected, what made it all bearable.

Before Micah could say anything, the call came to line up. I doubted the order to move out would be much behind it. I quickly kissed both Micah and Zeke on their cheeks, wished them well in whatever was to come, and ran with Gideon for our place in the column.

"You think Zeke will be happy with that sisterly kiss?" he asked as we ran.

I grinned. "I think you're jealous you didn't get one."

The march continued and though we moved swiftly and

with no breaks, we had spent a year building up our endurance with long runs and extended hunting excursions, so we were prepared. Building the embankment had strengthened us too—and not just physically. Learning to keep going even when we were tired was serving all of us well.

We hadn't been moving long when the front lines of the column began veering off the road into the trees. After a few moments we arrived at the point where Shem was turning the column. He talked earnestly to Seth, Gideon, and the captain of Seth's other fifty, Japeth, who had all run up to meet him. As Gideon came back, I caught the grim determination on his face.

When our captains were done realigning us and turning us toward the wilderness so we walked into it, the column was twenty men across with two units in each row. Our instructions were simple: spread as far as necessary to march between the trees, and move twice as fast as we had previously been moving.

The sense of urgency was so great that I found myself glancing back over my shoulder several times to see if Ammoron's army was right on our heels. They weren't—not that I could see.

Fortunately, the hills had tempered into a gently sloping grade that angled down to our left and probably slipped right into the West Sea South. Our pace on the road had been a fast walk. Doubling it put us at a jog. We were in our eighth hour with just the one break at midday. Despite the faster pace, it actually felt better because I was using different muscles and working through the stiffness that had begun to set in during the late morning.

Seth ran us for an hour and then decreased the pace back to a brisk walk for the next half an hour. We were to repeat the pattern until Seth received a command to halt.

"Are we to keep this up even into the night?" I asked Lib who jogged beside me on the soft ground of the forested terrain.

"If necessary," he confirmed.

We were in a full-fledged retreat.

But all we had to do was do that well. All we had to do was stay ahead of the enemy until reinforcements arrived. All we had to do was run through the forest, and that was one of my favorite things to do. I was here doing it with friends and doing it for a noble cause. Together we were just one part of this stratagem against the Lamanites. I knew a time might come when we would have to turn and fight, but for just now we merely had to run.

A year ago it might have been a problem for some of the boys, but I didn't—truly didn't—think there were any boys in the militia that couldn't run until nightfall. And with God's help, well there just wasn't a limit to how far and fast we could run.

We kept up this pace until twilight covered the forest. After we had walked slowly for a time to cool off, we sank down with our units to rest and eat. We ate another cold meal and then settled down to sleep. No fires glowed in the camp. I wanted to find Kenai and ask him how far back the Lamanites were, if they had turned off the road as we had, if Antipus had been spotted. But I was asleep before I could even complete the thought.

Ethanim woke me before dawn.

"The spies say the Lamanite camp is already moving. We have to go," he said quietly.

Before I even sat up, I reached into my satchel and withdrew a corn cake that was cold and hard and dry, but I started taking bites of it immediately and swallowing as quickly as I could.

I had filled my water skin last night so it was ready to go—for to be without water in the wilderness was to die—but I went to the small creek and drank deeply. In fact, I drank so much I thought I would probably get a cramp in my side when we started to march. But my body needed the water—I was feeling signs of dehydration—and I didn't know how available water would be during the day. I didn't know what the day would hold.

We began moving swiftly through the trees again. This was the third day of our march and fatigue was setting in. I could see it in all the boys around me. I could feel it in my own limbs and in the heaviness of my eyelids.

Every once in a while I could glimpse the shining green sea through the trees. The Sea Road I had heard about must be just below us. It would have been nice to travel on it instead of through the wilderness, over the uneven and sloping terrain as we were, but we were much better hidden in the trees.

We didn't talk much through the morning, except for Reb, who told joke after joke which everyone within hearing distance laughed at half-heartedly.

We had only been moving an hour or so when we saw that the column had stopped. When we neared the gathering group of striplings that were drinking from their water skins or were bent over, hands on knees, catching their breath, Isaiah, the chief captain over our thousand, directed us to loop around and make a wide crescent around Helaman.

"We've come a long way north," I remarked to Gideon as we sat on our heels and waited for further commands. "Do you think we're as far north as Melek?"

"I doubt it. We only turned north yesterday."

"But we ran half the day."

He shrugged and bit into an apple. He passed one to me. "Eat. It will help with the thirst."

Lib sat on my other side. "Haven't you been drinking?" he asked. Was that concern or anger?

"Of course I've been drinking." I usually allowed myself only a ration of water, but I always drank when needed.

The tartness of the apple seemed to do the trick. I wasn't sure about hydration, but it eased my thirst. I ate it hungrily as I watched Gideon eat his in five big bites.

A messenger ran past us calling for captains, chief captains and the council to assemble to the north.

Gideon chucked his apple core, got to his feet, and held out his hand for me.

"But I'm not a captain," I protested, shrinking from his hand.

"Helaman's been inviting you to council meetings for a while now. That makes you in the council. You're so dumb sometimes."

I shot to my feet. "Dumb?"

He laughed, took my hand in a firm hold, and set off to the north at a jog. I tried to drop his hand, but he held it tightly and I might have seen a small smile. It was a very poor time to be teasing me. Gideon walked me directly to Zeke, squeezed the hand he still held, let it go, and walked away.

"Did he really just do that?" Zeke asked, with more disbelief than anger.

We both stared after him. I didn't bother answering.

"Sometimes that guy is so weird," Zeke muttered under his breath.

It had become a strange situation, the three of us, and I thought Gideon just dealt with it in his own way—blatant refusal to hide our friendship.

"You should go stand with your captain," Zeke said.

I looked up at him. He meant it.

"My captain brought me here. He wants me to stand with you."

He scoffed. "I only care what you want." He looked hard into my eyes a moment more and then he nodded his head in Gideon's direction. "Go."

"Don't be a bully." I sidled up to his shoulder and turned to face Captain Helaman who was calling for our attention.

"The Lamanites have stopped pursuing us," Helaman said, getting right to the point. He turned to Kenai to confirm this.

Kenai nodded. "We saw them move out this morning but

they did not pass the checkpoint we set."

I wondered if Kenai had slept at all since we had left Judea. There was darkness under his eyes and a gauntness to his face I had not seen on him before.

Helaman spoke again. "Perhaps they have halted their march so they might catch us in a snare."

He let that sink in for a moment. We all knew the risks of turning back. We could continue on, circle back around to the West Road, return to Judea in safety, and know we had done our part in the plan. We had discussed all this before as a council, and I knew what the others would want to do.

"Therefore what say ye my sons?" Helaman asked into the silence. "Will ye go against them to battle?"

I heard the crunch of the bark and leaves on the forest floor as Zeke stepped forward. I felt the brush of his skin as he stepped away from me. "Father, behold," he said, and he swept his strong arm out to indicate the circle of boys. "Our God is with us, and he will not suffer that we should fall." I looked around at the council and the two thousand faithful warriors they led. He was right. God had protected us so far.

"Let us go!" called Seth suddenly, his kohl-rimmed eyes filled with excitement.

All eyes turned to him, but someone else called out, drawing all eyes back to the other side of the circle.

"We would not slay our brethren if they would let us alone!"

I turned to see who spoke, but I couldn't see over the boys behind me. I caught Gideon's eye as I turned back around. He folded his arms and looked between me and Zeke.

Micah stepped into the center of the circle. He was looking at me too, but he turned his eyes to our commander when he spoke.

"Our fathers made an oath that they would never take up their weapons in battle, but we have made no such oath."

As he spoke, I thought of our father leading his people out to battle. Mother often said Micah was like him, and as he spoke with quiet power, I could see what she meant. He was the eldest son of the dead king, and each of these boys knew it— except perhaps Micah himself, but surely he had heard the rumors, surely he could remember being very young.

He looked around at the council of boys. "We have promised instead that we will never give up our liberty, and that we will fight in all cases to keep ourselves and the Nephites out of bondage." His voice rose as he drew each boy into his words. "We will protect the land unto the laying down of our lives!"

Kenai stepped up behind Helaman and gave the most convincing argument. "Let us go, lest they should overpower the army of Antipus."

Were Antipus and his army here then? I tried to see the answer in Kenai's eyes. They shone with determination, but I couldn't see the answer.

Helaman nodded and frowned. Then he turned to look at me. Three quick steps brought him to face me. "And what is your opinion, young Keturah? Should we march out to meet the Lamanites in battle?"

Chapter 15

Did he want me to temper the zeal of the boys? Was he looking for fear? For caution? For faltering faith? If he was seeking those things in me, he wouldn't find them.

I looked at Zeke, who stood next to me utilizing the moment to secure his hair back. He was preparing for battle. Gideon regarded me with his determined black gaze. He stood with Enos, Seth, and Eli, and their hands each gripped the hilts of their swords. They stood ready. I found Kenai in the center of the circle, his steady gaze and slight nod indicating he knew a lot more about the situation than I did. I had always trusted his judgment. Beyond him Micah stood with his arms folded, his hands gripping his biceps, and his head bowed. I knew they all worried for me, but they all stood like stone pillars, confident in the same knowledge I had.

I licked my lips and turned my eyes back to Helaman. My voice rang out, so different, contrasting the male voices, complementing them, and I knew why Helaman had invited me to join the council. It was not because he wanted me to be a reasoning voice among reckless boys.

"My mother taught me to believe there is a just God," I said to him. "And if I do not doubt it, I will be preserved by His marvelous power." Helaman had been in my home when Mother had spoken those words, and his eyes sparkled now with approval.

I drew my beautiful broadsword from the scabbard on my back and raised it in the air, the obsidian blades glinting deep purple in the morning light, the blue words standing in stark relief against the bare wood. I raised my voice so all could hear. "Let us turn and fight!"

A battle cry went up and more swords, spears, and bows blazed toward the sky. Two thousand warriors behind us waited for the decision, and when they heard me they got to their feet and took up the cry as well.

At last Helaman held up a large hand. "Ephraim! Isaiah! Line them up facing south."

Ephraim and Isaiah and the other chief captains moved immediately to give the orders.

When I turned to follow them, Helaman stopped me with a large, heavy hand on my shoulder.

"Where did you get your sword?" he asked.

I glanced at Zeke, but returned my gaze to Helaman. "Joab gave it to me. It was donated to the striplings. Kalem did the fine finish work." I held it up so he could examine it. All around us, boys hustled to re-form the ranks. Helaman fingered the strange symbols.

I remembered Micah had said the prophets could read the languages of the plates and ancient records. "What does it say?" I dared to ask Helaman. "Do you know? Can you read it?"

He slowly shook his head. "But I can find out if it is the will of the Lord." He looked up suddenly. "Quickly now, my children. We must hurry."

Zeke didn't even walk me to my unit. He stopped at his own and gave me a nudge toward the front of the column. He looked me in the eye and said simply, "Go with faith, Ket." Then he turned to his men.

I joined the men of my unit in the column facing south—facing the Lamanite army. Where had they halted their march and why? How long would it take us to find them? And what would happen if we did? No one asked these questions out loud. We just lined up and moved out.

Perhaps the Lamanites had deemed us no longer worth their continued effort and simply retreated. But even if they did, they would run into Antipus at some point. If Antipus had overtaken them, we would wade into the fray and fight. But if they had not retreated and Antipus had not overtaken them, then we were marching assuredly to our deaths.

If we found Antipus engaged in battle, it meant that he and his men had covered the same distance we had in half the time, literally running through the night to keep the Lamanites from attacking us. Helaman had sent messengers to inform Antipus he must leave earlier, but it was a full day's run just to deliver the message. Antipus had left Judea no earlier than midday yesterday. I remembered running through the forest. We had been allowed short breaks to walk, but had still covered a great distance. If Antipus and his men had overtaken the Lamanites, they were exhausted.

I turned to Lib as we marched quickly along, dodging limbs and leaves.

"Antipus's army won't be prepared to fight, will they?"

"If they caught up to the Lamanites?" He shook his head. "No."

"This is such a mess. If only I hadn't run into those spies."

"A mess? It's just war, Keturah. It's what we came here for."

I looked at my unit captain, really looked at him. He always knew what was happening even if he hadn't been given all the information. He had a way of just figuring things out. All the boys in our unit liked him, though I wouldn't have said he was a natural born leader. I had thought more than once that he might have preferred to be in the background. He was handsome, too, the way his light hair fell over his forehead, the way the green in his eyes could remind you of the forest.

"Lib?" I asked.

"Hmm?"

"Do you have a girl at home?"

He shot me a startled look. "No."

"No one special?" I asked.

"No one at home. Why?"

There was no reason why I asked. I just noticed he was handsome, wondered if he had formed an attachment to anyone, and opened my mouth before I thought about how it would sound. He wasn't one of my brothers. He wasn't Zeke or Jarom or even Gideon. We were barely friends, and what I had asked was none of my business.

"Anything to keep your mind off of whatever lies to the south?"

I glanced up at his profile again. "Yeah, I guess."

He moved closer to me. "Don't worry, Ket, you're totally prepared. And God is with us, can't you feel it?"

"No," I said. "I don't think I can." I realized with a measure of despair that it was true.

"That's just because you live so close to the Spirit."

"What do you mean?"

"You're used to feeling the peace and comfort of the Holy Spirit. Sometimes that can make you think it's not there, because you've never known what it feels like to be without it. You kind of take it for granted."

I thought about this as we passed through a small clearing where the units merged back in together to form a loose column. Just before we entered the trees again, we started to register familiar sounds, sounds we recognized from the training ground. Lib and I slowed and looked at each other. So it was true. Antipus must have arrived.

I looked around. The other boys were slowing too, anticipating orders. I thought the place we had camped last night lay just ahead over a small rise that hid us from the battle. The captains' arms began to shoot into the air, calling a visual, silent halt that traveled back through the lines quickly and efficiently. The noise that drifted over the rise was a roar that sounded a great deal like the rush of water in the river, but I could hear distinct grunts and shouts too.

I caught a glimpse of Kenai edging away from the rise back toward Helaman at the head of our small army. When he reached Helaman they exchanged a few brief words, and Kenai made motions to indicate the position of the enemy. Helaman turned to Shem and issued a command which Shem relayed to the highest chief captains, Isaiah and Ephraim.

Then, through a break in our loose column, I saw them turn as one and draw their broadswords from the sheaths on their backs, their cimeters from the scabbards at their waists.

Seth ran along our lines calling out commands to his hundred.

"Flank right!" he bellowed. "On command!"

We were to sprint in formation to the right side of the battlefield—a battlefield we couldn't even see yet. I drew my sling from my belt and took a long, slow breath. I cast a glance at the boys who had surrounded me. I was in the middle of them all with Lib on my left and Ethanim on my right. My eyes found Gideon, but the only boy who looked at me was Reb. He gave me a slight nod, no goofy grin this time, and then we were running forward.

As we crested the rise, I looked down on the battlefield. At the distant end where Antipus had overtaken the Lamanite army, men fought each other with swords and spears. At the closer end of the field, enemy soldiers actually stood and waited their turn to fight.

Antipus's men were covered in their thick, protective clothing, which had surely made their march terrible. Most of the Lamanites wore simple loincloths, some with buckskin leggings beneath. Some, but by no means all, even wore articles of armor over their chests. Their clothing, while it shielded them from little, offered more freedom of movement than the thick garments most of the Nephite army wore. But the differences, besides the fact that they both held advantages, made it easy to discern between friend and foe.

And this made it simple to choose my targets.

A calmness enveloped me. I slung stone after stone as easily as if I had been on the training ground slinging at targets. I struck man after man with lethal hits, as did all my brothers around me.

We hit as many men as we could. They were standing still. It was easy. The men on the field began to notice something happening, and when they looked to see what it was, Micah's men picked them off with their arrows. They aimed for vital organs to make death as quick and merciful as possible. Sometimes in the smaller skirmishes, our aim had been only to incapacitate our foe, but today our aim was death. We had to conquer this army. There was no safe place of retreat.

I chose each victim as I fed his rock into my sling with sure fingers. I marked the men in the middle who were rushing toward Eli's hundred now with their spears raised, and I slung my rocks at them.

The swords Eli's men wielded were too short to fight off the spears effectively. For a moment I was terrified for Darius and Kenai and the others, but the calmness returned an instant before I saw them break ranks, split down the middle and flank to the sides of the battlefield, allowing Enos's hundred, who specialized in fighting with the spear, to rush in behind them and engage the spear-wielding enemies.

But Eli's men didn't fall back. They ran forward, hewing down hulking grown men, experienced soldiers, as they advanced. I saw Darius charge forward with my father's shield before him on one arm, and his broadsword striking and slashing with the other. Jarom and Kenai were at his side. And then I lost sight of them in the fray, amid legions of soldiers and the angels that assuredly fought beside them.

My unit was still up on the rise slinging in quick regular intervals. There was no return fire, but I had already thrown half the rocks I carried. There were more on the ground here, but picking them up one by one would require taking our eyes off the enemy. Covering each other as we gathered and shared them would be our only option when we ran out.

At a glance I saw that the hundreds who had trained to use the javelin-throwers had foregone throwing their javelins and had been commanded instead to go forth into the battle to fight beside Enos's men in hand-to-hand combat. The enemy there began to fall back.

Micah's hundred moved forward, shooting from the cover of the trees. They were accurate, deadly, and difficult for the enemy to find. They would not run out of arrows. We had made thousands upon thousands during the last year of preparation, and we had soldiers whose task it was simply to carry and supply the bowmen with arrows.

I remembered telling Zeke that hauling arrows for other soldiers didn't seem like an important task. It wasn't difficult, dangerous, or exciting, nor did it require much skill. He had replied that he would like to see me use my bow without an arrow.

A lot of rocks pinged off of breastplates and headplates, falling with dull thuds to the ground, but many more hit fleshy targets. They cut as deeply as arrows and could cause great damage, especially if they hit vital organs, which Seth had taught us to aim for. Foreheads, eyes, lungs, hearts, and something he called kidneys were all high on our priority list.

When I ran out of rocks, I fell back so the other boys could finish slinging theirs. I looked around to see that none of the enemy returned fire. They were all engaged in hand to hand combat now with Helaman's army. I took a breath and inspected the larger battlefield.

Between the striplings, the Nephite warriors, and the soldiers of Antipus, we had the Lamanites surrounded. Antipus should have been at the forefront of his men, but he wasn't. In fact, he was nowhere in sight and his men looked to be scattering at the distant end of the battlefield.

But as I watched, the Lamanites turned, one by one, to see what was occurring at our end of the battlefield. When they saw thirteen-year-old boys like Darius slaughtering their kinsmen, turning the battle, their confusion quickly turned to fear. Yet, despite it, they turned to fight the forefront units of stripling warriors who had slain their way across the battlefield. I grudgingly admitted the Lamanites fought with courage, for they were truly afraid.

When the Lamanites turned toward us, I saw Teomner, a Nephite captain from the council of war, yell at the man who held the Title of Liberty. The man waved it fiercely back and forth, and it snapped through the air. Teomner rallied the exhausted troops, commanding them to renew their attack, which they did with fierce savagery, and man after man fell before them.

Seth ordered us to stop slinging and draw our swords, but we never got the order to advance toward the battle's front. Before long the fighting had ceased. We watched in near disbelief as the commander of the Lamanites, with a disgusted look on his face, surrendered to Helaman in the center of the battlefield.

I scanned the battlefield quickly but I didn't see any of my brothers. I didn't see Zeke or Jarom.

I sent a worried look to Gideon, but Lib intercepted it and came to stand beside me. He put his arm awkwardly around me, something he had never done before, while we watched the action down below.

Helaman commanded the Lamanite soldiers to throw down their weapons, and as they began to file forward toward the center of the field, we stayed on the rise but held our swords at the ready.

The battle was over.

Antipus had fallen. Word shot through our ranks swift as an arrow—and cut to the heart just as painfully.

He had sustained many wounds. His guards had propped him up against a thick tree while they fought all around him, fighting mightily to protect their commander. He bled out onto the ground. His men assured Helaman that he had lived to see the surrender, and whether he had indeed seen it in body, or just in spirit, I knew Antipus gloried in the victory.

The Lamanite commander had ordered his men to cut down the chief captains first and work their way down the ranks, a tactic that had worked. It threw the rest of Antipus's men into confusion. Their ranks broke, and they began to retreat.

But the Nephite reinforcements that had come up from Zarahemla had done much the same as Kenai's men, rushing up the sides of the enemy's lines in order to engage more men in battle. They might have done better to rest while the people of Antipus fought first because many of them fell due to their fatigue from their long march, but with their efforts, we had successfully surrounded the Lamanites.

It was late afternoon by the time things settled down. We moved back into our column so our captains could count us and determine how many had been wounded and who had been slain.

No one in my unit had suffered so much as a scratch. We had stayed a distance away on the rise and none of the Lamanite men had even attempted to disable us.

Micah and Zeke were probably safe as well. From what I

had observed of the battle, the bowmen had stayed in the trees and shot from behind them. This had given them both cover and time to choose the most immediate targets and aim for them.

It was Kenai, Darius and Jarom I worried for. They should be near me in the column, ahead just a few rows, but I couldn't see any of them. Perhaps they were lying with the wounded under the cedar trees where we had placed them out of the direct rays of the warm sun. A detail had gone out onto the battlefield and separated the wounded from the dead. I had not been on that detail, but I almost wished I had been so at least I would know if my brothers were alive.

I started hopping in place, trying to see them. Gideon came to stand next to me. He was over a head taller than me— the top of my head hit just below his shoulder—and he could see ahead of us much better than I could. He put a hand on my shoulder.

I stopped hopping and looked up at him. I could feel the worry all over my face.

"If you're trying to look like a hardened soldier, I see right through you," he said, attempting humor.

I dropped my eyes.

He sighed and squeezed my shoulder. After a moment he said, "I see Kenai."

"You do? Is he okay?"

"He's standing."

"Standing," I said to myself. That was good. "What about Darius and Jarom? Can you see them?" I craned my neck to see over the shoulders of the boys in front of us.

"Wait here," Gideon said and then walked along the outside of the column up toward Kenai's fifty.

While I waited, I inspected the boys in front of me. The boy who normally stood in front of me was not there. In fact, there were many holes in the lines all around me. All of the boys I could see had cuts and the beginnings of large bruises. Some of their shields were broken. Some of them cradled their arms as though they too were broken—which they probably were.

My throat got tight as I waited to know what had happened to my brothers. I thought of my father's steel shield with the jaguar on the front. I hoped it had protected Darius. I closed my eyes. Jarom didn't have a steel shield.

Lib was looking at me. I felt his gaze and turned to meet it. I thought he might say something, but he didn't. He just stared deeply into my eyes and finally turned back toward the front of the column.

"Can you see anything?" I asked him.

"The captains are reporting their counts to Helaman. His eyebrows rise higher with each report. His left arm is bandaged and bleeding through bright red."

"He needs to apply pressure to it," I said urgently.

Lib gave me a faint smile. "Ket, he knows that. He's busy."

Gideon shouldered his way past Ethanim then and stood next to me once more.

I looked up at him expectantly.

"Darius and his friend—"

"Jarom?" I cut in.

He nodded. "Darius and Jarom are both fine." He shook his head and couldn't hide his smile. "Both were unharmed."

I stared at him. "Unharmed? What do you mean?"

"I mean there is not a scratch on them," he said as if he couldn't believe it himself. "Kenai has some cuts and a head wound, but the boys, the youngest boys—they're untouched."

"Untouched," I repeated. "How is that possible? I saw them rush toward the enemy lines. Did they not engage anyone, do you think?"

"They're both splattered with blood and exhausted, but still running on adrenaline." He glanced around, sweeping all who could hear into our conversation. "Their entire unit is the same—bloodied, exhausted, excited, and untouched by the enemy's weapon."

Just then, we heard Helaman's deep, strong voice call for our attention. He reported the numbers of dead and wounded among the people of Antipus and the Nephite reinforcements who had come from Zarahemla just a month ago. We waited anxiously for the count of Ammonites.

"None of the striplings have been slain," he boomed across the battlefield.

A deep silence filled the forest while we all wondered if we had heard him correctly. Then a cheer went up through the trees, a war cry that echoed from the heavens.

Chapter 16

After the column broke, my unit made camp on the rise. We rested while Ethanim and Reb cooked the evening meal. Lib and I sat apart from the others.

"I should go to the wounded," I said.

The sun had lightened his hair almost to match his faded yellow tunic. His eyes were green like the forest with flecks of brown. He stared into our fire for a moment, his arms locked around his drawn-up knees. "I don't think you should."

"I could be of some help," I said halfheartedly.

"They've got enough men there—men who have experience treating battle wounds."

"You think I would just be in the way."

He let his eyes drift toward the infirmary station where he and the others had carried the wounded while I had gathered the enemy weapons. "It's rough over there. I think you should keep the images of those wounds out of your mind." His jaw was firm and he looked at me. "Don't go, Ket."

I nearly said, "Watch me," but I held my tongue for a moment and actually thought before I spoke.

I had already seen so much today, so many gruesome

wounds, so much violence, so much death and pain. So much hatred. Why would Lib say this? The Lib of a few months ago wouldn't have cared.

"I won't stop you," he said quietly, and I knew he wouldn't. It was my choice.

I drew the tip of an arrow through the dirt at my feet. "I'll stay."

We left it at that, and I didn't go to see the wounded. I would have to deal with wounds eventually, but for now, there were others here who had experience. A year ago I would have insisted I needed the experience so I could learn. But now I knew that God handed out experiences when we needed them, and not before.

"Finish your water. I'll go get you more," Lib offered.

The small river that flowed past camp was a bit of a walk to the east. It was a good offer and because I was fatigued, I let Lib do it for me. Our eyes met as I took the last swallows from my water skin. I held it out to him, but he didn't look at me as he took it.

He made the same offer to everyone else, and Corban and Cyrus went with him to help carry the full water skins back.

I took a breath and let my eyes drift closed. My mind went over and over the battle from beginning to end. How many stones had I slung? A hundred? Two hundred? How many targets had I hit? How many men had I killed? How many children had I made fatherless?

It was troubling, but I consoled myself with the knowledge that I hadn't killed any man who wouldn't have readily killed me.

I knew I had fallen asleep because Gideon woke me after a time. My cheek was on my knees when he shook me lightly on the shoulder.

"Your brothers are hiking up the rise." He turned and walked to the other side of the cook fire, went to his heels, and

174

stared at me, his eyes pensive, until my brothers entered our camp. Then he glared at Kenai and wouldn't look at me at all. But I shrugged it off. I was used to Gideon's moods, and the battle had everyone drawing into themselves.

I could smell that our dinner was almost done cooking over the fire. The noise and ruckus of the battle had scared away all the game, but Corban and Cyrus had snared us some fish from the river to accompany our rations. I knew that many of the units were eating well from the provisions we had carried with us. Still, I felt blessed to be eating hot fish with my unit.

I called out. "Dare!" He was climbing up in front of Kenai, who had a bloody bandage tied around his head. "Kenai!"

I hugged them both tightly and they both let me. I checked them over for cuts and bruises, but just as Gideon had claimed, Darius had none.

Kenai, on the other hand, was bruised and cut everywhere. But, on inspection, most of the cuts were superficial and shallow. He would be sore for a while, but he would recover.

I glanced over their shoulders.

"Jarom is unhurt, like Darius," Kenai said, anticipating my questions. "We haven't heard from either Micah or Zeke," he continued with a hitch in his breath as I fingered a particularly sore bruise on his shoulder. "But they are not among the wounded."

I nodded. "You're lucky your collarbone didn't break with this blow," I told him.

He shrugged. And then he cringed. "You're remarkably unconcerned about Zeke," he practically accused, not loud, but loud enough.

I glanced at his eyes. Heat creeping up my neck in tingles, very aware of Gideon behind us, I returned my attention to the jagged cut that ran from his collar bone halfway down his chest. "They shot from the trees. You said yourself they are not among the wounded."

He snorted. And then he groaned.

"Here," I said. "Sit down. Have these cuts been cleaned?"

"No," he said softly. "The surgeons and healers are caring for the badly wounded."

I nodded as I rummaged around in my satchel for the medicines I had brought with me. I glanced around for my water skin, but Lib had not returned with it. "Do you have water in your water skin?"

Darius quickly offered his. "I do."

"Good. Get the cup from my pack and set some water on the ashes to heat." I turned back to Kenai and began rubbing Mother's salve into his cuts. "This is Mother's. It will curtail infection."

He nodded and gritted his teeth against the sting.

When the water was steaming, I dropped in a handful of ground willow tree bark to steep. I glanced at his still gritted teeth and dropped in another handful. I felt his head with the inside of my forearm. No fever as yet. "Have you had any sleep in the last three days?"

He gave a very small shrug, but the flatness in his eyes told me the truth.

Two deep cuts split his left arm. I washed the blood away to check for debris inside.

"Hold on," I muttered as I dug out some shards of stone and wood. "Sorry," I whispered when I was done.

He didn't acknowledge the pain. I almost chastised him for his silly stoicism, but he shifted and extended his leg toward me.

"Did you pull that out?" I exclaimed, drawing the attention of everyone in our quiet camp.

Several of the boys moved closer as Darius brandished a bloodied arrow. Joshua took it from him and the boys began to pass it around.

A slight smile crossed Kenai's lips, but his eyes darkened.

"Gideon." I craned around to see him inspecting the arrow with the others. "Yarrow. Do you know what it is?"

"Yes."

"I've seen it around. Find me some."

He glanced at Kenai, nodded, and left the rise.

I wanted to ask my brother what was going on between him and Gideon. It had started before the morning of the march, the morning he hadn't had a blister on his foot. There was definitely something. The question was on the tip of my tongue, but Kenai caught my eye and shook his head.

Not in front of these boys, his eyes said.

"This will ease the aches," I told him instead. "Mother gave it to me every day during my first detail in the trenches." I shot a self-deprecating glance toward my unit. I hadn't told them I was that bad off, though they had to have known. "Drink it slowly," I warned.

Gideon returned with two handfuls of white yarrow.

"Thank you," I said, barely getting the words out before I had the yarrow in my mouth, chewing it into a paste I could make a compress from. My entire unit moved in and watched closely as I tended to the arrow wound that went completely through Kenai's leg. At last, I had it bandaged. I handed the rest of the yarrow to Darius.

"Did you watch closely?"

He nodded.

"Do it each morning with a clean bandage." I looked between my brothers, meeting both of their eyes, thinking of Kenai pulling that arrow out himself. "And if it forms puss, tell me immediately, but don't take him to the surgeons." I waited until they both nodded. "Now, let me have a look at your head."

I unwound the bandage. The cut was on the side of his head, and I had to sweep his hair away to get a good look at it. "Darius, bring me your water."

After I washed away the blood, I could see the cut was

very shallow. I breathed a sigh of relief.

"The wound is not large," I told him. "But you might suffer some effects from the blow to your head."

Kenai looked at the ground. "I didn't receive a blow to the head. I think I either caught the edge of someone's weapon or else scraped it on the branch of a tree."

I laughed, more out of relief than anything. I let the wound air-dry, covered it with Mother's salve, and then re-wrapped it with clean bandages from my satchel.

Jonas, one of Kenai's men, jogged up the hill. He too had cuts and bruises, but like Kenai, he would heal. Kenai looked up at him expectantly, his focus sharpened and his clenched jaw visibly relaxed.

"The support teams will make it to camp late tonight," Jonas reported. "They thought to camp, but we told them they were almost here—and that we needed them."

Kenai nodded. "Thanks. Go report it to Helaman."

"Mahonri is doing so as we speak."

Kenai nodded again and looked between Darius and me. "I've got to get back."

Darius jumped to his feet. He offered his hand to Kenai and helped him to his feet. I noticed they were both careful to use the arm that was not badly bruised at the shoulder.

I gave Darius my jar of salve and most of my bandages. "Take this to the men in the units around you. It only takes a little on each cut. When you run out you can use wine or vinegar from the provisions to clean the wounds. Deep wounds must be bandaged until they knit."

He knew all that, but he nodded and started away, walking closely to Kenai as if he thought his brother might fall over.

I was sure Kenai had slept very little since leaving Judea almost three full days ago. Hopefully the willow bark would work and he would be able to get some restful sleep.

That night we slept in shifts, taking turns guarding our Lamanite prisoners. The Nephites left at dawn to take them to Zarahemla where they could be secured within the walls at the fortress there.

The rest of us slept deeply and did not rise at dawn. The horn did not sound for us to wake up, a luxury Helaman allowed us after our long march and battle. At midmorning when we all began to stir, I thought I saw Mother pass by on her way up the rise.

"Gideon," I said to his still reclining form on the ground. "I thought I saw my mother. I'm going over the rise to check."

He rolled out of his bedroll as I had known he would, and rubbed a hand over his face. I could hear the rough scratch of his stubble as his hand went over it.

When we had gone only a little way, we saw the woman and it was indeed Mother. She was staring out toward the sea, which was visible here through a break in the trees. Her small hands held her arms crossed in front of her. She looked so pensive I hesitated to go to her.

But then she turned toward us, and Gideon, seeing it, gave me a small nudge in her direction. That was all it took, and I ran to her.

"What are you doing here?" I exclaimed into her hair as I held her tight. "I thought you weren't coming."

"I made Kalem bring me. I couldn't stand being safe in the city without knowing my children were okay." She pulled away from me, holding me at arm's length so she could look me over. "You're fine," she said. "I thought—this morning when I got a look at all the wounded—I thought surely I would find you all there. I could hardly believe it when they told us none of the striplings had been killed." She heaved a burdened sigh. "Though there are some who are badly injured."

I bit my lip. I should have gone to help them. "Have you seen Micah yet?"

"No. I've been tending to the wounded since the third watch. I've come up here for a small respite. I haven't seen any of the boys." Her tired eyes were filled with worry and stress and questions.

"Helaman allowed us to sleep this morning. The boys are probably still abed."

"Well, none of them are among the wounded, so that is a worry off my mind. And you! How did you manage to come through the battle unscathed?

"We shot from here, from the rise, and never received any return fire. Darius and Kenai were on the front line and charged through the Lamanite warriors."

Her eyes questioned me still, and I knew I was keeping her in suspense so I hurried on.

"Kenai has only cuts and bruises. He's got one bruise on his collar bone that is particularly bad, and a shallow cut on his head, though he says he only scraped it on a tree branch." I bit my lip. "He took an arrow in the leg." Her eyes tightened, but I hurried on. "I smoothed your salve over the cuts and bandaged the deepest ones with yarrow. I did not have anything to treat the shoulder."

She nodded slowly, her eyes showing a measure of relief. "And Darius?"

"Completely unscathed. You should have seen him, Mother! He fought with Jarom and they hewed down the enemy as if they were avenging angels!" And I wasn't entirely sure I hadn't seen angels fighting beside them, but I didn't say that to Mother. I would let her draw her own conclusions.

She gave me a disbelieving look.

I looked around, suddenly remembering Gideon, who leaned casually against a tree a short distance away trying to guard me and still afford me my privacy. But I knew he couldn't help but overhear.

"Tell my mother Darius is unscathed," I said.

He narrowed his eyes at me, nearly scowling, but he turned to Mother and said, "Keturah speaks the truth. Darius has nary a scratch."

Mother glanced between us and then walked toward Gideon, who stood up straighter when he saw that she approached him. "I see you too have weathered the battle unharmed," I heard her say. Then, astonishing us both, Mother stretched up and wrapped her arms around Gideon's neck.

He looked to me but lightly wrapped his arms around her in return, uncomfortable with the show of affection. She said something softly to him that I didn't hear and he laughed and hugged her more tightly, actually laying his cheek on top of her head for a moment before releasing her. She spoke to him again, and he nodded.

I remembered how stiffly he had hugged his father all those months ago, and I wondered if that was how he normally hugged his mother as well. Perhaps hugging did not happen much in their home. I tried to picture his mother, the woman who had accepted the Gospel, left the land of her inheritance, taught Gideon to be strong and faithful.

Gideon waited while Mother told me goodbye, and then he walked me farther into the woods so I could take advantage of the privacy of the bushes.

"What did my mother say to you?" I asked him when we were headed back to camp.

He took a deep breath and let it out. "Does it matter?"

Feeling dumb for prying, I shook my head. "I suppose it is between the two of you."

He hid a smile. "She said not everyone can scowl at you and get away with it, Rabbit."

I punched him, but he only laughed. I whirled to view the place Mother had been, and then I whirled back to Gideon.

"What did she mean?" I demanded.

Gideon shifted, reached up to smooth down a strand of

my hair between two of his fingers.

I caught and held my breath.

"I think your secret is out," he said softly.

What secret?

My lips moved to form the words, but someone called out to us.

"Gid! Keturah!"

We both turned at the sound of Ethanim's voice. All of the other boys of our unit were with him.

Gideon dropped his hand, but let it rest on my back as we turned. He edged closer to me as the boys drew near.

Lib glared at Gideon, but most of the others seemed to be either looking into the trees or down at their sandals, hiding smiles. Ethanim looked between us, hands on his hips.

"This isn't what it..."

"Looks like?" Lib finished for me, color flushing his fair skin. "Because it looks like you and Gid snuck off together before dawn."

I laughed because dawn had been so long ago, but regretted it when I saw a flash of hurt in Gideon's eyes.

"Lib," Ethanim warned.

Lib gestured to us.

Gideon edged even closer to me.

I cleared my throat and lifted my chin. "I had to *go*."

The color slowly drained from Lib's face. "We're digging graves," he said at last. He moved away and the others followed him.

"You don't have to explain yourself to him," Gideon said quietly as we made our way to the field of graves after them.

I sighed. "He's my captain."

"There is some information he is not entitled to."

Like the fact that we were falling in love, he meant. Even my mother had seen it at a glance. "They all know."

"They don't know anything." His voice was low and

confusing. "Come on, we're late."

We spent most of the afternoon digging graves for the fallen soldiers. When our time in the graves was done, we went to the river to wash off the grime. I was combing through my wet and tangled hair when Lib motioned for me to follow him. I glanced in the direction he pointed, away from camp, and hesitated, so Lib took my hand and tugged.

"Where are we going?" I asked. "And why are we holding hands?"

"Oh. Sorry," he said sarcastically and instantly dropped my hand.

"Well, I didn't mean it like that," I said.

"Like what?" Lib was irritated today. It was unusual for him.

"I didn't mean you had to drop my hand like it was a hot coal."

He looked at me curiously as we walked along, but didn't say anything more.

We walked east for several minutes before I saw Zeke standing beyond a small thicket of underbrush. He was pacing. When he heard us, he looked up. I glanced at Lib, who gave me a sad smile that I wouldn't wonder about until later, and said, "Go on. I know you've been dying to see him." He scratched the back of his head. "At least, I thought..."

"I am," I rushed to say. "Thank you."

He shrugged off my thanks and gestured me to go on.

I flew into Zeke's arms, and when he caught me up I suddenly burst into tears.

"Oh, hey, what's wrong?" Zeke asked. He set me gently back on the ground and held me close to him.

I shook my head, which had the effect of burrowing my face further into his chest and tangling my hair in his long fingers. "I'm just glad you're okay," I sobbed through broken breaths.

"It's alright." I felt his arms tighten around me. "I'm alright. I'm right here." I felt him laugh a little. "It's the adrenaline wearing off, Ket."

"And relief," I mumbled into his chest. I held him tight, breathed in the smell of leather and insect repellent. He was here. He was whole and unharmed. He was mine and nobody else's.

"It is nice to see your true feelings once in a while," he said into my hair.

I didn't even know my true feelings anymore.

I drew away and looked up at him with wet eyes. With anyone else I would have been embarrassed by my tears, by their suddenness and their intensity and my inability to control them, but I was not embarrassed with Zeke.

"I asked Lib to bring you here. I can see now it was wise to meet in privacy." He brushed away more of my tears.

I glanced back over my shoulder. "Is he waiting?"

"No. I'm going to walk you back."

"One of Lib's conditions?"

He smiled. "Yeah."

"Lib gives me conditions all the time."

"He's in love with you, you know."

I felt my face get hot. "I've begun to suspect as much," I admitted.

"I told you they would all fall in love with you."

"One is hardly all." But it wasn't just Lib, and we both knew it.

"Do you return his affections?"

Was he asking about Lib? I turned away from him. "What time are we marching out?"

"I actually feel sorry for him," Zeke persisted. "Being in love with a girl who is in love with someone else—it's not easy. Only the best of us can bear it."

"Try being the girl."

After a moment he put his hands on my shoulders. It was such a familiar action, protective and brotherly. I closed my eyes with the ache of it—of both wanting and fearing more.

"Forgive me, Ket," he said quietly as he smoothed my damp hair back over my shoulders, drawing a shiver from me. "I never thought how it might be for you. I'm sure it's confusing." I felt him kiss the top of my head, lingering, breathing hot breath into my hair. But Micah kissed me on top of my head. Didn't Zeke feel any more passion for me than that? Was I destined to marry a man who felt nothing for me but obligation?

I turned to him suddenly. "Zeke, why did you bring me here?"

I felt the intensity in my eyes as they searched his for an answering intensity. And they found it.

"So I could do this."

His kiss was not like the kisses he had given me in Melek. Zeke was firm, confident, and possessive—I could sense it in the touch of his hands. He held me and kissed me with the heart of a Nephite warrior who took back what was his. For just this moment I didn't want to be familiar and comfortable with him. I wanted this new feeling, this emotion that should have been there all along.

I wanted to be swept away in something I couldn't control. This world and this war with its killing and death were so finite. Life—mine, his—could end at any moment, and I let Zeke sweep me into something infinite, something that wouldn't end even with death.

"It's okay," he said again. He wiped my tears away with his thumbs, and when they didn't stop forming in my eyes, he kissed them away. "It's okay. I'm right here."

"If you had died," I choked. "If you had died—"

But I was afraid that was not why I was crying.

"I didn't." He kissed me again. "I could never leave you."

Chapter 17

Over the months that followed our first battle, Kalem and the other men eagerly studied the Lamanite weapons we had taken in our victory. In the afternoons, since I had little else to do once my training and daily chores were completed, I looked over Kalem's shoulder while he worked.

"They haven't changed much in fifteen years, but there have been some innovations," he said.

The Lamanites, though base and lazy, had extraordinary weapons because that was where their interests and obsessions were. As Kalem studied them he tried to develop new ways to defend against them. His interest in weapons had been fostered in the Lamanite lands, but it was serving us well in Judea.

The oath he had made not to bear arms sometimes seemed like such a struggle for him to keep, but I thought that made it all the more meaningful. It wouldn't be much of a sacrifice, an offering, or a commitment if it was easy to do. Although, Mother said offerings that were easy to make counted too. They were just as important. They had a value all their own. And I did believe that in keeping commitments over time they eventually became easier to keep.

I was coming to realize the level of commitment to the oath that our parents had made relied a lot on personal interpretation. Each person had a different extent to which they were willing and able to uphold their oath.

There were many men who had been willing to break it to assist the Nephite armies in defense of our country and our freedom, for God had said we should fight for our families—even unto bloodshed. But Helaman had talked them out of breaking their promises, and he told them they could serve in other ways by providing food and provisions for the soldiers. He believed, as we all did, that God would bless us for keeping our covenants.

There was Kalem, who wouldn't kill, but he would make weapons. They weren't his personal weapons of war and he was not wielding them in defense of his own life, but I always wondered if he might wield them in defense of Mother's life.

There was Mother, who had kept Father's weapons, reasoning that she kept them symbolically buried in the ground. And there were many more like Mother. Though they wouldn't fight for their lives, they let their children do it for them. Gideon's parents were among these. They let Gideon and Jashon protect them, fight for them—and in fact, I wondered if they expected it of them.

And there were those like Leda's parents, who believed that God would protect them, even when they took no steps to protect themselves. My father had felt this way. Or perhaps he had not expected to be physically protected, but had wished to seal his testimony with his death.

I believed all the levels of commitment, all the sacrifice and offerings were acceptable to the Lord. Weren't we all different, and didn't God teach us all in different ways? In the way and time that was right?

"Step back," Joshua said as he and Noah raised a thick log and held it in place.

I moved back, making way for them to work.

Reb lashed the log to the one next to it, and after Lib measured to be sure it was straight, he climbed the wall and lashed it at the top. Ethanim and Corban scooped cement into the hole at its base. Gideon and some of the others were lengthening the trench in which the logs would be set.

I bit on my thumbnail as I watched them work.

They had only placed four logs into the breastwork of timbers atop the embankment, but they were all sweating and dirty. The boys had dropped a log, which was still at the bottom of the trench thirty feet below us, and it had nearly hit Cyrus in the head as it toppled down. Most of the boys had splinters already. I had seen them all try to suck them out, and I thought only a few had been successful. I looked at the huge pile of logs we were to place today, and I wished they would let me help.

But I stayed out of the way because it wasn't like before. They weren't excluding me. Something in my heart told me they were protecting me. This wasn't the hardest job we had ever done, and I still didn't want to be treated differently, but I accepted that I was different and none of us could change it.

"Keturah."

I looked up to see Lib approaching me. He held a bucket and a trowel.

"Not all of the logs are straight," he said as he motioned me toward the completed area of the wall. He offered me the bucket, which was filled with cement, but kept the trowel for himself. After scooping some cement onto it, he showed me how to fill in the cracks, pushing the cement all the way through the wall between the logs. "Got it?" he asked. When I nodded and took the trowel from him, he said, "Some of these holes are big enough for the Lamanites to put an arrow through. We want the wall to be impenetrable."

"I suppose you're going to tell me there are no small jobs."

He laughed and shook his head. "Only jobs that hurt worse than others." He held up his hands. There were splinters from today's work, but also bruises and calluses from practice, burns from cooking, and cuts from fashioning weapons.

Taking his hand in mine to examine the wounds, I said, "I can help with those. Are the others' hands like this too?"

He looked at his hands and shrugged. Then he glanced behind him where the boys were erecting another log. "I've got to check that before the cement sets," he said, and he turned and left.

That night after the evening meal, I tended to everyone's hands. I used a needle to dig their splinters out, cleaned their wounds, and bandaged their burns. After that, they all came to me privately with their wounds. Word spread, and many of the striplings showed up at our camp with all manner of afflictions, small wounds, bruises, stomach pains, fevers, muscle aches, twisted ankles—any small thing they weren't too embarrassed to seek help for.

"Maybe I should have come as a healer instead of a soldier," I said to Kenai as I bandaged a deep cut on his arm, which he wouldn't tell me where or how he had gotten.

He snorted. "They are not coming here because you're a healer," he said.

"I know." I blushed. "I think they all want a bit of mothering."

He outright laughed. "They are not coming here because you remind them of their mothers."

"Don't be so sure," I said. "You have your mother here, but think of the others."

He stopped laughing but said, "You know better than that."

I twisted my lips to hide my smile. "You're done." I glanced around the empty camp. "And I think I am done for the day."

Kenai shouldered his gear and left, but I wasn't alone long before I saw Corban and Cyrus coming toward camp, and they were carrying Mathoni. I stood as they approached.

"Keturah!"

"What's wrong? What happened?"

I could already see that Mathoni's ankle was swollen and starting to discolor.

"You've hurt your ankle," I said.

"At the river," Corban supplied. He helped set Mathoni down on a bench at our cook fire, and ducked out from under his arm. "He slipped on a wet stone."

I nodded. "Why didn't you take him to the healers?" If they were coming from the river, they would have passed the healers' camp on the way to ours.

They looked at each other and shrugged.

I sighed and gave my attention to the ankle.

Mathoni was the youngest of the boys in our unit, and he sometimes got treated as such, but he returned my concerned gaze with a stoic one, and I couldn't help but smile.

"It's broken," I said. "I can't set it." I turned to Corban. "You'll have to run for my mother."

I heard the crunch of gravel on the road behind me. "Is it broken? I can set it."

I looked up to see Zach entering camp with Ethanim, Lib, and Joshua.

"Are you sure? If it's done wrong he could become crippled." I glanced at Mathoni.

"I can set it."

Mathoni nodded, and I relented. It was his decision. I moved away and let Zach have some room to work. I watched as he felt the bones for a moment and suddenly twisted them into place. Mathoni grunted in pain, but Zach kept his hands on the ankle, fingers prodding until he had assured himself all the bones were in place.

Zach turned to me. "Bandage."

I passed him what I had left, several lengths of clean bandages. I could wrap the ankle, but I watched as he prepared a splint and bandaged it himself.

"I'm going to start referring the men to you when they come seeking a healer," I said to him as we ate our evening meal.

He kept his eyes on his food. "They would stop coming."

Reb snorted, and after a minute, a few of the others joined him in laughter.

I sighed. "Well I can't very well turn them away."

Lib held up a hand. "We'll do it for you." He looked to the others, and they all nodded.

One late afternoon when I came back to camp after talking weapons with Kalem, when we had been in the soldiers' camps with no action for what seemed like months on end, Kenai stood near our cook fire consulting with Lib.

I walked toward them. Lib wore a look of concern, but he nodded his agreement to whatever Kenai was saying.

Lib answered the question in my eyes. "Kenai wants you for a scouting assignment."

I looked to Kenai.

"You and Gid," he affirmed. "I'm moving out at dawn. Bring your camping gear. And it's cold at night. Wear a tunic." He paused. "No tent, though."

I grimaced. We were almost to the rainy season again, and there was a good chance it would rain while we were gone.

"Where are we going?"

"That's all I can say for now." He threw a glance at Lib.

I knew better than to ask about his spy missions.

"Lib, you'll get a break from guard duty," I said to change the subject.

He nodded. "But not yet. Come on. I'll walk you down to get the rations for dinner."

"Meet me at the south gates at dawn," Kenai said, and

with a nod to Lib, he left.

"I don't like it, Keturah," Lib said when we were headed together toward the ration tent.

"Don't like what?"

"It sounds dangerous."

"Going with Kenai? He's the best at what he does. I'll be fine."

"He said his other team got wounded while they were out. That's why he needs a new team."

"Oh."

"Tell him you won't go."

"You tell him."

"He's my superior. I'm not going to refuse him requested soldiers."

"How about Gideon? Should he decline to go?"

"Gid? Of course not. Gid will be fine."

I slugged Lib in the arm.

He stopped walking and looked at me.

I tried to keep my voice even. "Lib, you have never said I couldn't do something because I'm a girl. Don't start now. I like you, and I want to keep liking you."

He started walking again and rubbed his arm. "Ow. Did you have to use the knuckle?"

"Lib," I said. "I'll be fine. It's just one trip, right?"

He nodded.

"That's what I thought. Gideon and I have worked with Kenai before. He needs us because he knows he won't have to train us. I know he wouldn't want to train someone for just one mission. His regular guys will heal up and be ready for the next one."

"He could take any man in this camp. I don't like it."

"Why? Because you won't be able to spy on me all the time? You won't know where I am at every second? You won't be able to control my every action?"

I knew those weren't the reasons, and so did he.

He frowned. "Do you really view it that way, Keturah?"

"No," I said quietly. "I do appreciate your vigilance."

He just nodded, but I could see it was the right thing to say.

Lib took the third watch instead of the first that night so he could see me off in the morning. Sensitive to his feelings, I gave him a quick, hard hug before I walked out with Kenai, Gideon, and Jonas.

"Get some sleep for a few days," I said to him.

When I was walking with Kenai outside the south gates, he said, "What was that all about?"

"With Lib?"

"Mm-hmm."

"He worries about me."

"Giving him a big hug is going to stop that?"

Gideon glanced at me, but he and Jonas pretended not to notice our conversation.

The nights were getting warmer now, more like the nights in Melek, but the early morning just before dawn was the coolest time, and it felt good to be moving. It felt good to be outside the city walls. I spared a look back at the city, taking pride in the embankment, barricades, and towers I had helped build.

"Yeah, it's going to stop it," I said, knowing there was nothing that would stop Lib from worrying about me while I was gone.

We followed Kenai up through the green hills, and he gave us directions and specific instructions as we went.

"Always pause in the trees before you enter a clearing," Kenai said when we came to the first one.

I know that, I wanted to say, but Kenai kept talking like he had the instructions memorized, and I could tell it was just what he told all the new spies he trained out here.

194

He pointed to my wrist where I wore a thick leather bracelet with metal adornments. "Take off anything that will reflect the sun."

"And Gideon and Jonas too, right?"

"Well, sure," he said vaguely as he helped me up and over a large fallen tree. His hand was moist with sweat, but firm and gripped mine tightly. "Gid and Jonas too, but that goes without saying."

I rolled my eyes as I slipped my bracelet off.

Kenai was becoming a little bit of a stranger to me, and obviously he didn't know me anymore, either. I had seen him plenty in the past year and a half, but we didn't live together anymore. I lived with Lib and Gideon, Ethanim and Reb, and all the others. He lived out here in the wilderness with the constant threat of discovery. Now I understood why Helaman called the warriors his sons, and why he had told us the boys in our units would be our brothers.

In a way, it was strange to me that Kenai helped me over the rough terrain because for the past year and a half Gideon and the other boys of my unit had been doing it. They were as much like brothers to me as Kenai was. Though with Gideon, my feelings went much beyond sisterly affection.

I looked back at Gideon, hopping easily down from the tree Kenai had just helped me over, his long legs making it easy for him. I wondered if he felt the same way about me.

My mind roved back over the time we had spent together since that day in early spring when I had claimed I was indifferent to him. I remembered his hands adjusting my aim, his quiet words of encouragement, the intensity in his eyes when we had sparred on the training ground. I remembered him admitting that he missed our time together at the falls. I remembered his kiss, the slow and tentative kiss I tried never to think about because the memory only confused me.

It's not that I love you.

There were so many different kinds of love. How was I to sort through them all?

The four of us trekked quietly through meadows and mountain valleys, but none of the journey seemed to follow an established path. Much of the time we traveled straight up the mountainside.

"Don't leave signs for someone to follow," Kenai told me. Kenai seemed to have forgotten all the time we spent together in the woods while growing up. He and Micah had taught me to hide my own trail long ago. I watched him for a moment, his face closed, his movements quick and deliberate, and I decided to take his instruction as a reminder. A reminder wouldn't hurt me, and anyway, maybe he needed to give it more than I needed to hear it.

About midday we came to a summit. Before we crested the top, Kenai halted and said, "We don't want to skyline ourselves, so we're going to creep low up the rise until we've seen what lies on the other side."

"Don't you already know what's on the other side?"

"A valley full of Lamanite soldiers," Kenai said curtly, and the prickle at the back of my neck told me he wasn't joking.

He was never joking anymore.

"Where are we going, Kenai?" I planted my feet, bracing them against two jagged rocks. "And why?"

He paused and then gestured Gideon and Jonas closer. He stood with his arms folded while we all gathered around him.

"We're relieving a detail of spies that are watching Antiparah. For obvious reasons, we aren't taking the road. The city is on the far side of the valley that is beyond this peak." He gestured up to the peak that loomed above us to the south.

"And why?" I asked again after considering for a moment.

"Because I said so, and I outrank you."

None of my captains had ever said something like that to

me, commanding me to do something that way, with sharpness and unyielding in his voice. But when they gave an order, I complied. Maybe it wasn't Kenai that was acting strange. Maybe it was me. I wouldn't have questioned an order from Seth or Gideon or even Lib, though lately his over-protectiveness had been getting worse and I knew some of his orders were because of it.

"Oh, Ket," Kenai said, backing down. "Don't get all stubborn on me. Let's eat before we cross the summit. Come on." He held out his hand to me.

I stared at it. Did he want me to take it? I didn't, and instead, I clasped my own hands in front of me and looked around.

"Where?" I asked tersely.

"Where what?"

"Where do you want me to eat, Captain?"

"Keturah." Kenai was more perplexed by my question than exasperated, as I thought he would be, as the old Kenai would have been. He really had forgotten the way we used to be together. Something was bothering Kenai. He had the weight of a lot of responsibility on his shoulders. Perhaps his duties required him to do things he didn't like doing. I knew he would do whatever was necessary. Kenai was going on nineteen now, but I thought this war had aged him more than that.

Persisting in my teasing, I raised my eyebrows.

He dropped his hand and led the way to an area protected in the trees.

"This rock okay?" I asked, indicating a stone I intended to sit on.

Gideon and Jonas were not oblivious to the tension between my brother and me. They each sat on their heels and eyed us warily as they got their food from their satchels, portions of cold meat, cheese, and bread.

Kenai considered me for a moment, narrowed his eyes,

and then said, "No, that's where the captain sits."

Exactly what I was looking for. I grinned widely, punched him in the arm, and flounced over to sit near Gideon, who sent me a questioning look. I shrugged and pulled my own rations from my satchel.

Kenai sat on the rock and tried to hide his smile from me.

When we had eaten, Kenai said, "There's a stream down that way. I'll go fill the water skins."

Gideon and I emptied ours, swallowing quickly, and tossed them to Kenai.

"I'll go with you," said Jonas.

Neither Gideon nor I spoke while they were gone, but Gideon reached behind us into the deep shade of the underbrush. He picked a moonflower that still bloomed and passed it to me in silence. He held my gaze for a small moment, but then looked away.

I looked around and realized the area was covered in moonflower vines. At night, this place would look ethereal with so many white blooms, and their perfume would drift on the breeze for half a mile.

I tucked the large white bloom behind my ear, and lay back in the vines to rest until it was time to go.

I lay very still, even when I felt Gideon's fingertips touch mine. I felt his gaze on my face and opened my eyes to meet it. The way he only held my gaze for a moment, the way he looked down, smiling, and then looked back at me because he couldn't help it told me exactly how he felt.

When Kenai and Jonas returned, we set off for the summit. Kenai passed me with his long stride and tugged at my hair.

As Kenai had said, when we crossed the summit we could indeed see the city of Antiparah in the distance. It looked to be another half a day's journey, but we didn't travel that long before Kenai sounded the margay's call and we walked into a grove where a unit of four of his men waited for us.

Kenai introduced Gideon and me to Jacom, Levi, Eliam, and Mahonri.

"So this is your little sister," said Mahonri, looking me over in a way none of the striplings had ever done. "Kenai's sister. The great woman warrior. You were right, she's perfect."

What was that supposed to mean?

I glared at him and fingered my copper axe at my belt, but Kenai ignored his comment and demanded, "Give me your report from Antiparah."

Jacom stepped forward. "There is movement inside the city. The people are gathering, preparing for something."

"Preparing for what?" asked Kenai.

"For battle?" asked Gideon. "They must know we're making preparations for war."

Eliam shook his head. "I don't think so. It's the women and children who bustle around the yards and gather the herds in."

"Perhaps they are sending the women and children to safety," suggested Jonas.

"We'll find out," said Kenai. Then he turned to the four boys we were replacing. "Tell Helaman all that you've seen. Meet us on the northeast side of the summit in a fortnight at the start of the second watch."

The four of them gathered their things and set off toward Judea. They wouldn't make it back tonight, but they would have a good start before it hit full dark. Kenai and his men were skilled at traveling by the stars so they could utilize the cover of darkness, and they might just travel all night and walk into Judea at dawn as Kenai had done the morning of the last campaign. Only a half moon would shine tonight, but it would be bright. The air was clear and the sky cloudless, making travel easy.

Unfortunately, the absence of cloud cover also meant the temperature would fall during the night. And with rain sure to come in the next few days, it could have made for a miserable fortnight.

Much of the fortnight was wet and cold, but it wasn't miserable. We made a base camp high in the hills above the city and Kenai sent Gideon and me out scouting together on the west side of the city while he and Jonas kept their watch on the east side.

Before we departed, I went to the stream to fill my water skin. When I returned, I heard Kenai speaking to Gideon. Kenai had been so different and secretive on this trip that I thought maybe he was giving Gideon the real instructions he intended to keep a secret from me. I stayed partially concealed on the opposite side of a large mahogany tree. I peered around it and listened.

"They patrol a perimeter close to the city, but they seldom patrol this far out. Just keep alert for scouts. The gates are open and the people are allowed to come and go as they please. If a traveler comes across you, pretend to be traveling also. I hear you speak Lamanite."

"I do."

Kenai nodded. "If you run into anyone, tell them you are married and traveling to see family."

"I can come up with my own story."

I watched then as Kenai folded his arms over his chest and gave Gideon a level stare. In a low voice he never intended for me to hear, he said, "I'm sending Keturah with you because you work so well together. I know she listens to you. But I hope I don't have to remind you that the girl you will be alone with is my sister."

Gideon had been standing casually, listening to his orders, but his fists clenched reflexively against the insult on his honor.

"And remember that she is spoken for."

Gideon made no reply. I would have burst from my

hiding place in outrage but for Jonas, who appeared at my side and placed a restraining hand on my arm.

He gave the slightest shake of his head and said, "Don't," under his breath.

"And I expect her returned to me in safety. If she is harmed while under your protection—"

"You question my honor?" Gideon demanded suddenly. "I would protect your sister even to the giving of my life!" He bit the words out, barely controlling his anger. "I would protect her even from myself."

Kenai studied the strong warrior for long moments. I wondered if Jonas could hear my heart pounding. I had never witnessed any of my brothers act this way concerning me.

Kenai shifted back and his voice softened. I didn't think he had intended to anger Gideon. But he seemed satisfied, as if he had confirmed something to himself.

"I could never question your honor. I am not concerned about you stealing her virtue, Gid. I am concerned about you stealing her heart."

Chapter 18

"I am not spoken for," I told Gideon later when we sat on an outcropping overlooking the city. There was indeed movement happening, though we couldn't determine what they meant to accomplish by it.

Gideon didn't speak right away. Nearly twenty, he was clearly full-grown. I felt like a child sitting next to him. Seventeen now, I wasn't a child—but sometimes I still felt like one.

"Your family has expectations, Kanina," he said matter-of-factly. "And your heart is divided," he added with aching surety.

"I do not think Kenai was speaking on behalf of my family." Gideon turned to look at me, but I kept my head turned away when I confided, "Kenai is Zeke's best and oldest friend. His loyalty does not know bounds."

"Does Zeke still intend to marry you then?"

I did look at him then. "Of course." I frowned. "Why wouldn't he?"

The idea that Zeke might change his mind had never occurred to me, and I wasn't very comfortable with it.

"Did you never think he might want his wife to love him?"

Love him. His wife. Gideon couldn't know, but that question cut very deep.

"I do love him," I admitted quietly.

He placed his hand over mine. "I know."

We spent three nights in the hills together. The first night was cold, as I had predicted. We could have no fire, and so, when my teeth began to chatter, Gideon sat against a tree and let me lean back against him in the warm circle of his arms and sleep while he kept watch.

The next two nights were warmer but rainy, and we built a shelter from broad evergreen leaves at the base of an overhang and took turns sleeping in our bedrolls tucked up against the rocks.

Beyond what the spies already knew, we didn't learn anything from our time together on the west side of the city. We were too far away.

When we met up again with Kenai and Jonas, Kenai said, "We still can't determine what they're doing."

We were all quiet.

"Have you ever tried sending someone into the city?" Gideon asked him.

"No," said Kenai gravely as he leveled a look at me, and a long silence dragged out between us.

"You want me to go in," I said suddenly, realizing what that look meant.

"No," he said quietly. "But you're the only one of us who can."

I looked to Gideon. He was looking at Kenai with a measure of suspicion in his narrowed eyes, but he agreed with Kenai—none of them could enter the city. They looked like Nephites, and they looked like soldiers. A glance at Jonas told me he wouldn't argue.

"Okay," I said, raising my chin. "When? How?"

Kenai's face showed both relief and regret.

Gideon took a menacing step toward Kenai. "That's the reason you chose her, isn't it? The whole reason you brought her here."

Kenai shifted uncomfortably, but he gestured to me and said, "Just look at her! She looks exactly like our mother. Her dark hair and eyes will get her through the city gates with no one the wiser. Neither you nor I could do that."

"She's a young girl—she won't even be challenged," added Jonas.

"She won't attract any attention," insisted Kenai.

"She's your sister!" cried Gideon.

"She's a soldier!" Kenai shot back.

I stepped between them. "I said I'd do it."

They both looked at me. Gideon's throat worked.

Kenai spoke to Gideon over my head. "Maybe Ket's heart wasn't the one I should have been worried about."

Without a word to any of us, Gideon turned his back and walked angrily away. I knew he hated when his feelings for me got in the way of his responsibilities. They confused him, and he felt guilty when they compromised his sense of duty.

I watched Gideon walk away, then I turned to Kenai. "Tell me what to do."

It had rained again during the night, but the morning was beautiful and clear when I approached the gates of Antiparah. I eyed the guards nervously, but kept a pleasant smile on my face.

Unlike our tightly guarded gates at Judea, Antiparah had an open gate. Kenai had been watching the city for a long time and if he said the gate was open, I believed him. Because the people here had no need to fear the Nephites would take their women or children—they knew we wouldn't—and because their army was strong enough to discourage enemy soldiers from venturing near, the people didn't fear going outside the city walls.

But we had weakened their army, and I was making

myself uneasy thinking about what that might mean regarding how strictly the gates were guarded.

I wished Gideon was there with me. I had been wishing it since leaving the boys in the trees. He was the one with the gift for languages. What if someone asked me a question I could not answer with a nod?

Before we had left our base camp that morning, the four of us had knelt in prayer. The boys had walked me down to the city and even now waited in the trees behind me with their bows loaded, not that three dead guards would necessarily be helpful if something went wrong.

Kenai had reminded me what information I needed to listen for, and Gideon had taught me some Lamanite words, making me repeat them over and over. Added to the words my mother had taught me, I was walking into a Lamanite holding guarded by their largest army with about ten Lamanite words in my arsenal and nothing but my father's blade strapped to my thigh under my long tunic as a weapon.

"Bak betul eh nah?" asked a guard with a smile and a nod as I approached. There were only four guards standing casually to the sides of the gates. This one was young, a year or two older than Gideon maybe, and handsome with dancing, dark eyes and a smile that took me off guard with its friendliness.

"Shalal," I greeted, and it was not hard to blush and smile at him, which Kenai, Jonas, and Gideon had all agreed would help me get past the guards.

"Shalal," he replied. "Bak betul eh nah?" The guard pushed off from the wall he was leaning against and came toward me.

"Cumeni," I said without really knowing why, but still smiling.

His eyebrows rose and he glanced at the sun in the sky.

I covered a pretend yawn, as large as I could make it.

He smiled.

"Lachum nah ahche?"

What was my business here today?

I understood him! Overcome, I looked down at the ground where the toe of my beaded boot made trails through the dirt. I understood, but I didn't have the words to reply.

He stepped closer to me and spoke again.

Yes, I nodded, I was visiting family. I was leaving today. Yes, I was traveling alone, and yes I did know it was not very safe to do so. What was my name?

The other guards were grinning at us, and it occurred to me that perhaps not everyone got questioned this much at the gate.

I blushed more deeply when I realized this, and why, but I made myself look him in the eye—I was a soldier like he was, after all—and tell him my name. "Keturah," I said.

"I'm Muloki," he said and placed his hand on my shoulder.

I had not been greeted this way—the proper way to greet a woman—in a long time, not since I had joined the army, and it surprised me that the Lamanites shared the same polite custom. It had always bothered me that there were different ways to greet men and women. Why should they be different? But Muloki's hand lingering as it did on my shoulder felt so personal and so flattering.

His thumb brushed along the skin at my neck and sent chills skittering down my arms, and I knew it was intentional.

"Shalal, Muloki," I said, my eyelids fluttering down again, this time my gaze falling on my entwined fingers. When I realized I was twisting them nervously, I stopped.

One of the other guards laughed and called out to Muloki. "You'll have to gain permission from her kinsmen to court her if you detain her any longer!"

I thought of my kinsman in the woods behind me with an arrow notched into his bow. I didn't think he would give Muloki his permission.

Muloki winced a little as he held my gaze, but then rolled his eyes and smiled, sending a quick glance back over his shoulder.

Then he gestured me through the open gate.

I walked through the gate before I let myself take a deep breath and release it slowly. I pulled my hair over my shoulder and looked curiously back at the gate. Had I really gotten through so easily? Muloki was staring after me, and he turned quickly away when he saw I had seen him. I couldn't help but smile.

Then I looked around for the well.

It was morning and all the women would be fetching water from the well. If not a well, then a river. And if not the women, hopefully some girls old enough to know what was going on in Antiparah.

I wasn't even sure I would be able to understand anything once I got to the well. I said a quick prayer—about the tenth one since leaving the boys—that God would guide my steps.

Kenai had said I must walk confidently as if I was walking toward the well at home or shopping in the market with Mother. I tried to. I held my head high and I didn't glance around like I had never been here before. In truth, the city looked much the same as Judea.

And if it was in fact like Judea, there would be a well in the center of the city.

I kept my path straight down the main road until I saw a stream of Lamanitish women with water vessels balanced on their heads. They were dressed in sleeveless tunics belted at the waist. They looked beautiful in soft greens, blues and reds, with straw colored baskets or terra cotta water pitchers on their heads and black-haired little ones at their feet.

When it was warm, I preferred to wear a sarong tied at my shoulder. I knew it was not a coincidence that Kenai had advised me to wear a tunic instead. Still, it was not sleeveless and I felt out of place. I balanced no pitcher on my head, and no children danced around my feet. I fingered my water skin and felt sure someone would notice I didn't belong here.

I studied the well and the women around it as I approached. A spring flowed from the earth into a pool where the women knelt and filled their containers.

Just as I was about to pull my water skin from where it hung on my satchel and kneel at the pool, I saw a little girl about Chloe's age carrying a small vessel up a side street toward the well. I watched her for a moment. She was alone, and even the small vessel was too big for her to carry.

Go to the girl and offer to help her.

I felt a presence next to me, but I knew by the tingle running up my spine that if I looked around there would be no one there. I wasn't sure if I had heard the words or felt them, but I did not wait to be told twice.

When I got close to the little girl, I squatted down so I was on her level. I looked into her big brown eyes. "Shalal, little Kanina," I said.

"Shalal," she replied, her brown eyes wide with curiosity.

I gestured to her clay pitcher and said the word Gideon had taught me for water. "Ha'a?"

When she nodded, I took the pitcher from her and reached out with my other hand, which she took trustingly, and we walked together to the pool.

I knelt at the side of the pool and dipped the pitcher into the cool, clear spring. I set it down and wiped the excess water from the outside with the bottom of my tunic just as I had done so many times at home in my village. It was a small vessel, but filled, it would be too heavy for the girl. I wondered why her mother had sent her alone. I would carry it home for her.

"I'm Keturah," I said to the girl, placing a hand on my chest.

She smiled.

I asked her what her name was.

"Susanna," she replied.

I didn't know how we understood each other, but I balanced the pitcher on my head like the other women, held out my hand to Susanna, and told her to lead me to her home.

She placed her hand in mine and began walking back down the street from which she had come.

We walked to the outskirt of the city before she turned into a small yard surrounded by a fence. Moonflower vines grew over the fence. The yard was neat. A tidy herb garden grew to the side of the hut.

Susanna let go of my hand and walked through the flap at the door. After hesitating for a moment when she didn't return, I went to the doorway and rapped on the frame.

"Shalal?" I called.

"Come in," said a thin voice from beyond the mat.

I pushed it aside and stepped into the dim hut.

After my eyes adjusted, I could see that it was very similar to my hut back in Melek. A stove sat in the corner with shelves above it for the storage of dishes. I could see that no fire burned in the stove.

I found Susanna sitting on a mat near a pallet on the floor, upon which a frail woman lay—a woman who looked exactly like me.

Well, more accurately, she looked exactly like my mother.

"Oh!" I said.

The woman looked at me for long moments in confusion. Finally she asked, "Leah?"

I stepped closer and fell to my knees next to her pallet. "No," I said. "Leah is my mother."

When she didn't reply, only looked at me, I asked, "Are you sick?"

She nodded. "Stomach pains."

I hesitated and then reached out and placed my hands over her stomach. It felt normal. I felt her head. Fever.

"Just the flu, I think," she said and smiled the same smile Mother did when she was tired.

"Have you any hyptis?" I asked.

She shook her head.

I reached into my satchel and withdrew my plant book. I opened it and showed the picture of hyptis to Susanna. "Does this grow here?" I asked her. When she nodded, I said, "Please go pick me some and bring it here."

Her mother nodded and Susanna ran out the door, reminding me so much of Chloe, only without the laughter and the skipping.

"What is your name?" I asked the woman.

"Hannah."

"How do you know my mother?"

"Leah is my sister."

I had gotten up to move to the stove, but I stilled. I wanted to ask her many more questions, but she was so weak and breathless I didn't ask them. I would ask Mother. Instead, I set about building a fire and heating some of the water I had carried. I made a strong broth from the things I found in the hut—dried meat, roots, and herbs. Hannah lay still, but her eyes followed me.

"Why are you here?" she asked breathily.

I knelt beside her again and smoothed her hair back from her forehead. She was burning hot.

"I need to know what is happening in Antiparah. Why are the people gathering their flocks and loading the grains for travel?"

"So it's true," she said.

"What's true?"

"The Ammonites have come to avenge their God."

"They have come to reclaim the Nephite cities."

She closed her eyes and sighed weakly.

"What is happening here?" I asked quietly.

"We are leaving. They say in the city that the Nephites are preparing for battle. The Lamanitish people here do not want to be caught in the middle of Ammoron's fight. We are leaving." She paused to breathe. "We are yielding up the city, falling back to Manti."

I stared at her for a moment, and then I got up to prepare a tea from the herbs in my satchel that would take her fever down.

I stayed long enough to administer the medicines and prepare the hyptis for use. I gave instructions to Susanna, kissed her on top of her head, and went to the door. I wished I could stay longer, much longer, but Kenai, Gideon, and Jonas would storm the gates to come in after me if I did not hurry back.

"Tell Leah," breathed Hannah, "I love her."

I nodded. "Good-bye Aunt Hannah."

Our eyes met, and I left.

As I hurried along the main street and out through the gates, where Muloki gave me a friendly wave and a playful wink, I was thinking that Mother had a lot of explaining to do.

And I was hoping I never had to meet that friendly guard on the battlefield.

I stayed on the main road out of the city until I was sure I was out of view of the guards at the main gate, and then I surreptitiously searched for any other guards on the walls and in the towers who might be watching. When I was sure no one was watching me, I veered off into the forest and jogged toward our meeting place.

I sounded the margay's call and heard it in return. Then I saw them through the trees. Kenai and Jonas sat on a fallen log. Their heads perked up at my call. Gideon was pacing the tiny clearing.

When Kenai saw me, he shot to his feet. "Where have you

been?" he exclaimed. I went into his arms, and he hugged me fiercely. He would never say it, but I knew it had been hard for him to send me into Antiparah alone.

"I'll tell you," I said, but I turned and went to Gideon. He had ceased his pacing. He stood stone still, the look on his face giving away everything. He bent and wrapped me with unrestrained affection in his thick arms and straightened, lifting me gently so my feet came off the ground. He held me in silence for long moments. No, I hadn't mistaken that look on his face—I recognized the feeling in his embrace.

Kenai said nothing, but I felt his eyes on us.

I told them everything about the friendly guard and how I had told him I had come from Cumeni that morning. I told them how I had yawned to indicate the earliness of my departure.

"Why were you delayed so long at the gate?" Kenai asked. "Did you have trouble?"

I sent a glance to Gideon who was watching me intently. They had seen that? "No trouble," I said. "The man was nice."

Suddenly, Kenai grinned. "How nice?"

I didn't want to blush again, so I got defensive. "Just nice. He let me pass."

"He lets everyone pass. What did he say to you?" Kenai insisted.

"How could she know?" asked Gideon.

But I did know, though there was no way I could explain how. "He introduced himself. His name is Muloki. He was flirting with me, I think."

"You would be the last to know if a man was flirting with you," Kenai laughed. He was about to say something else, to tease me about the guard, but Gideon shifted closer to me and a severe look stifled the words before Kenai said them.

I told them everything except that Hannah was Mother's sister, that she looked so much like me. I didn't know where to begin. I was confused, and I was mad at Mother. She had not told me of Father's nobility—my own nobility—and she had not told me about her twin sister. Why would she hide these things? I wanted to think on it before I told anyone.

"She didn't think it strange that you didn't know what was going on in the city?" asked Kenai.

"No, she knew I was Ammonite."

A look of alarm shot into Kenai's eyes. "How?" He demanded. "From your speech? How did you understand each other?"

"I don't know," I said. "She spoke like me."

He thrust both hands into his hair and turned from me. "She'll tell them our spies breached the gates!" he accused as he whirled back.

I knew she wouldn't. She wasn't pleased that the Ammonites had come to "avenge their God," but she had seemed resigned to it.

"No. She was sick in bed. She couldn't even get up to start her fire or cook herself something nourishing."

After a full explanation, Kenai seemed satisfied, but Gideon gave me a strange look. He knew there was something I was holding back. He knew me so well by then, I was sure he did sense me hiding something, but he couldn't know it had nothing to do with the information Kenai needed.

"So the Lamanites are abandoning Antiparah." Jonas let out a whoop that reminded me of Darius.

Kenai gave a genuine smile and then turned to Gideon.

"Gid, you and Ket can keep watch on the west side again. Move south around the city tomorrow, and meet us back at the main camp the day after that. We will leave for Judea at the new moon."

No warning. No reprimand. No admonishing Gideon to remember who I was. Just trust.

Kenai held out his hand and after a moment, Gideon

clasped arms with him. Then he pulled me aside while Gideon and Jonas strapped on their weapons and supply packs and prepared to move out.

"I know you follow the Spirit," Kenai said. He glanced at Gideon. Then he looked into my eyes. *I just hope you know what you're doing.*

I wanted to tell him that I didn't, that for once, I would welcome advice.

"See you at the new moon, Ket," he said aloud, and gesturing to Jonas, he turned abruptly, and they left.

Things were different between Gideon and me. As we traveled up into the hills, the new feeling deepened. We didn't speak about it. We couldn't. But when I closed my eyes I could still see the expression on his face when I had walked safely out of the enemy stronghold. I could still feel the urgency in his embrace and the relief in his deep sigh, and I knew I would never be the same girl I had been before.

We kept watch on the city until it was time to meet Mahonri, Eliam and the others. The movement inside the city— they had actually begun moving provisions out through both gates by the time we left—made more sense now that we knew what they were doing. I wondered if Hannah would be well enough to travel to Manti.

I walked with Kenai when we set out to meet his men beyond the summit. The grasses were wet from the rain, making my feet cold even in my moccasin boots, but the air smelled fresh and clean.

At a time when Gideon and Jonas were a short distance ahead of us, Kenai said, "I've been thinking, Ket, about Lib."

"Oh?"

"You can be a really sweet girl, and I know you're trying to spare Lib's feelings or whatever," he began. He was uncomfortable, I could tell, but not as uncomfortable as Micah sometimes was when he had to talk to me about boys.

"He's my captain. He worries about me," I said.

"It's more than worry, and I think you know that."

I made a noncommittal sound.

"He hides it well, but I see it because it is my duty to help Micah look for it." He sighed. "You're just going to confuse him, and he'll see it as teasing. You'll lose his trust, Ket, like with Zeke. If you really like him—that's fine I guess—just be honest with everyone. That's all I'm saying."

"I am honest," I protested. I was.

He snorted softly. "Sometimes your actions can lie even when your mouth tells the truth. And sometimes," he went on more quietly, "your actions tell the truth."

I thought about how I had embraced Gideon so tightly, so desperately when I had walked out of Antiparah, of Kenai watching it and seeing a truth he didn't want to recognize.

"Okay," I said. "I'll think about that." I paused. "Zeke doesn't trust me?"

He shot me a sideways glance. "Do you blame him?"

If anyone knew Zeke's true feelings, if anyone knew him better than I did, it was Kenai. I didn't answer, not out loud. But after a few moments, I asked, "Kenai?"

"Yeah?" he answered distractedly, glancing at the sky and judging the time by the depth of the sun on the western horizon.

"Do you think he still loves me?"

Kenai's silence scared me.

Things had changed after Zeke kissed me. Gotten weird. He never came around camp to see me, and when we did see each other at council meetings, he barely said anything to me. But I knew I still meant something to him, or he wouldn't have been so deliberately avoiding me.

Was he deliberately avoiding me?

Who was I if I wasn't Zeke's best friend? If I wasn't the girl he loved? I didn't want to define myself by how Zeke felt about me, but he had been such a large part of my life. It would be impossible to just extricate him from it—not without creating an empty space.

But Kenai looked down from studying the surroundings. "Of course he does, though I've no idea why."

He yelped playfully when I punched him.

"Did Mother ever tell you anything about having a sister?" I asked, venturing on another sensitive subject.

He stopped walking. "We have another sister?"

"No," I said quickly, laughing a little. "Did she ever say that she had a sister?"

Kenai frowned. "No. I'm not aware of any family—neither Mother's nor Father's."

"Don't you think that's strange? They must have families."

He shrugged. "They left their families when they joined the church of God—like Eli did."

I contemplated this. It was not the truth. It couldn't be. Mother's father had taught her the healing ways. When she spoke of him, she spoke fondly. Had he not joined the church of God? Had he just let her walk away from Middoni with the Ammonites after Father had died? Had he let her take her children and go alone?

It was already dark when we approached the summit. The clouds were thick in the sky covering the stars, and there would be no moon tonight—just the barest sliver, and that was already setting. Traveling under the new moon decreased the chances of being spotted by the Lamanite spies. We could all easily navigate by the stars, but the darkness made it difficult to see the things around us.

We walked through the darkness together. Kenai stopped and tried to get his bearings.

"Any idea where we're at?" he asked finally in a low voice, and I knew it wasn't easy for him to admit he didn't know.

"Sound the margay. See if they reply," suggested Jonas.

"Wait," I said and lifted my nose in the air to better catch the perfume that floated there. Moonflowers. I slipped my hand into Gideon's in the darkness. "We're almost there."

Chapter 19

I watched from my position on Judea's training ground as Teomner led a thousand soldiers out to secure Antiparah.

We did not go with them.

Corban nudged me. It was my turn to spar. With one last longing glance at the retreating backs of the soldiers, I turned and faced my opponent, the boy who stood in front of me in our column and still had yet to smile at me.

I had come back to Judea from the scouting mission anticipating more action—battles, small skirmishes, hunting parties, anything. Even though it had been rather boring work watching an entire city from a distance, it had still been more exciting than maintaining the fortifications in Judea and repeating the same training over and over.

But there was no action, and I fought jealousy as even the sound of the army's footsteps faded.

One afternoon after we had finished our training for the day, Mother came by our camp with Kalem. Most of my unit had been playing ball, but when they saw Kalem, they rushed to get their weapon-making materials.

Kalem's knowledge had proven to be an immense asset

to our army, and I was glad that he had found friendship and acceptance here.

Mother handed a cloth sack to Lib. She often brought the boys extra treats when she could get them, though an arm around their waist, a smile, and a few motherly words worked just as well in gaining their affection. None of them ever said they missed their own mother, but I was sure they all did.

I watched as Lib began pulling apples from the sack and tossing them to the men. They all chorused their thanks to my mother as she walked toward me.

"Hi, Kanina," she said pleasantly.

"Hello, Mother," I replied.

Since Antiparah—since meeting Hannah—I had planned to tell her I had met her sister, but every time I tried, I lost my courage. To tell her anything, I would have to divulge all the details of my mission into the enemy city, and I knew she would not like that I had done it. Why was I still protecting her from the things I did and loved that made me the person I was?

But I knew. I thought I would disappoint her, and so in a way, I was protecting myself from her disappointment. And it wasn't just that I had been inside the city that would upset her. It was the fact that Kenai had been the one who asked me to go in. So maybe I was protecting Kenai, too.

Asking me to walk into the enemy stronghold had been a difficult thing for Kenai to do, but I wished he had known he hadn't needed to manipulate me. He should have known that once I recognized the necessity of the mission and knew the possibility for me and only me to make it work, I would not say no. That was the reason he had waited until I had seen for myself the futility of watching the city from the hills before he asked me to do it.

And it was the reason he had brought Gideon. Zeke, for instance, would never have let me walk into the city alone. Kenai knew Gideon would see reason, would do what had to be done.

Kenai knew Gideon could convince me to do it if I failed to agree to the plan.

I know she listens to you.

Now I understood better why Gideon didn't want to love me.

My mother stood by me and surveyed the boys of my unit. "They miss their families, I think," she said.

I took a breath. "Do you miss yours?"

I didn't know what I expected, but she just sighed deeply, regretfully and said, "Yes, very much. But the years have a way of tempering the sting."

"Do you have a big family?" I asked.

"No," she said.

I bit my lip. "Mother, there is something I want to tell you."

She looked at me expectantly.

"When I went on that mission with Kenai, I met your sister, Hannah. She's at Antiparah. She was anyway, before they left."

A look of confusion stole over her face. "Hannah?"

"Kenai, he asked me to—"

"But my sister is dead," she said before I could go on.

I stared at her. "No," I said, as confused as she was. "I met her. Inside the city. She was ill, but certainly not dead."

Tears welled in my mother's eyes. "No, Keturah, she died when we were very young."

My chest tightened suddenly and my stomach dropped. I thought of the voice that had spoken to me, directed me to help Susanna draw water and carry it home.

"How young?" I asked.

"Oh, around Chloe's age, I'd say. Chloe reminds me of her sometimes with her big brown eyes. Except, my sister never skipped around like Chloe does." She smiled at her memories.

My mind was turning things over and over. What had

happened? Who had that woman been? Why had she looked like my mother and known of my mother? Why had she spoken my Nephite dialect so flawlessly?

"Where did you meet this woman who claimed to be my sister?" Mother asked after a silence had settled around us for several moments.

I looked at her and she must have seen the concern and confusion in my face because she touched my arm and asked, "Keturah, what has happened? What is it?"

I started with Kenai requesting me for the mission. That part she knew already. Then I told her everything. I told how we could not determine what was happening in the city. I told how we determined someone must infiltrate it and find out. I looked her in the eye and told her how I had walked boldly into Antiparah, past the guard, and toward the well.

And then I told her every single thing I could remember about Susanna and Hannah. "She said to tell you she loves you."

Mother closed her eyes. "I do not know what happened, Kanina. I am only glad that it did."

I wanted to ask about Father, too, about his royalty—something I had not yet been brave enough to do for surely she had some reason she had not told us. I opened my mouth, but Kalem motioned us over and we joined the rest of my unit. The moment was gone.

It was not many months after we had secured Antiparah that we received six thousand more soldiers from Zarahemla and the lands around it. This might have put a tremendous strain on our provisions, but we received additional provisions with the men and their families. Added to the supplies we received from the government at Zarahemla and the regular supplies we received from the people of Ammon, it was sufficient.

The months went by and still we trained and fortified. We had to be satisfied with some small skirmishes and intrigues with rogue bands of Lamanites, hunting parties, recon missions, messenger assignments to the cities round about, and guard duties. But we had yet to see another battle or major stratagem. It had been a year now since the decoy past Antiparah, and for that time we merely held the line.

Next to hunting, my favorite job in Judea was manning the watch towers. The thing I liked about it was that even on the hottest days, the tower provided shade. They had the potential to be stifling inside, but they never were because a breeze blew through the slim windows.

I sat with one other man from my unit and we watched the terrain. We watched for enemy movement, but none of us had ever seen anything. It was boring work unless I got paired with Reb, and then I laughed the whole time. Perhaps I also liked to be the one on the watch instead of the recipient of it.

I liked when Lib paired me up with himself, which he was careful to do only once in ten times, but with so many towers around the city and a full time guard that fell to the Ammonites, it came often enough. We would sit together in the cool breeze and have long talks about so many things of which he had great knowledge while we kept a close eye on the beautiful valley and hills around us. I let him school me in ship-building, art, farming, armor, the words of the prophets—it seemed there was no subject about which he didn't have some useful knowledge. I felt I didn't know anything when I listened to him talk, but he never made me feel that way on purpose. The only area in which I could rival him was plants and medicines.

One late afternoon when I was on duty with Gideon, the rain poured down on the sturdy roof of the tower. That was another good thing about watch duty—it was dry. Well, mostly dry, I thought as I watched a small puddle form in the corner where a leak let in drizzles of water.

Gideon lay on his back with his head propped on his satchel trying to catch up on the sleep he had missed during the night—when he had sat awake outside my tent while I slept. He was so indefatigable that it was strange to see him resting—though I knew he wasn't asleep. His long legs were crossed at the ankles, his hands lay over his chest with his fingers loosely entwined, and his face relaxed into the lines of a face that was no longer a boy's.

No one was going out in that rain if he could help it, so I glanced at the terrain regularly but let my eyes roam over Gideon.

I loved him so much.

I had known since Antiparah. I had known from the instant I saw his battle-worn face and the wound that would leave a new kind of scar there. His face had shown the same raw relief that I had felt, and he had been unable to restrain his feelings, even in front of Kenai.

I knew he warred within himself against his feelings for me. He had this idea that the call to arms would be a lifetime call for him. I did not fit into his plan.

But wasn't love supposed to conquer those kinds of obstacles?

My fingers itched to sweep back the lock of hair from his forehead, but I wouldn't be able to bear it if he stopped my hand in its gentle caress again. The night on the march to Judea when I had traced his scar seemed so long ago now—over two years. Though it no longer stung and had been balmed by many tender moments, the confusion and rejection I had felt still made me hesitate to reach for him.

I clenched my fists so I would not do it. I would not hurt him by making his war more difficult.

I turned my eyes back to the terrain.

"Gideon, what do you make of this?"

He was up instantly, and I smiled to myself—he was a soldier to his core.

"I don't know," he said after he had gotten a look through the narrow window.

A small band of men had emerged from the canyon and rounded the hill that hid Judea from the West Road. If we had been in the tower near the west gate, we would have called down to the guards to alert them that a band of men approached, but our tower was so far from the gate that protocol only required us to stand at the ready until their business here had been determined.

So we stood at the narrow window, and before long I felt Gideon softly smoothing my hair down my back. I had stopped my own caress, but I was not strong enough to stop his. That was not my war to fight.

We stood like that for a quarter of an hour waiting, as all the guards in the towers would be, until we could see the band of men better. And all the time Gideon stroked my hair, my neck, and down to my shoulder in slow, forbidden caresses.

At last I could restrain myself no longer. I reached back and took his hand. It was rough and hard and dry. I brought it around to my lips and smoothed them over the rough places and the scars. Finally I placed a lingering kiss in the middle of his palm and returned his hand to my shoulder.

"We have to talk about it sometime," I said with my eyes turned again to the band of men approaching us, resigned already that he would not admit his feelings or discuss what we were to each other.

"Kanina," he said, the timbre of his voice low and just loud enough to hear over the rain. "Don't ruin this moment with talk of the future."

I rounded on him, losing my temper and my good intentions with it.

"And when there is no future, Gideon, what will this moment mean? What will I remember about the soldier I once knew? The man whose fierce eyes saw past the girl with the hopeless dream? Whose hard hands taught me a fatal aim and whose warrior heart," my voice broke, "beat as mine?"

225

I searched his face and when I didn't see any warmth, only the stone-cold mask of indifference I had come to hate, I pushed hard against his chest, but he barely moved. My emotions were swirling out of control, and I continued vehemently with both my voice and my chin raised.

"Will I remember that he knew he loved me and spoke the words—that he owned up to his love like the unyieldingly honest man he was? That he valued the gift of my love in return? That he kissed me with everything in his soul? That—"

He pulled me so suddenly to him that my head fell back, and Gideon, my incredible Gideon, was kissing me before I could finish my tirade.

His soul was there in his kiss, his heart in his hands as they urgently clutched my waist, the pressure of his fingers wavering between gentle and desperate. For long moments he was the warrior who fought for what he wanted, the boy who recklessly took it, and the man who hungered for his woman.

The rain beat down on the roof and the band of men approached our stronghold. The puddle had grown larger and threatened to nip at our heels. The gray light had grown dim and our time in the tower was coming to an end.

These were the things that I remembered.

When eternity had passed, the warrior straightened. He looked down into my eyes. His were as black and sharp as my obsidian blade, as if they would either take my life or save it.

"I can't love you," he ground out.

I searched his eyes. "But you do."

He gave a slight nod of his head and then pulled me fiercely against his hard chest, encircling me with protecting arms and we stood for long moments shielded from the war around us.

"You have got to be kidding me," Gideon said to himself after a moment, the emotion in his voice replaced with sarcasm.

"What is it?" I asked. I looked up and followed the line of

his gaze through the window to the men below who approached the city, whose leader was even now calling out to the guards at the gate. I turned toward the window again so I could get a better look.

Gideon stood behind me and watched over my head as fifty or sixty striplings slogged toward the gate.

"Are units out today?" There were too many men to be a hunting party, and the day was too wet besides. "Who is it?" I asked.

He groaned. "My little brother."

"Your brother? Are you sure? Can you see well enough?"

"I'm sure."

"Your little brother. Not Jashon then?"

He gave a little laugh. "No."

"Then that leaves only your youngest brother at home to protect your parents," I said, turning to study his reaction.

He glanced at me and gave me a brief, sad smile, probably glad he didn't have to explain what it meant that his brother had left home, but he turned his eyes back to the band of men below.

"Do you want to go see him?" I asked as we walked back through the city toward our camp. The rain had slowed to a drizzle. It was dark and Gideon did something he rarely allowed himself to do. He took my hand.

"Nah, I'll catch him in the morning."

"How old is he?"

"Lamech is barely twelve."

"Not that much younger than Darius," I observed.

"When he first joined the militia, but Darius is fifteen now."

"The same age I was when I joined the militia."

He squeezed my hand.

Lib had saved our rations for us, but they were long since cold. Noah had cooked a pheasant, and the meal was delicious, as I had come to expect when Noah cooked. Lib was already sitting up outside my tent when Gideon said, "Goodnight, Kanina."

I made a point not to watch him walk away.

"Anything exciting happen?" Lib asked, completely unaware that the entire world was different.

I pulled the strap of my satchel over my head and rubbed my shoulder where the weight had rested. "Nothing ever happens on guard duty," I said. "Goodnight."

"I'm going with Gideon," I informed him the next morning when Gideon was walking out of camp.

Lib looked at Gideon's retreating figure and then back at me with a dubious expression. "Does he know that?"

I grinned. "He will." And I took off running.

"Hey," I said when I caught up. "I want to meet him."

He glanced down at me and didn't say anything, which I took for permission.

First we went to the command tent to find out where he was.

"Sixty new recruits," said Shem as he ran his finger down the list of names. "We divided them among existing units."

Lamech was in Micah's hundred. The head of his unit was a boy I didn't know named Boaz, but I had heard of him.

Gideon set off in that direction, but I didn't move. He had gone about ten paces when he turned slightly and looked down at his side, lifting his elbow as if he were looking for me there. I couldn't help a small laugh.

"Aren't you coming, little rabbit?"

"Boaz is Zeke's unit leader," I said bluntly.

Gideon put his hands on his hips and heaved a sigh. "It will come up eventually. We might as well face it now."

I walked toward him. "Okay, but no holding my hand."

"Why? Are you afraid Zeke will see? Are you ashamed of our friendship?" he teased. But when he teased me about Zeke, there was always an underlying current of jealousy and tension.

228

"Not as ashamed as you are," I teased him back—something I didn't normally do because I loved Gideon and respected how difficult it was for him to love me in return.

"You're a brat," he said as he turned and fell in beside me.

"I am both bold and deadly, qualities you find irresistible in a woman."

He hooked an elbow around my neck and tousled my hair, an action completely at odds with the way he wanted to hold me, I knew.

I saw Zeke immediately when we approached their camp.

"Go to him," said Gideon.

Zeke looked warily at us as I walked toward him and Gideon hung back.

"You're a nice surprise this morning," Zeke said. He was sitting on a log near their smoldering cook fire adjusting a bow string. He glanced at Gideon. "He's not."

"Your new soldier," I said, ignoring the gibe. "Lamech."

He looked at me, waiting.

"He's Gideon's brother."

His brows rose skeptically, but he met Gideon's eye and pointed out Lamech's tent. He didn't look at me, just frowned and returned his focus to the bow.

"I came to meet him," I said and sat on my heels beside Zeke's log. I picked up one of his arrows and ran my fingers over the thick black stripe and two thinner red ones—it was the way he painted all his arrows.

"I'd never have guessed they were brothers," he said as he glanced toward Gideon and Lamech. "They don't look a thing alike."

I didn't tell him why. "Do you think you can handle it?" I asked instead.

He rolled his eyes toward me and his look stopped just short of a glare. "Do you really think I would take out my feelings about you and Gid on a twelve year old kid?"

"No!" I protested but added, "Maybe unintentionally."

He turned fully and looked me in the eye. "I will treat Gid's brother fairly. Happy?"

"I know."

"Then why did you ask?"

"I didn't ask about how you would treat Lamech. That is where your own mind went," I pointed out. "I asked about you."

His eyes narrowed. "Why would you care about me?" he asked wryly.

It had been close to a year since the decoy and battle of Antiparah. Close to a year since those stolen moments we had shared together in the woods, and rather than improving our relationship, those emotional moments had started to break it down.

At first I hadn't understood why. But I had thought about it a lot in the past year while I was on work details, while hunting, while staring at the terrain from the tower window, while lying on my back in my tent fingering the soft leather that protected me from the elements. Since Kenai had said those hurtful words, that Zeke did not trust me, I had thought about it.

I had confused Zeke.

Sometimes your actions can lie even when your mouth tells the truth. And sometimes, your actions tell the truth.

I had shown him the emotion, the passion, the love I truly did feel for him, and yet he saw me with Gideon so often laughing and touching and staring into his eyes. I knew he had even seen what was written on my face every time I looked at Gideon—I adored, admired, and loved him, and trying to hide it only made it more obvious.

What was Zeke to think?

But what were any of us to do?

"Zeke—" I began to protest, but Gideon and Lamech approached, their long, early-morning shadows falling over us.

I stood, and after Zeke set the bow down, leaning it

carefully against the log, he stood too.

"Lamech, this is Keturah. She is in my unit, and she is Zeke's best friend," Gideon said to his brother.

That was hardly an apt description of my relationship with Zeke these days, but I didn't refute it, and neither did Zeke. I looked at Lamech and smiled.

He was taller than me, though that was not a large accomplishment for a boy. He was slender and sinewy with hair so black and shiny it reflected blue in the sunlight. It was long like Zeke's but unlike Zeke's soft, loose hair, Lamech's was thick and hung in two fat braids at the sides of his head. He was not as handsome as Eli and Joshua, but like Gideon, he definitely wasn't ugly and even at twelve looked dangerous and calculating. His dark, deep-set eyes looked as if they would never reveal his true feelings.

"She's in the army?" Lamech asked his brother doubtingly after regarding me for a moment.

"And a better warrior than you. Do not underestimate her. She is not like Mother."

"It's nice to meet you," I said to Lamech.

He nodded at me, then, dismissing me, turned to Gideon with an obvious bit of hero worship in his eyes. "Mother and Father sent some things for you. And a letter. Come on, I'll get them."

Gideon gave his young brother a look. Lamech interpreted it correctly, rolled his eyes, and laid his hand briefly on my shoulder. "It's nice to meet you too," he said.

"You go catch up with your brother," I said to Gideon. "I'll go back to camp."

Gideon turned to Zeke. "Will you—?"

"Don't." Zeke held up a hand. "Don't ask me that like it is your place to ask it."

The four of us stood silently together for an uncomfortable moment. Lamech looked between his captain and his brother, two men he clearly respected. Then he looked at me with narrowed eyes.

I licked my lips. "Zeke, do you have some time to walk me back to my camp? Lib will pitch a fit if I walk in alone."

"Yeah," he said. It looked like he couldn't get his breath, but he put his hand on the small of my back and led me away from Gideon and Lamech.

I wanted to say I was sorry. I wanted to assure Zeke I loved him. I wanted to comfort him, hold his hand, make things easy again.

Instead of any of those things, I said, "I've been weaving a shawl for dancing. I'm making it to match my beaded boots." I held out a foot so he could see a boot, hopping beside him when he didn't stop walking.

He tried not to, but he smiled.

Chapter 20

I was eighteen before we began to plan the siege of Cumeni.
With the new supplies and men, our armies were strong and Helaman felt the time was right for another major campaign.

"You coming?" Seth asked one night when he was on his way to a council of war.

"Just let me tell Lib."

He waited while I did, and then we left. We were halfway there before I ventured the question, "Is Gideon coming?"

Seth cast me a sidelong glance. "He is. We'll meet him there."

The council met with the men of Antipus. We all felt his absence still, but Helaman presented his plan with authority, and this time he did not ask for a vote on it. He would take the striplings to lay siege on Cumeni and leave Teomner, Antipus's highest captain, in command at Judea.

Shem gave assignments to the captains before we left the fire. I waited on the outer edge of the light for Seth and Gideon to walk me back to camp.

Gideon joined me first. He smiled when he saw me, and

I couldn't help a smile in return. He took my elbow and pulled me farther away from the others. The light was dim, but the fire glowed in his eyes.

"What is it?" I asked in a hushed voice.

He leaned down so he could keep his voice low as well. "Helaman has entrusted me with a mission."

"You already command fifty. Has he given you more men?"

He shook his head. "But the authority to choose the right ones."

I searched his eyes. This was what he wanted. Recognition. Responsibility. Rank.

"What kind of mission?"

He glanced quickly over his shoulder. No one was near. "We're to remove the guard from the Cumeni Road."

"We?"

"Of course I'm taking you. You're stealthier than anyone, Ket."

I had worried a nail while the council talked about removing the guard from the road. Kenai had said the guard was large—over a hundred men—and I knew it would involve fighting.

Seth found us in the dark. "You walking back with me or what?" He looked between us.

The captains had dispersed and most of them were gone. Micah was standing in the firelight with Shem, Isaiah, and Ephraim, Helaman's highest captains. Helaman lingered to confer with Teomner, but when he left, Teomner and one of his men approached Micah and the others. I wondered if Micah stood among these men because of his age, his skill, or because they knew who he was.

"Ket, are you coming?"

Seth and Gideon had turned back when I didn't follow them.

"Yeah," I said. "Sorry."

When I got to my tent, most of the others had gone to sleep. Lib sat up near the fire writing something on a piece of parchment. I went closer and saw that he was not writing, but drawing.

Seth continued on toward his camp, and Gideon got into his tent and pretended not to notice that I sat down next to Lib at the fire. I saw him kneel for prayer before the flaps of his tent closed for the night.

"What are you drawing?" I asked.

He folded it over itself. "Nothing. Go to bed, Keturah."

"It looks like a boat," I persisted.

"It's nothing. Just something I used to do with my father. I'm just passing the time."

"You should use the time to sleep. I don't need a night watch."

"Goodnight, Keturah."

I yawned. "Goodnight, Lib."

I let the flaps of my tent fall and slowly tied them closed. Then I knelt for my own prayer.

My mind raced. Gideon would choose the army over me. Micah would marry me to a boy who thought he loved me but did not. Kenai would have to go into great danger to find out when the Lamanites would deliver supplies to Cumeni. Mother had never told us who we really were. It was one of those prayers that I felt more than said, and I finally lay down and drifted off to sleep.

It wasn't until the morning we left Judea for Cumeni that I recognized a new face in the line behind mine. He was one of the sixty new striplings and was about the same age as Lamech, though the last time I had seen him, he had been a boy of nine.

"Onah!"

He eyed me curiously for a moment before his eyes lit with recognition when he realized where he had seen me before.

He had come to my village seeking the midwife, my mother, not long before the stripling army had left Melek.

"How is your mother? And the baby?" I asked.

"Mother has had another child already and the baby is no longer a baby," he replied, seeming relieved to know someone— even if we had only met for a few minutes years ago.

That baby would be a three-year-old toddler by now, the age Chloe had been when I had left the village. She was six now, I realized. Would she even remember me when I returned? Sarai was eight now and Isabel ten. No, eleven!

That was all the time we had for conversation. The horn sounded, and we were marching.

Unlike Antiparah, which lay in a large valley, Cumeni was situated in the hills, which had to be reached by traversing steep inclines and crossing ridges. The narrow road that led into the city had been cut into the hillside and was heavily guarded.

We had to get past the guarded road and camp where the people could see us because inciting their fear and fostering the hopelessness of rescue was what made a siege successful.

We neared the road to Cumeni within two days and our first operation was to take out the band of men who guarded it.

We halted well before we reached the Cumeni Road. I knew why, but most of the boys didn't. They knew only that we planned to move into position around Cumeni during the third watch. Our orders were to eat well and fall asleep early.

When the sun was setting and the light began to dim, Gideon caught my eye.

It was time to leave.

What few of the men knew was that Gideon would lead a secret task to remove the guards from the Cumeni Road so the rest of the army could enter the valley unchallenged. Helaman had let him chose fifty men to take with him, which I knew he had done through prayer and inspiration. Most of the men were from the fifty he already led, but there were many exceptions.

Neither Onah nor Lamech were coming, for example. Gideon's cousin, Enos, who was a chief captain in his own right, was coming, along with several of his best men. Gideon had also chosen Kenai and his unit of spies.

Gideon and I got up first, leaving camp as if he was walking me into the forest as one of my unit did each night. Later, as more boys drifted off to sleep, each member of Gideon's team would quietly walk away from camp and join us in the woods.

The moon was high when everyone had assembled, a round white orb that reminded me of the melons we had practiced slicing in the training ground. I felt once more for the knife I wore on my arm. Cold, hard, reassuring. Tonight, it would both take lives and save them.

We knelt together and prayed for success, and then we were off silently, more silently than even the breeze, through the night.

When we neared the road, Gideon's arm went up to call a silent halt. He and Kenai began wordlessly directing us into position. Several hundred Lamanite soldiers guarded the entrance to the valley. Since the area was so steep, most of them slept on the road. The only guard was here at the crossroad. And it was just a heavy guard, not an army of men.

Several guards sat awake, talking quietly to each other now and then, but the Lamanites clearly did not expect an army to descend on them. Had their spies not noticed we marched down the West Road toward them? Why were any of them sleeping? Were they not on duty?

I thought perhaps there were enemies we could not see hidden somewhere, waiting to ambush us, but I knew Kenai had quartered the area and searched it thoroughly for spies. My eyes went to him as he picked his way silently across the field of men. It suddenly occurred to me why no Lamanite spies had reported our presence, why the lazy soldiers felt safe enough to sleep.

I took a deep breath and placed my trust firmly in Kenai, who had more information than I had and more experience in the terrain.

Gideon had sent Kenai and two of his men, Eliam and Mahonri, to take out the sentries who sat awake. I did not watch. I watched Gideon for the signal to move. While I waited, my eyes flicked quickly to the four men that lay sleeping on the ground. It would take me less than a minute to complete my silent, deadly task. I held my father's blade in my hand and kept my eyes on Gideon until I saw the signal, the sign that Kenai had killed the sentries. Then I stole silently forward and began to work in the exacting way I had been taught. I did not think. I would think later.

I looked up to see Kenai standing there in position to help me if I needed it. When he saw I did not need it, he glanced around for anyone else who might need help. All around, Ammonite boys were stealing for the cover of the trees to regroup. My brother gathered me in a glance and we ran together for the forest. One unit of boys stayed behind to clear the road before the rest of us returned with the army. It had gone off without a single hitch.

We stopped at a stream to wash, but the moon hadn't moved a full hand's width across the sky before we walked stealthily back into camp and quietly sought out our bedrolls. My hands were icy from the water, and my stomach churned as I crawled under my blanket between a silent Lib and Ethanim who did the same. The rest of my unit settled in quickly, and for once, Reb was not telling jokes.

Gideon, however, had gone to report to Helaman, to tell him the way was clear. He did not come back before we got the call to line up, and even when the call came he stayed at the head of the column with the commander. I was glad. It gave me a measure of security knowing Gideon helped command our movements because I knew of his expertise and skills. When it came to warfare, Gideon knew what to do. I trusted him completely.

When the sun began to rise, the guards at Cumeni saw us camped around the city, and unless they decided to come out to battle against us, camping was all we had to do until the supplies arrived.

On the third morning I stood next to our cook fire and stretched. I looked to the city walls, beyond an arrow's distance, but not so far away I couldn't see the guards in the towers pacing and ruminating. I could see one man scratching his ratty beard. I could see another leaning on his spear, looking out at us. Beyond them, I could see the tallest of the buildings inside the city.

I thought of the women and children in the city. There would be many. The one thing I did not like about this plan was that it would cause the children to suffer. They would go hungry, perhaps even die with it, before their leaders gave in. And they would give in. They would have to, for we would not allow sustenance into the city.

And I would not let myself think about the wives and children of the guards on the Cumeni crossroad whom I had deprived of their protector.

Instead, I thought of Mother. I thought of Dinah and Hemni, Cana, Isabel, Sarai and Chloe. I thought of those who could not fight, whom I fought for. I thought of having a family of my own someday and how I couldn't do it until I knew they would be safe.

I hadn't seen or talked to Zeke in several weeks, so when I heard his voice next to me I was surprised.

"Nice day for a siege," he said.

"Unless you're inside the city," I returned, but I smiled. It was good to see him, no matter what our circumstances were or where our relationship stood. He was still and always would be my friend.

"Feeling compassion?" he asked.

I sighed deeply, unable to hide my melancholy mood. There was no point in trying to hide something like that from Zeke anyway. We might have been separated by thirty units of boys physically and by a chasm deep as the West Sea emotionally, but Zeke would always know when I was unhappy.

"The families," I said. "There are families inside those walls. I didn't come here to starve children and take their fathers. The men who I—" I stopped and swallowed hard.

Zeke knew about the guard on the crossroad, and everyone knew about Gideon's promotion to higher captain. He had probably figured by now that Gideon had taken me with him to clear the way for the rest of the troops.

I felt him take my hand. He began walking toward the woods.

When we were alone on the steep slope, he said, "Do you want to tell me about it?"

I couldn't speak. I didn't know where to begin.

He waited for a long time. "Ket," he said softly at last. "Is this what you wanted—these images, these feelings—when you insisted on being in the army?"

I swallowed the lump in my throat. "Don't say you told me so."

"I would never do that."

That was maybe the second time I had ever heard him lie. I smiled weakly and tried to think of the words to describe what I was feeling.

Zeke continued to patiently wait, shifting occasionally on the incline.

"It's not the images, the blood, the faces of death, what I did—killing those men," I made myself say, "that bother me."

He was motionless, listening.

"It's the far-reaching effects of their deaths that I can't get out of my mind."

He shifted closer to me. "I think I understand," he said. "You're thinking about your father?"

I nodded. I had known he would understand. Kalem had killed my father almost sixteen years ago, and no matter how much he did in restitution, there was one thing he could never restore and that was a lifetime of experiences with my father. "Yes," I choked out and, to my dismay, tears began leaking from my eyes.

Zeke didn't reach out for me. The muscles in his jaw clenched. "You should have stayed home with Mother and Cana."

My tears stopped forming suddenly, though my face was wet, and my eyes shot to his. "I have to make this world safe for my family, for my children!"

"That is not your responsibility—to protect them, to die for them! It is my responsibility to die for our children!" he said forcefully. He took a breath and softened his voice. "It is your responsibility to live for them."

I didn't understand. How would life be better if Zeke died? Was he saying it was Father's responsibility to die for me? But he hadn't needed to die at all. Had he?

I shook my head. Zeke was wrong. I felt like the little girl he had always known growing up when I folded my arms and pouted.

I didn't understand why responsibilities and roles had to be different like this, why they were so defined. I had been doing a man's duty for the past three years, and I had done it well. Though, I had been wondering lately what I was accomplishing by it. I was starting to realize that when I did that which was Zeke's to do, I robbed him of the blessings that came with it.

After a long silence, Zeke spoke. "Are you mad because I said *our* children?" He looked at the ground, his arms folded across his chest. "Was it too presumptuous?" I could hear the disgust in his voice. Of all the things for me to look at as he spoke,

I couldn't take my eyes off his long fingers gripping his biceps. "Have you made a commitment to...to someone else?"

"No," I conceded quietly, "I'm not mad about that, and no, I have made no other commitments. Even if I had done so and didn't have the decency to tell you—and you obviously think I don't—Micah would have."

It was not relief I saw in his eyes, though I sensed it. It was a measuring, a considering. I did not understand why our roles had to be different, and Zeke did not understand me. He did not understand why I wouldn't allow him the privilege of protecting his future family, as was his right and duty.

And to be honest, I was starting to wonder why myself.

But one thing he did understand about me, I thought with sudden realization, was that saying something to anger me stopped my tears.

You should have stayed home with Mother and Cana. That hadn't been what he meant at all. Could I be right? Did he fight with me on purpose? I looked at him curiously for a moment, a look which he misinterpreted.

When he bent down and kissed me gently on my lips, I didn't kiss him back—but I yielded to his sweet reassurance and did not protest in any way.

That night was the first night the Lamanite army came out from the city to try to kill us in our beds. But we had already employed that tactic ourselves and were prepared against it. We all slept upon our swords.

"Keturah! Your weapon!"

I was instantly awake when I heard Ethanim's warning, my eyes searching the darkness, my other senses pitted against it.

I slipped out of my tent and scanned the moonlit camp. I saw movement everywhere around me. No sooner had I seen that half my unit fought with Lamanite men in loincloths, than I began quietly and efficiently slipping my blade between their ribs as Eli had once shown me on the training field.

The enemy had tried to sneak in quietly, but we were all awake now, and shouts and grunts and cries of pain sounded in the night.

Ethanim fought off a man with his sword. I snuck up behind the man and stabbed between his ribs. I pulled my blade from him and went from man to man repeating this method of death.

I had just stabbed the man fighting Joshua when I saw a man about to cut through a boy I thought was Onah.

I grabbed for my axe at my belt and threw it.

It hit the man and he went down at Onah's feet, but when I turned, I saw the arc of a sword coming at me from above. I grabbed for my own sword in its scabbard on my back, but my hand hit only air. My sword was still on my bedroll.

I didn't have time to panic because a strong arm wrapped around my waist and pulled me out of the way quickly and forcefully. I fell to the ground with Lib as Reb took the full brunt of the blow on his own sword with his thick, strong arm. Corban kicked the Lamanite hard with the foot I had healed for him so that the man stumbled and fell backward. I turned my face to Lib's shoulder—but not before I saw that every boy in my unit— Ethanim, Reb, Corban, Joshua, Cyrus, Mathoni, Noah, Zachariah, and Gideon—stood between me and the dead Lamanite who had tried to harm me.

Lib pulled me into a sitting position and held me close. I only let him hold me for a moment because I was mindful of Kenai's warning to keep my actions toward Lib consistent with my feelings for him. But that was the only reason I got to my feet when I did. The fight was over.

Our army had guards who watched the camp at night, a guard duty that we took when it was our turn, but my unit kept their own guard each night. For the first time, I was more than accepting or tolerant of it—I was grateful for it.

My unit formed a circle and when Lib had seen that none of his men were wounded, he hurried away to find Seth so he could make his report.

"Gideon had just taken the watch and I had nearly fallen asleep," Ethanim said, "when the camp's guards sounded the alert."

Gideon was still breathing heavily from his exertions, his broadsword held down to his side. In the silver moonlight that seemed so beautiful now falling over us, I met Gideon's eyes.

I thought of the first time I had ever seen him.

I am quite indifferent to you.

Could anything be farther from the truth?

Chapter 21

The Lamanites tried this unsuccessful tactic many times. I thought it was a testament to their increased desperation as the days went on, but Gideon said it was likely they were getting messengers out during the confusion.

"They are dogs," he said. "But they are not stupid when it comes to warfare. What is that you're beading?"

We were sitting outside my tent in the late afternoon, and I glanced at him. "It's for Zeke," I admitted, and then I told him how he had given the old tie-back to Eve. I didn't tell him how tenuous things were with Zeke or that the beaded tie was intended to be a peace offering or that it made my heart ache to think of him giving the old one away.

Gideon was silent.

"I'm...sorry," I said. For so many things I couldn't even name.

"Love does not happen to everyone. Don't be sorry for it."

A lump formed in my throat, and I couldn't reply—even if I had known what to say. I kept my eyes on the black and red beads.

"I am glad to know you will not be alone when the war is

over." He lingered for a few moments, but then he got up and left without another word.

After that, I worked on the beading inside my tent.

We waited many days for the Lamanite provisions to come. We had a lot of time when there was little to do. Sometimes I went to Darius's camp and played ball with him and his friends. Sometimes I worked quietly in my tent intricately beading the tie for Zeke's hair. Sometimes I tramped through the forest hunting or fishing with my unit. I always felt guilty about that and at the same time extremely grateful that I had the freedom and ability to find food.

Late one night when we had been camped outside Cumeni for many days, I couldn't sleep so I sat up with Reb, my watchman for the night. Sometimes it was just easier to stay up until the Lamanites attempted their raid, but that wasn't why I couldn't sleep.

I had heard the wailing inside the city earlier that day. People were beginning to suffer from hunger.

But my troubled mind kept me awake, and it was because I was awake that I saw Jacom dart by on his way to the command tent. Something was happening.

After a short time, during which Reb and I made our speculations, a messenger ran past calling everyone out of sleep and to attention. When everyone was awake, Seth gave us our orders.

The Lamanites were trying to sneak supplies in under the cover of night. And we were going to take them.

We had actually trained during the long days for just this situation—it was our main tactic after all. My unit, along with others, was to sneak around through the forest back to the West Road and come in behind the supplies on the Cumeni Road so we surrounded them. It was a simple plan, and if everything went according to the plan, our purposes would be easily accomplished.

When we got into position, we waited quietly in the darkened forest for a long time. Nobody seemed nervous. I wasn't even nervous. We had traveled the route many times in preparation so that even in the dark it was familiar. We were only a small part of the ploy and only had to perform our part to the best of our ability. Besides, by that time those types of actions were common and prowling between the trees on the steep terrain with the boys in my unit, my brothers, felt more like a drill than war.

That was, until the Lamanite supply party passed by us in the dim light, and then the excitement thrummed through our ranks. This was the key element to our plan to take the city Cumeni, and it was happening that night. Finally!

We waited for Seth's signal and then drew our swords and crept onto the road behind the supply party in silent, stalking ranks.

I marched silently between Lib and Ethanim, both tall, strong, handsome, valiant, and lethal. They were eighteen like me and full grown men now, though Lib still seemed to get taller every day. By the time we approached the Lamanites they were halted before Helaman.

The supply party expected to meet the Lamanite guard—the one I had helped eliminate—on the portion of the Cumeni Road that had been cut into the mountain, but instead, they met us.

Or rather, they met Helaman and a hundred men with drawn swords—and five hundred bowmen hidden in the trees.

Because of the slope of the road, I could see Helaman clearly in the moonlight. He gestured to the woods and back toward us, probably explaining to the captain how many arrows he had pointed at his heart. I saw the Lamanite captain's head crane around toward the rear of his column.

And that seemed to be all it took. His men yielded up their weapons, dropping them at Helaman's feet. Then Helaman

escorted the men who carried the Lamanite provisions back to
our camp. The rest of us followed, and my unit and several others
gathered the abandoned weapons as we passed. Helaman
commanded the Lamanite prisoners to leave the provisions near
our supply tent. Then he sent them to make camp, and he
commanded soldiers to guard them.

My unit would not be on guard duty until sometime the
next day, so we marched together to the supply tent and
delivered the weapons we had taken from the enemy.

Another week went by and they still had not given up the
city.

"Hurry," Gideon said. "The council will not wait for you
to fix your hair."

Actually, they probably would, but I began walking with
him even while I finished braiding my wet hair and coiling it at
the nape of my neck, securing it with a long tie I had made to
match Zeke's.

Gideon touched the tie and smiled sadly.

I flushed, but said, "Why are you in such a rush?"

"I'm not."

But I knew he was. He had been summoned to the
command tent earlier in the day, and I figured he already knew
what would be happening at the council meeting. And from the
lightness in his step, I figured he was excited about it. No one
else would see his excitement, but I had learned to recognize it.

"You are," I insisted. "Why don't you just tell me what is
going on?"

"It is not for me to tell."

"So there is something going on. Come on—tell," I plied.
"Hey, isn't Seth coming?"

"He's meeting us there."

"Good, so it will be our secret. Just tell me."

He only laughed and shook his head.

"What?" I asked defensively when I got the feeling he was

laughing at me.

"Alright. Zeke said you could be wheedling, and he was right. I've seen you be persuasive before, but I've never known you to be quite this wheedling."

"Wheedling? Why would Zeke say that?" I pursed my lips.

"I think he might have been trying to talk me out of wanting you at the time," he said and tried to put me in a headlock.

I dodged his arm and frowned. "Talk you out of...wanting me? Like I was a mediocre horse or the last corn cake?"

He laughed again. "Something like that."

"I'm sorry," I said suddenly. "For all the trouble with Zeke and my brothers. A lot of trouble you don't deserve."

"Don't be sorry," he said frankly. "I can take responsibility for my own actions. Besides, I've always been glad to know you have men who will protect you." He held up a hand before I could protest. "Men who will protect your best interests. And besides, I like Zeke. I'd never have gotten to know him if it weren't for you."

We had come to the outer edges of the council area where men were gathering. This was so similar to the conversation we had had about the hair tie, except this time, Gideon did not lose control of his emotions and walk away. I reached up and placed my hand over his forehead. He stopped walking and gave me a questioning look.

"I'm just checking for fever. I think you're delirious."

"Yeah, Gid, you look ill. Hideous, really."

Gideon turned his head. "Hey, Zeke," he said and punched Zeke harmlessly in the shoulder.

I stood motionless with shock, but Zeke punched Gideon back.

Could these two ever be friends?

Zeke gave my hand a squeeze and went to sit with Micah.

Gideon and I found Seth, and I didn't have to wait long after the meeting started to find out what had Gideon so pleased.

After the prayer, Helaman said, "We have possession of the Lamanite provisions, but they can see them from their towers. They will try to recover them before they ever give up the city. The men are still strong."

He stopped so we could consider this.

"But their desperation is increasing. They will surely act on any hope of obtaining food. I have determined to send the supplies to Judea and the men of the supply column, which we have taken prisoner, down to Zarahemla."

A murmur went through the men, but they quieted quickly.

"Then their leaders will see that there is no hope for it and yield up the city." Helaman spoke gravely, resigned to accomplish our designs. The siege was not as bloody as a battle, but it weighed heavily on him, as it did the rest of us.

"How can we help?" called Eli.

Helaman smoothed down his tunic and looked around at all of us. "As most of you know by now, I have made Gid a chief captain. He draws his men from each of your units as needed, depending upon the nature of his assignment. Give your troops to him willingly, my sons—he chooses them for their particular skills and by the Holy Spirit. Gid will conduct the prisoners to Zarahemla and guard the provisions to Judea on his way. The rest of us will wait here and see this siege to its end."

We walked slowly back to camp with Seth. I wanted to ask Gideon if he was taking me with him to Zarahemla, but I didn't. "You could have just told me," I pointed out instead.

"Ket," said Seth. "Do you want me to walk you into the woods before we go back?"

"No," I said. "I want to go alone."

Seth and Gideon laughed. I caught Gideon's eye, and I wished he was the one walking me back.

"I can wait," he offered.

Seth shook his head and waved Gideon on.

Gideon hesitated. "See you later then," he said and turned to go.

Seth sometimes walked me into the woods for my necessary tasks, but not very often. I thought he occasionally took a night watch near my tent too, but I couldn't have said for sure.

When I was done and emerged from the trees, Seth was sitting on a tree that grew straight out from the side of the hill. He was hunched over, staring down at his hands in the twilight. He didn't make a move to leave.

"I'm done."

He looked up, frowning. "Come sit down," he said.

We weren't going back to camp? "Is that a command?"

He shook his head. "No. Do you need one?"

"No," I said as I joined him on the tree. "Did you have something you wanted to talk about?"

"Mmmm," he said.

Was that a yes or a no? I couldn't tell, so I just waited.

The sun had just set, but it was already dim here in the trees. It hadn't rained in days, and I thought we were probably due for some. The storms here in the mountains could be torrential. I looked up at the sky through the trees, but I didn't see any clouds.

"Pretty," Seth said.

"Hmm?"

"The night. It's pretty."

"Seth, I wish you would just tell me what this is about."

"Gideon," he said abruptly.

My jaw tightened. I had already had this conversation with Lib—a number of times. I didn't say anything.

"It's just that Gid, well, he's not going back to the barley farm after the war, if you know what I mean."

I frowned, and heat rose in my chest.

"I mean, he's a soldier. Gid was born to be a soldier."

"He told me he wants to stay in the army once the war is over," I told him. "Is that what you're trying to say?"

"Kind of," he replied.

I could tell he hadn't said what he wanted to say. I looked at him. The thin tattoo lining his eyes was so striking that I couldn't look away once I caught his eye.

"I'm a distraction." That was what he wanted to say.

His eyelids fell, and he looked down.

"I'm aware, Seth. He doesn't want a wife and family. I know that."

"But, I think you still hope for it," he said gently.

I wanted to blurt out that my feelings for Gideon were none of his business, but while Gideon and I were both in a unit under his command, they absolutely were his business. And he was right—my heart ached with the love I couldn't give to Gideon, the love he wouldn't accept. I could not stop myself from hoping that he loved me enough to change his mind in the future.

"I cannot help the way I feel," I said.

"No, I guess none of us can."

I met his eyes again and his quiet stare said a great deal.

Blushing deeply, I let my own eyelids fall.

"You're saying *you* will be returning to Melek when the war is over." I wanted to sound accusing, but the truth was I felt much more tenderness toward him than that. But I felt tender toward all the boys. I loved them all.

He was quiet for a moment. "I could be dead before the war is over. I'm not saying anything. I'm not asking anything. I shouldn't have said that."

"You didn't," I pointed out.

He smiled so charmingly my heart melted. Had I never seen him smile before?

"Anyway, it's not about me," he said. "I just wanted to say

be cautious with Gid. For yourself, but for him too, you know?"

I nodded.

"He can go far, Keturah."

"If I don't hold him back, you mean," I replied as I jumped down from the tree.

He jumped down too. "I didn't mean it like that. I shouldn't have said that."

"You didn't," I repeated with a smile I did not feel, one that I hoped hid my heartache. "Will you walk me back now?" I had to get back to my tent where I could be alone, suffer alone.

"I'm sorry," he said. He hesitated, but pulled me firmly into his arms. "Not for what I said, but, you know, for the way things are."

At first I did not return his embrace. I remembered Kenai's warning and how well it had worked to keep things friendly and appropriate with Lib. But I knew that what Seth offered, he offered only in friendship, so I relaxed into him. I let him comfort me, and to my surprise, it helped.

"Did Gideon ask you to talk to me?" I asked into his shoulder.

His arms tightened. "No." The word was muffled in my hair. I didn't know whether or not to believe him, but I told myself he was an honest man and turned toward camp.

He grabbed me by the elbow to keep me from going. "Ket." He swallowed and searched my eyes. Here it came. This is what he really wanted to say. "Did you ever think Gid might be using you to get to someone else?"

I recoiled. Who could I possibly assist Gid in getting close to that might move him closer to his military goals? He already had the approval of Helaman. My lips moved to ask who, but it suddenly came to me.

Micah. He meant Micah.

"No."

I would never believe that.

It took Gideon just two days to assemble his men and move out. He did not take me. It was a disappointment I didn't hide from him.

"I'll be back in a fortnight," he said in an effort to placate me, but he was so eager to go, it didn't work.

I hated that I made him feel he had to placate me. It was exactly what he didn't want. It was exactly what Seth and Lib cautioned me against.

We were standing in camp with boys busily moving and working all around us. "And just think," Gideon continued. "You'll get to be here for the surrender."

I tried not to smile, but the idea of a surrender was appealing.

"Good luck then," I said. I couldn't even spare him a smile before I turned and walked away toward the bright rising sun, the glare of it making my eyes sting.

"Keturah!" he called from behind me, his voice coming from deep in his chest.

I stopped, but I did not turn around. I clenched my fists into my skirt as I listened to him walk toward me. I could hear his feet parting the long summer grasses. I could hear the other boys in camp, a shout of laughter, the distant groan of the city gates.

I could hear him breathing behind me.

"You know this is what I want, to rise in ranks of the army. I thought if anyone understood that, it would be you."

He was right. I did understand. Oh, how I understood.

"I do," I said tightly through the lump in my throat.

"Don't be angry," he said into my ear. I could feel the warmth of his body on my back, though he did not touch me.

"I'm not angry," I said.

"Then those are tears of sadness?"

I squeezed my eyes shut and shook my head vigorously. "No." I quickly swiped the tears away.

I was sad. Because he was leaving? Because he wasn't taking me with him? Because he didn't love me enough to...what? Take me away from Zeke? Micah wouldn't even allow it.

I smelled the sweet fragrance of a moonflower, and when I opened my eyes, I saw that Gideon held one in front of me, the stem between two rough fingers.

I took his offering and mustered a smile for him. "Go. Do your duty."

He lingered for a moment. "Goodbye, Kanina," he said, and I listened to him walk away.

I stared at the moonflower for long moments, gaining my composure, willing my tears to stop, but they wet my eyes and clung to my lashes. He would be back. This was foolishness.

When I looked up at last, I saw Zeke. He stood a few feet away. And then my tears did fall because he was always there when I needed him.

I went to him, but he did not have waiting arms. The moment I touched him he jumped away from me as if he were throwing off a sword-wielding Lamanite warrior.

I looked at his angry face. What did he mean by nearly pushing me away from him?

"You come to me when you mourn for *him*?" he growled, gesturing in the direction Gideon had gone. "You reach for me with his favor still in your hand?" He looked at the flower with a sneer. Then he grasped my hand and shook the flower from it. "No, Keturah." His voice was rising in intensity, shaking. "You go too far. You abuse my loyalty. You have tortured me beyond what I can bear."

He backed away from me and then turned on his heel and walked away with his head high, his long stride putting a distance between us I wasn't sure I could ever close.

I didn't know what I would have done or how long I would have stood there crying, gazing after Zeke, mourning

Gideon's military success, if Reb hadn't clapped me hard on the back nearly knocking me off balance.

I turned to look at him, at all my brothers standing behind him. He handed me my bow.

"Let's go hunting. You look like you need to kill something."

Chapter 22

When the Lamanites gave up Cumeni a few days later, it was anticlimactic. Most of us didn't even know they had surrendered until we got orders to go in and guard the men.

The women and children filed out of the gates and traveled to Manti or one of the other Lamanite holdings. I stood stonily and watched them go, weak, bedraggled and showing signs of malnourishment. But they were proud. Even as I passed them parcels of food, I garnered more than a few looks of pure hatred. I didn't know if that was because I was a Nephite, a soldier, or a woman.

"Even without the women and children, there are more prisoners than we can guard," said Lib as we surveyed the large square where the men mostly sat or stood idly talking to one another and sneering at us.

I nodded.

"Gid should be back in a few days," he said.

Gideon had been gone five days when the Lamanites

surrendered, and it had been six more since. It had taken a full day alone to confiscate all the weapons, and another day to distribute rations among the prisoners.

"Lib, let's not talk about it, okay?"

They had all seen what had happened with Zeke. After he had stormed away and Gideon had taken the prisoners of war to Zarahemla, my unit had taken me out hunting. Nobody mentioned Zeke or Gideon. They all liked Gideon, but since Zeke had started taking a watch at night, they had become friends with him too. They had all seen this coming.

Lib studied me, but I kept my eyes on the prisoners. "Okay." He paused. "I just hate to see you so miserable."

"I'm not miserable."

"Lying doesn't become you."

I snorted. "Why do I have to be becoming all the time? Can't I just take a day to grieve?"

"To wallow in self-pity, you mean?"

"I'm fine."

"You're as much of a prisoner as they are." He nodded to the Lamanites in the square.

I watched one of the prisoners making marks in the dirt. He moved idly as if he was just killing time, but I began to notice others look at the drawings as they moved past. I had been watching this all afternoon, but slowly, I began to think something strange, something deliberate was happening.

"Do you notice anything weird about the man making the drawings?" I asked Lib.

Lib squinted in the man's direction. "He's in the middle of the square."

"That's not it," I mumbled, staring at the man.

"He hasn't moved all day."

"And the others have." I looked up at Lib. "The others are moving around him."

Lib glanced back at the man. "So?"

I shrugged. "Could he be their leader?"

"The chief captains are being held within the prison walls. I think you're changing the subject."

I sighed. "Lib, I can't talk to you about Gideon."

"You could if you wanted to."

"Are you sulking?" I laughed. "What could you possibly want to know?"

He straightened. "I don't want to know any of it. I just thought you might want to talk, that's all."

I shook my head and smiled sadly. There was nothing to talk over. My choices were already made. My future was already arranged, and Gideon would not be in it.

The day Gideon got back to Cumeni, though I didn't know he was back at the time, was the day the prisoners rebelled.

The uprising began after I had been off duty for several hours. Obviously, they had been planning something while we stood by and watched. The prisoners had reportedly all stood together, rushed at the guards in all directions, and broke through our lines. Once beyond them, they picked up anything they could get their hands on and began to fight.

We heard the noise from our new camp inside the city walls.

We had barely time to look at one another in question before Lib ordered, "To the square!"

He drew his sword and ran, never looking to see if we followed. He knew we would.

The battle was in full sway when we arrived along with every other soldier in our army, and we waded in swinging.

The Lamanites had been weak, but we had been feeding them a simple ration for days and they had begun to get their strength back. Because we had starved their families, their vendetta against us became personal, their hatred raw and seething, and their attack was vicious.

But they had been the ones to resist surrender. Instead of

waging a battle, we had offered them their lives, and the price was simple. We asked only that they yield up their possession, a city that was ours anyway.

But even after being forced to yield, still they fought against us. Their great pride prevented them from seeing the straight path out. Seeing them fight with little more than their bare hands against men with swords, I could honestly say it was a magnificent pride.

But it cost them their lives.

Unlike in the aftermath of the battle with the army at Antiparah, this time I was among the units ordered to go out and separate the wounded from the dead. Some of the striplings were wounded superficially, but the prisoners hadn't had much to fight with—just their hands, stones, or anything they could use as a club. By the time it was over, we had slain almost two thousand of them.

I looked down at all the blank faces that had chosen death, whose pride had spoken for them. Lib had said I was a prisoner too. Would I fight in vain? Or would I yield up what was not mine to begin with?

Micah's men and Seth's dug the graves outside the city, huge holes where we buried the prisoners piled so high that we had to mound the dirt up over them. This was accomplished in much the same way as we had built the embankments around Judea, and I wished for the time in the trenches when we had done this without stinking, dead bodies under our feet.

When all the dead prisoners had been buried and the ones yet alive were on half rations, Helaman held another council.

"Gid has returned," he said, "and I've asked him to escort the remaining prisoners to Zarahemla, sword in hand." He turned and found Gideon among the captains present. "Take Enos, Kimner, and Seth and their hundreds."

Gideon nodded.

I went to say goodbye to Micah before we marched out the next morning.

Zeke walked past us. He nodded to Micah, but he did not look at or talk to me. He did not acknowledge me in any way.

Micah watched his back for a long moment. Then he turned to me, worry and speculation in his eyes.

I answered the question he didn't ask. "Gideon."

"You have to stop this nonsense with Gid," he said bluntly.

"It is too late. It has already gone too far."

He was quiet for a moment. "Did you never think of forgiveness?"

"Zeke won't forgive me," I said hopelessly.

He looked hard at me, taking my measure. "Do you even want him to?"

"Yes, of course!"

"I know you don't want him to be angry, and you don't want to lose his friendship, but do you want his trust and love back?"

"Yes," I insisted.

"Perhaps it's better this way. Perhaps he can finally let go of you and be ready to find someone else when he gets home— someone who will really love him in return."

The thought of that happening brought the sting of tears, but I did not allow them to fall. Could another woman know him like I did? Could another woman love him? Or was Micah right? Could I even love him?

"Of course," Micah went on, "that is not what I want. Zeke is my choice for you."

"Why not Gideon? He's strong and faithful. Why not Seth or Lib or anyone else? They are all handsome and brave and good."

"It is not a matter of good qualities measured against bad," he said. "It is a prompting I feel inside. I do not need to know more than that. I do not need to weigh anything else."

I believed him, but why could he feel it when I could not?

"I said once that I would respect your opinion, your choice, if you would respect mine. Gideon is a good man, one of the best. I would never turn him away if he spoke for you. But here is my opinion." Our eyes caught. "He won't, Keturah," he finished gently.

"Because you have all poisoned him against it!" I cried. "You've all threatened him!"

He shook his head sadly. He spoke with both understanding and sympathy when he said, "Nobody has done that. You are seeing only what you wish to see." He heaved a deep sigh and frowned. "We have spoken to him of his intentions—that is true. But if he has intent to marry you, he has not been honest in it. And Ket, I believe he is an honest man." He reached out and tugged on my hair as Kenai often did. "It is not the time to arrange these things anyway," he said, but after a pause he counseled, "Reconcile with Zeke, Keturah."

"I told you, it is too late."

Micah put his hands on my shoulders and looked into my eyes. Then he pulled me into a brotherly hug.

"I'll speak to him," he said.

I didn't protest because I knew Micah would do what he wanted. But I knew his words to Zeke would have no effect. He hadn't seen the look on Zeke's face.

Dry-eyed, I reached into my satchel and withdrew the tie I had made for Zeke to tie back his long hair. "Will you give him this for me?" I asked my brother.

He hesitated with his hand poised to take it. "Why don't you give it to him?"

I shook my head. "Please?"

After he accepted it, I kissed him on the cheek and left.

The prisoners dragged their feet, and we did not make a lot of ground that day. The rebellion still in the prisoners' eyes prompted Gideon to divide the night into only two shifts and keep half our men on guard while the other half slept.

When morning came, we got a late start because the prisoners refused to move. Gideon was busy, but I found him and handed him four warm corn cakes. He nodded his thanks as he strapped his gear onto his back.

"Did you employ so many guards on your last trip to Zarahemla?" I asked.

"No. They weren't needed. It wasn't their families we had half-starved."

I nodded. "What's Zarahemla like?"

He shifted a piece of cake in his mouth and grinned. "You're going to love it."

There was a commotion at the edge of camp, and Gideon's attention shifted immediately. Four men ran full out toward us over the grassy knoll we were camped against.

Kenai.

He ran with Jonas, Eliam and Mahonri. As they got closer I could see that their hair was matted against their heads and sweat was streaming down their red faces.

Gideon shoved the last uneaten corn cake into my hands and ran to meet them, calling over his shoulder, "Enos, Kimner, Seth!"

He hadn't called my name, but I thought it had been an oversight, and I raced after him, dropping the cake in the deep grasses.

By the time I arrived on the knoll, Kenai was already talking, even as he gulped for air.

"A force of Lamanites...marching...on Cumeni," he said breathlessly.

"Where have you run from?" Gideon asked.

"Zeezrom," Eliam gasped out. "To inform the army there. Send reinforcements."

"You ran here from Zeezrom?" I exclaimed.

Gideon glanced over his shoulder at me. He wasn't surprised to see me, but he didn't appear annoyed either.

Kenai nodded.

"Good," said Gideon. "Drink," he commanded Kenai and his men, and then he turned to the rest of us.

"Ideas? Quickly."

"We could make it back," said Enos.

"We are only three-hundred. The two thousand from Zeezrom," said Kimner. "They will be enough."

"But three-hundred they don't know about could make a difference," Enos insisted.

Gideon looked to Seth, but Seth was looking with troubled eyes at me.

"Seth?" he prompted.

"We have to go back," Seth said.

"I doubt we can rush the prisoners back," I put in. "You saw them yesterday. They were like petulant children."

"You'd know all about that," said Kenai, gaining his breath back, and he pulled my hair right before I punched him.

Kenai obviously thought we should go back or he wouldn't have run all those miles. He had run the entire distance we had covered yesterday—which thanks to the sluggishness of the prisoners wasn't extremely far—after he had already covered the distance between Zeezrom and wherever he had spotted the Lamanite troops, probably near Manti.

A shout came from behind us, then more shouts until it became a roar. We turned around quickly and when we saw what was happening we drew our weapons and ran.

The prisoners had broken out again against our line of guards. And still, except for the few who got their hands on a stone, they had nothing with which to fight. We watched from the knoll as droves of the prisoners ran upon the swords of their guards. Some broke through and fled—wounded, weak, and hardly worth pursuing, though many of the guards ran after them.

Seth and I drew up at the same time and began slinging. I called to my commander for his order. "Subdue?"

"Death!" Gideon called back over his shoulder.

I adjusted my aim. Freedom or death was the obvious desire of these men, and Gideon did not have the authority to extend them their freedom.

It did not take long. Seth grabbed my arm and pulled me with him down to where Gideon questioned his men.

"They heard the spies," Lib was saying. "They heard that Lamanite reinforcements had been deployed, and they just went berserk. We couldn't stop them."

Gideon gave a curt nod, and seemed to give no more thought to the prisoners. He reached over and took my obsidian blade from the rawhide tie on my arm and signaled the guards that had pursued the prisoners to return. "It is a gift from God," he said. "Line up in a column. Seth's men, Enos, Kimner. We leave for Cumeni."

Our march was swift, reminiscent of the march that had lured the Lamanites out of Antiparah. At that time we had fled from danger because our force was small. Now with an even smaller force, we ran toward it in the hopes that we might save our brothers and retain the city we had taken.

I wondered how Kenai, Eliam, and Jonas were holding up. They had already run so far. I didn't care how Mahonri was holding up. I was still getting over the insulting way he had looked at me in the hills above Antiparah, though I understood now what he had been looking for—my ability to get inside the city walls. Still, we were never going to be best friends.

The Cumeni Road was not blockaded when we arrived. The forest was silent. If a battle was raging, we couldn't hear it yet. Perhaps we had made it in time to be of some help, but the natural sounds of the forest were absent and so we proceeded with caution, stealing as silently as it was possible for three-hundred men to steal toward Cumeni.

It was not long before we heard the battle. Gideon's arm went up and we fell still behind him. He held up his water skin, reminding us to drink, which we did and ate a little too so we would have strength and mental clarity after our hasty march.

Gideon spoke to Reb. When he moved to talk to Lib, Reb took Corban, Cyrus, and Mathoni and ran into the woods to the north.

"Lib, take the rest onto the hill far enough above the city to get a view of the battle. Go quickly. I need a report in less than a quarter of an hour."

Lib's eyes shot immediately to me.

"She's with me. Go."

Lib did not hesitate a moment longer, and he did not look back after he had gestured to the boys and taken off up the steep slope to the south.

Gideon spoke briefly to Seth, who then ran along the column speaking to unit leaders. Immediately, units began kneeling together in prayer.

I looked to Gideon. He dropped to his knees in the moist earth. He tugged on my hand and I followed him down and bowed my head. Gideon thanked the Lord for the actions of our prisoners which freed us to come to the aid of our brothers. He asked for protection. He asked for strength beyond our own. He asked for the mantle of wisdom as he led his men. And he asked for the angels of God to fight with us for the cause of freedom, our families, our lands, and our religion.

As he spoke, his familiar voice touched me—it fell over my hair and neck and shoulders, over my chest. A hot lightness began to spread from there out to my elbows and my fingers, my knees in the dirt and my feet that would carry me toward my enemy.

When he was done, I was so overcome it was a moment before I could open my eyes and raise my face to his.

I hardly recognized him.

I couldn't describe the change in him. His dark eyes shone like pools of living waters. He was bigger—stronger if it was possible. His handsome face glowed with light and lit with determination. He emanated the Spirit of the Lord so obviously, so boldly that I finally saw what everyone else saw in him. There would be few commanders with his level of intellect and intuition, his mantle of inspiration, and his natural skill. There would be few commanders with his mix of compassion and justice. The world would be better and safer if Gideon led righteous men in the cause of freedom.

He stood and looked down at me. We stared at each other for long moments. Slowly, he reached out for my hand, which I gave him. He pulled me to my feet.

"Behold," he said softly, a small smile playing at his lips. "The daughter of Helaman."

He held my gaze with stormy emotion as he kissed the hand he still held in his.

Then he let it go.

We both turned and faced forward, looking out together at the short road which had only war at the end of it. He issued me a quiet order. "I want you to fight with the broadsword today."

I swallowed. "Yes, sir," I said.

"You're a brat," he said.

And we didn't say any more until Lib and Reb came to report on the battle.

"There are no places of retreat," Lib said. "The enemy has forced our men back to the walls of the city. They fight valiantly to protect the gates, but the Lamanites have the clear advantage."

Gideon looked to Reb, who nodded.

"Fall in rank," he said, and we did it quickly while he jogged over to Enos, Kimner and Seth who waited a short distance away. When he had given them their orders, they broke away and ran back to their hundreds.

Gideon shook his head at me. Taking my elbow, he pulled me out of my line and to the front of the column with him. "You're with me," he repeated.

I glanced back, but nodded.

"Volley first. Then draw your sword. When we get to the lines, I want you to kill every enemy you see. I want you to do it fast and hard, just like we practiced in the woods."

He didn't wait for my reply. He lifted his arm in the air to call the charge, and we began to run.

Chapter 23

When we came into the clearing where we had camped during the siege, we saw that thousands of men fought, and that thousands had already died.

Gideon and I halted and waited a short moment while the men behind us fanned out around us forming a single row around the rear of the enemy lines. The moment the last man was in place, Gideon gave the command and we charged forward.

Ammoron certainly had sent plenty of troops. Most of the enemy soldiers we could see faced away from us watching the battle, waiting for their turn to fight, but this was to our advantage. We had a chance to take out as many men as possible while their attention was engaged elsewhere.

I fingered a rock into my sling on the run and threw it. A man went down before he could even grab at his head where the rock was now lodged in his skull. I saw others go down in the same way, and I knew that my brothers had done the same. Three hundred men were dead before we even reached them. We sent another volley, and again, men went down. We were quick with our slings, accurate, and deadly. We hit many men before drawing our swords.

I pulled my sword from the scabbard on my back with my dominant hand and grabbed for my axe with my other.

I did not waste time engaging the first man in combat. I jabbed at his chest through his back, yanked my sword free of his flesh and vaguely noticed he dropped as I turned to the next man. The rear of their lines turned and engaged us in combat.

I fell on my next opponent fast and hard, thinking of nothing but the man I fought, keeping only a small area of awareness on the surrounding enemies.

Every man I fought hesitated for just a moment when he saw that I was a woman, and it gave me that extra edge I needed—one I used to my advantage. I made the men doubt their eyes, made them look twice when they should have been swinging their swords.

As I continued to fight, working my way through their ranks, I knew that I fought well beyond my ability, and even as I hacked with my axe and sliced through every man in my way with my broadsword I sent up a prayer to God in thanks for the companionship of His holy spirit that magnified me in my work.

I got caught in a sword lock with a man who was thin but very strong. His face was close to mine. If he hadn't painted himself in grotesque patterns and stained himself with what appeared to be blood, I might have thought about the family he had left at home. But he was disgusting—I didn't even want to be touching him—and I thought of my own family instead. I thought of the people in my village who could not fight for themselves, the people I fought for.

I snarled at the man, but he was so strong I couldn't break his hold. Suddenly he went limp, and he fell forward onto me. I rolled out from under him before he hit the ground, and I was back on my feet in a second, giving a grateful glance to Ethanim who caught it before he turned and blocked the blow of another warrior.

I repaid the favor and dragged my axe through the

warrior's gut, yanking hard when it caught on a rib, as I ran ahead to the next foe, who was already swinging at me. But he was so tall that it was easy for me to duck, roll past him, come up behind him and bury my axe from behind, taking at least one lung and a kidney.

I caught my breath for a moment and then fended another blow. It was so fierce I lost the grip on my sword and it clattered to the ground out of reach. It seemed that this should make me panic, but I withdrew my obsidian blade from my arm band and inserted it between the man's ribs as he lifted both his arms to stab downward with his sword. I got a direct hit to his heart, and it hemorrhaged as he went down.

I honed in on the next man, but Gideon engaged him, making their fight look like play. *Watch out for the cimeter*, I thought as I quickly retrieved my sword from the ground and shoved my axe into my belt. I almost felt sorry for the Lamanite, almost wished him luck. He would need it.

I took a moment to glance toward the city walls. We were halfway there.

All the men of my unit were still standing though most of them were bleeding. At times we fought together, teaming up on the enemy, and at times we fought alone, relying on the skills we had all learned together during so many early mornings on the training ground. We moved relentlessly forward toward the city walls where our army was falling by the sword.

I had just thrown a man to the ground, twisted his arm to force him to crumple after a hard blow to his head, when a sweaty arm encircled my waist and I heard—as I smelled his foul breath—the soldier's lascivious laugh. His hands began to roam all over me. I stomped on his foot and brought the back of my fist to his nose—but all that did was produce a gush of warm blood down my neck. I looked around. Did he really think he could assault me this way with all my champions around?

After another moment of struggle, he slumped as I had

known he would. I threw him off and looked quickly around for the man who had saved me. Everyone was engaged in fighting. There was no one around.

But there was an arrow in the man's back. A black bar and two red lines.

My eyes shot toward the walls of the city. Zeke wasn't there. I looked around toward the woods, craning for a glimpse of him. I couldn't see him anywhere in the crowded mass of shouting and bloody men.

A hulking Lamanite ran toward me, a spear in hand, pointed at me. I sheathed my weapons and reached out to grab the spear with both hands. I dropped to the ground with it, using my weight to pull the tip down as I slid past the man in the other direction. The point of the spear lodged in the ground but not before it stabbed through the flesh of my leg, essentially pinning me to the earth. I cried out. He sneered and kicked me in the ribs, and my wound tore as my body jerked.

Gideon fought a short distance away. In a glance he judged my situation. He turned, moved sideways and kicked a spear to me, one that had been abandoned when its owner fell to the earth. I caught it in time to block the downward thrust—what the Lamanite thought would be the death thrust—of the spear, which left me with only a shallow cut on my side. Angered, he struck again and again, but I fought precisely, with exactness, as Gideon had taught me in the mud of the training ground in Melek.

And thinking of that rainy day, I quickly cut behind the man's legs with all my strength, and he fell flat onto his back. I had temporarily taken his breath, and while he lay shocked, I took it from him permanently.

A hand came into view and I looked up to see Noah, sweaty, bloody, but solid and raring. He hauled me to my feet with one strong pull of his arm. Then he turned and waded back into the battle.

I followed him.

We were nearing the walls and I began to see more and more Nephite warriors, both fighting and lying on the ground dead or wounded. I began to see stripling Ammonites too, and I knew it wouldn't be long before the battle turned.

That didn't mean I could stop fighting. There was more fighting left to endure. I would have to fight my way out, and I sent up a plea for stamina. My strength was starting to flag.

The last man I encountered, who I came upon as we both threw off an enemy, was the friendly, handsome guard from Antiparah.

Muloki.

He hesitated like the others, first realizing I was a woman and then realizing with shock where he had seen me before, realizing I had been a spy in the city he guarded.

The parade of emotions on his face showed shock, then confusion. I expected betrayal, hatred, and determination to follow. But the guard stood with his weapon raised and his face showed regret. He made no move to attack. I made no move to attack, either, and we just stood staring at each other, letting the hatred between our peoples fall away as the battle raged around us.

He seemed to make a decision, and I could see the muscles in his thick arms relax as he began to lower his weapon.

But I failed to keep my senses aware, because I didn't notice the things that Lib described to me later. I didn't notice Zeke running toward us, didn't hear him yelling, dodging men and blades and pushing men out of his way to reach me, to stop the weapon he didn't know would not strike at me. I did not notice him hurdle the man I had just thrown to the ground, drawing his sword as he flew through the air.

The thing I did notice, the one thing I did notice, was the quick reflexive movement of the guard as Zeke sliced through his arm, breaking it, leaving it hanging awkwardly.

273

It was a good hit, one that debilitated the foe, except that it came an instant too late—an instant that changed my life forever, and left Zeke's hanging in the balance. An instant where the guard from the gate of Antiparah rounded with his weapon and cut up deep into Zeke's leg.

"No!" I screamed.

But he was okay. He was still standing.

The regret I had seen in the guard's eyes turned to malice when he looked at Zeke, when he retrieved his sword with his unbroken arm and took a stance to continue fighting. Zeke too drew a cimeter from his belt and prepared to continue the fight. He crouched, ready to spring.

An unfamiliar horn resonated above the din and the guard looked from Zeke toward the sound. He turned, gave a last glance toward me, and then fell back and ran, cradling his broken arm to his side. I looked after him. Then I looked in every direction, whirling my head to look to the walls of the city, the woods, the clearing, the gate, the Cumeni Road.

The Lamanites were retreating.

I watched as every Lamanite I could see turned and retreated, running for the Cumeni Road, disappearing like chaff in the wind.

I felt hands turning me, searching for my wounds.

"Keturah, are you okay?" Gideon's voice was gruff.

I looked to him and nodded. Then my eyes swung to Zeke.

He stood tall and proud, bloody, frowning at us, frowning at Gideon's hand still at my waist.

Gideon pulled me to his chest with his strong arm and pressed his cheek to the top of my head. Breathing heavily, he rasped out my name. I tried to pull away from him, but he held firm.

"Why did you stop fighting? Why were you just standing still?" he demanded, and finally he let me go to look into my face as if he would see the answer there.

But he wouldn't. I stared up at him, not knowing what to say. I couldn't describe what had happened with the guard.

My eyes shot to Zeke again. His frown had turned to a brooding stare. The tip of his sword cut into the dirt and he leaned on it heavily. He was pale—so pale—and angry with me. His eyes flicked to Gideon a second before he crumpled to the earth.

"Zeke!"

I broke free of Gideon's embrace and rushed to Zeke where he lay in a heap in a pool of dark blood that had been pouring from his wounds as he watched me in Gideon's arms. *No.* It was already soaking into the ground.

I felt the hilt of my father's blade hard in my hand, and I quickly eased it under Zeke's thick armor and began to slice. This blade would save a life today. It would.

The weave was difficult to cut, but I got the armor free and pulled it from his body, looking for wounds.

But there were none.

Then why was he lying unconscious on the ground?

"Here," said Gideon.

I hadn't even realized he knelt near me, his strong hands working over Zeke's body to find the wounds.

I looked in horror at the deep gash on his upper thigh, still pulsing out blood. How had I not seen the wound I knew was there?

No.

I heard movement to my side and flinched, my hand instantly on the axe at my belt. But then Lib was there next to me, bare-chested and pressing his wadded tunic into the wound with large, blood-splattered hands.

I looked away. I was going to be sick. How many men had I killed today? How many wounds had I seen? Inflicted? Received? None of them had made me feel faint like this.

Because this was Zeke. My Zeke, who had sacrificed himself to save me.

No.

I was not worthy of his sacrifice.

Zeke, don't die. Don't.

Seth appeared. He assessed the situation with one thorough look and quickly untied the raw-hide that held his knife secure to his thigh and re-tied it tight high on Zeke's. I winced as he pulled on the knot. He rested a hand on Zeke's chest which still moved up and down. He pressed two fingers to Zeke's neck and gave a slight nod.

There were so many others who were wounded. We should see to them, too. But this was Zeke, and the only wound that I could see because it was mine. It was for me.

Gideon's voice broke through my hazy mind. "Cyrus, Mathoni, go." He gestured toward the city gates. "Bring a stretcher."

"No!" I exclaimed. "No!" I shook my head vigorously and gulped for air. "There's no time! We've got to get him to the surgeons." Though they would probably cut off his leg completely, but all I could think about was getting him there.

I could not carry him. I was not strong enough to carry a man of Zeke's size. They would have to do it.

My whole unit had circled around me, bedraggled, out of breath, wounded but whole and victorious. I begged them all with my eyes.

They exchanged pitying looks and shifted uncomfortably.

"We have to get him there!"

Seth knelt beside me. He placed a hand on my arm. I flinched again, but he kept it there. "All they would be able to do is stop the bleeding, and we've already done that."

My eyes went back to Zeke's ashen face. I reached out and touched his cheek. My fingers slid over his temple and down to the back of his neck. I felt the knot where his hair was still tied back, and my fingers halted.

Slowly, tentatively, with shaking fingers, I eased the familiar tie out from under his head.

I knew all the boys watched me. I knew Gideon watched me closely, but I let my tears come, let them fall and mingle with the pool of Zeke's blood on the ground as I fingered the beads on the tie I had made for him.

I looked up at Gideon, my eyes pleading with him to do that which I could not do, to carry Zeke to the healers—to carry the burden I could not carry.

"Please," I begged him softly.

He glanced back down at Zeke. "Okay, Kanina."

I expected him to pick Zeke up and carry him to the healers inside the city walls.

Instead, he placed his hands on Zeke's head.

The rest of the boys who could, those that had the authority, knelt beside Zeke, edged in closer, and did the same.

I bent and laid my head on Zeke's chest as Gideon called down the power of God and pronounced a blessing on him—that he would live, that he would heal completely and suffer no side effects, that he would marry, that he would become a father. The list of beautiful and miraculous blessings went on and on.

When I thought there were no more beautiful things to bless him with, Gideon said gruffly and earnestly, "Ezekiel, your heart will heal and you will love again."

When the last tender words of the blessing had been spoken, Lib eased me off of Zeke's chest and urged me to my feet. I watched Gideon shift and gently lift Zeke into his arms. Lib put his arm around my waist and I leaned on him—why had I ever resisted his protection?—as we followed Gideon, who carried Zeke across the battlefield to the healers.

Chapter 24

Seth was right. There was nothing the healers could do for Zeke. And the only thing I could do was stay by his side in the infirmary station, but after two days, Lib came and said I had to go back to our camp and rest.

"No." I shook my head.

"It's an order."

"You can't give me orders."

He smiled. "You know I can. But this one's from Seth."

I never disobeyed Seth's commands. Sighing, I scrubbed at my tired, grainy eyes.

"Come on." Lib held out his hand to me.

I took his hand and let him help me to my feet. Like Zeke, along with various less severe wounds, I had a good-sized gash in my own leg. It was painful, and I leaned on Lib as I limped along beside him. Here, two days after the bloody battle for Cumeni, wounds were a badge of honor, and I did not try to hide it.

"Zeke's unit will take care of him. More than anything, he just needs sleep now," Lib assured me.

There were so many wounded men that the healers

couldn't care for them all. They were working with the most badly wounded. Since Zeke's wounds were not among the worst, his unit was seeing to most of his care.

I wished Mother was there. Since we had not planned a battle, only a siege, most of the healers had stayed in Judea where it was safe, including Mother. But now that we needed them, Helaman had sent for the healers and support teams. I felt comforted knowing she would be here soon. It could not be soon enough for me because I knew that Zeke would get worse before he got better, and she was the only one I trusted to heal him.

I kept feeling his head for fever, but he was fine and cool so far. I had Mother's salve and some herbs, but there was nothing more I could do but wait.

I didn't fool myself that things would be back to normal when Zeke woke up—if he woke up. The last thing he had seen before collapsing was me standing in Gideon's embrace, and it had not been an embrace between a soldier and her captain.

I didn't know what to do about that yet. I just knew Zeke had to live.

It was true that Zeke's wounds were not many and mainly minor, but he had taken one blow that had bled quickly and much. My unit had stopped the bleeding, but not before he fainted. He wasn't alone. Two hundred other stripling Ammonites had collapsed from loss of blood during the battle. Every man, without exception, had wounds, and some were very serious. But so far, even though one thousand of the Nephite troops had been killed and at least that many Lamanites, none of the Ammonite warriors had died. I held on to that knowledge, praying it was part of God's plan, that He would not let any of them die.

"Hey, Ket," Noah greeted me cheerfully.

Good, Noah was cooking. I realized I was starving, and I couldn't remember the last time I had eaten.

"Can I help?" I asked, noting he was midway through his

preparations. If I helped, the work would go faster.

He shook his head and grinned. "Seth ordered me not to let you."

Clearly, Seth had a message he wanted to get across, so I went to find him. Lib gave a small sigh of resignation and helped me along. We found Seth in his own camp cleaning and refurbishing salvageable arrows. He pretended not to notice me.

I stood near him, letting my shadow fall over his working area. After a moment, I began to tap my foot. The action made my wound sting.

"Nobody's going to let you cook while you've got dried blood on your neck," he said at last without looking up.

Ew. My hand went to the crusty spatter on my neck. I'd forgotten about that.

When Seth did look up, he looked to Lib, not me. "Take her to get cleaned up, would you? Make sure she checks her own dressings. Feed her, and make her sleep," he directed.

Lib did exactly as Seth had instructed, and I made it easy for him. I remembered the man whose nose had gushed blood down my neck, and I was more than eager to wash it away.

"Here. You missed a spot." Lib took the cloth from me and dipped it in the river. Then he stood squarely in front of me and gently washed the remaining blood from the side of my neck. The river water was cold, and I felt goose bumps rise.

"Thank you." I tried to suppress a shiver.

His eyes were intent on my neck, but they flicked momentarily to mine. "No problem." He worked for a moment more. "I saw you hit that guy."

I shuddered. "He was disgusting."

His mouth was set in a grim line, and he clenched his jaw. After a moment he handed me the cloth and said, "Sit. Let's check that bandage on your leg."

My wound was high on the outside of my thigh, and even though I was a hardened warrior that had come through a very bloody battle, my face flamed as I inched up my sarong.

Lib was no longer the boy who had marched out of Melek three years ago. He was nineteen now and my captain and trying very deliberately to keep his touch impersonal.

When he saw the state of my bandage he sent me a stern, disbelieving look. "This dressing is filthy." He took his knife from his armband and began to cut the bandage off. "Is he worth letting your own wound putrefy?" he asked in disgust. His hands stilled. He took a breath, let it out. "Sorry," he mumbled.

He continued his work with steady hands that didn't falter even when I flinched at the tearing pain. When he finally uncovered the wound and saw that it was not as bad as he had feared, his clenched jaw relaxed some.

He cleaned it and applied a fresh dressing with no further comments about either my wound or Zeke, but I couldn't stop thinking of what he had said, of what his disapproval implied.

When I had finished bathing and eating, I knew I had to sleep. I was exhausted. I could care for neither Zeke nor myself if I didn't rest. Seth was right, and he knew me well enough by then to know that I wouldn't have left Zeke's side a moment before utter exhaustion set in.

For several days, nothing changed. Zeke didn't wake up, but he also did not get infection in his wound nor develop a fever, which was more than I could say for myself.

I was grinding willow bark to make a tea for Zeke when Zachariah appeared by my side suddenly and said, "Take some of this. It will help your friend."

I looked over at his large handful of wild angelica.

"I don't know what it's called," he said. "But it is helpful for loss of blood."

"Where did you find that?"

He shrugged.

I looked warily at the plant. I wasn't going to give it to Zeke on the recommendation of that shrug.

"You can boil the roots and put them right on his wounds. Feed him the stems." He moved closer to me so I could see the plant clearly.

"Are you sure that's not cicuta? Because cicuta is poisonous."

"Trust me, Keturah."

I took the plant. I wanted to trust him. I did trust him with many things—my life was at the top of the list. But I would ask Mother about this plant before I let it pass Zeke's lips.

"Thanks," I said.

Zach offered another plant with a grin. "And this is a much better pain killer than what you've been giving him." He gestured to the willow.

I took the plant he offered. The large green leaves were unfamiliar.

"You burn it. Breathe the smoke. Use it yourself." He gestured to my leg, and then he left as abruptly as he had appeared.

On the third morning after Lib had cleaned me up, I found Lamech beside Zeke's pallet. He was trying to get Zeke to swallow some water.

I knelt on the other side of the pallet and lifted Zeke's head a little. He swallowed, and I lay his head back down.

Lamech eyed me.

I eyed him back. He was a very difficult person to read, but I'd known that from the first moment I met him.

"You didn't die," he said.

"What?"

"You didn't die—in the battle. I thought you would die."

I frowned. "Well, I thought you would die."

A smile cracked his face, but didn't remain long. "We're just a couple of misfits they can't exterminate," he said.

I furrowed my brows. He was a weird little kid. "Sure," I said. "We're just two peas in a pod."

"No."

We both looked down at Zeke's raspy voice. Was he really awake?

"No," he rasped again. "One Keturah. Bad enough."

I grabbed his hand, and I was relieved when he squeezed it. I bent down and kissed his forehead.

"Zeke, I'm sorry," I murmured into his hair, but when I pulled away and looked at him, he had already fallen back into sleep.

Disappointed, I looked up at Lamech.

Anger burned in his dark eyes, but I stared back at him until he shifted on his heels and looked down at Zeke. He gave a cursory check to each of Zeke's bandages to see that they were tight and clean. I knew they were.

"Zeke loves you, you know," he said as he worked.

I bit my lip. Had he actually told that to Lamech? I let my fingers run over the blanket at Zeke's chest, the colorful one he had lent me to use in the dancing. "I know."

"What are you doing with my brother?" he asked without looking up, his voice tight but curious.

I watched my hands smooth Zeke's blanket. "I don't know."

"Then what are you doing *here*?" The restrained anger in his voice matched his eyes when I looked up into them. "You're hurting them both."

"It is no business of yours."

"You're being an idiot."

"It is no business of yours."

His eyes flashed again. "Leave him be. I can see to his care from now on."

"I'm a healer," I said indignantly.

Lamech snorted impolitely, but he gestured to the rows of wounded men around us, and I could see his point. I hadn't been much help to any of them.

"Keturah."

I looked up to see Lib approaching.

"He's right, Keturah. Let's go."

I got to my feet, but I didn't think Lamech was right.

Lib took me by the elbow and led me gently but firmly away.

"He's mine to take care of," I said.

Lib was looking over my head into the distance. "He's not, Ket, and from what I can see, you wanted it that way."

I couldn't argue, because he was right.

We walked in silence until I could see we were not going back to camp. Lib was leading me toward the center of the city, and once we were in the plaza, I knew he was taking me to the government building where the army had headquarters.

"To see Captain Helaman," Lib told the guard at the doors.

I walked through when the guard nodded but looked back at Lib who hadn't entered. He shook his head, turned, and left. I watched him for a moment then turned to the guard. "How do I get there?"

He was a stripling around my age. He had a narrow face and deep-set eyes, and I didn't think I had ever seen him before. He was probably under Ephraim's command because I thought I knew most of the men under Isaiah's.

"Left at the end of the hall," he said and let the doors fall closed.

Helaman was waiting in a large room and he smiled when he saw me.

"Micah says you've experience with plants." As I had come to expect, he wasted no time getting to the point.

"I do. You know my Mother is a healer. She has taught me many things, and I have listened."

"Rations are short," he said succinctly.

"I didn't know."

He sighed deeply. "Everyone will know soon. Does your knowledge of medicines extend to edible plants?"

"Of course."

"Do you think you could find some?"

"Out in the wilderness. Not here."

He nodded.

"But not enough for an army of men," I said.

"Show us what to look for. The men can do their own scavenging. It will keep them busy."

I nodded.

"Feeding our prisoners, even as little as we did, depleted many of our provisions. I've sent for the Lamanite provisions Gid took to Judea, but they are overburdened with men there also. There are no stores here and precious little space for fields and cattle within the walls." He held up a hand as he moved toward the door. "Wait here a moment."

I let my eyes wander to the window as I waited for him to return, and I could see the soldiers moving in the camps. What would happen when we ran out of food? Was it really dire enough to scour the woods for plants?

It was only a moment before he returned, and my eyes went straight to the soldier who was with him. Helaman didn't fail to notice it, though he pretended not to.

"I've put Gid over procurement of food. Show him where to find it out there."

"Yes, Captain," I said.

"Does your leg feel good enough?" Gideon asked as we left the building.

"Everyone has wounds." I could work as well as anyone else in Cumeni, though it was aching.

We left the city through the gates and entered the open area that had once been fields planted with grains and vegetables for the city. But we had camped there, fought a battle there, and anything that had been growing was trampled and dead now.

As we followed the Cumeni Road through the trees, I was immediately able to point out roots and bark, flowering plants, stems, and leaves that could all be eaten.

"But none of this will be filling," I said. "Much of it is bland. And this here," I said, stopping to point out a scraggly plant. "It has an edible root, but the plant looks very much like one that is poisonous. It would be simple for the men to make a mistake. How low are the provisions?"

"Low enough to have the commander worried."

I looked around. "I don't think we can scavenge enough from the forest."

"We'll find enough." Gideon leaned back against a tree, one of the tall ponderosas that grew here.

I moved closer and put my hand on the bark. "When I first met Ethanim, the color of his hair reminded me of this bark. It's edible. The inside." I looked up the trunk to the pine needles and then down at the ground. I picked up a pine cone. "These seeds are edible too."

"See? The forest is filled with these trees," Gideon said.

I shook my head. "No one will be happy on seeds and bark and roots and greens."

"We'll pray, and we'll find enough," he said again. Taking my hand, he pulled me up next to him.

I loved when he said things like this. He had faith, and he was not afraid to show it to me or to anyone. I let my head fall onto his chest, and he encircled my waist with his arms. I thought of the first moonflower he had given me. I thought of the kiss in the tower, so forbidden, so thrilling. I thought of the day Gideon left for Zarahemla and the day we fought together at Cumeni. I could never think of this war without thinking of him, and I could not live the rest of my life and never again think of this war.

"You're thinking of him." The words were murmured into my hair, but they were clear and sharp as a blade.

I wanted to say no, that I wasn't, but the reason the kiss

in the tower had been forbidden was because of Zeke. The anguish of the day Gid left for Zarahemla was because of Zeke. And the battle of Cumeni—there was no way to think of it without thinking of Zeke, who was at that moment lying unconscious because of a blow he took for me. That couldn't be ignored. It couldn't be overlooked or forgotten.

"You're fighting against it, Kanina. I'm glad. But don't make it about him or me." He took me by the shoulders and held me back away from him so he could see into my face. "Of all the things you fight for—your family, their freedom and religion, your God, your country—of all those things, Keturah, don't forget to fight for you. Fight for what you believe, fight for what you want."

"I don't know what I want."

He searched my face as he bent his head to mine. "I do," he whispered in the moment before he kissed me.

And he was right. He knew exactly what I wanted.

Gideon took me by the hand and led me through the forest. I didn't point out any more edible plants, and he didn't ask me to. But when we entered a little meadow where hyptis grew among the willows, I said, "This is a good place for medicines. I want to bring my mother here."

He arched his scarred brow. "Will you tell her I kissed you here?"

I laughed and tried to push him away, but it was no use, and I didn't want to anyway. Instead, I relaxed into his arms and pushed away thoughts of Mother and Zeke and everyone else.

"Come on. It's getting late," Gideon said after the long, forbidden, perfect moments.

We made our way back to the trail, but I stopped when I noticed Gideon was not following me. I turned, and I smiled when I saw him.

"There is one plant I know," he said. He held out his hand, and in it he held two moonflowers, their new blooms brilliant white in the fading sun.

I didn't know what this all meant, what Gideon intended. I didn't know what he wanted me to fight for if it wasn't for him. But I took the flowers and carried them with me back to Cumeni.

The End

About the Author

Misty Moncur wanted to be Indiana Jones when she grew up. Instead she became an author and has her adventures at home. In her jammies. With her imagination. And pens that she keeps running dry.

Misty lives near a very salty lake in Utah with her husband and two children, where they cuddle up in the evenings and read their Kindles. Well, she does anyway.

Connect with Misty on her blog at
http://www.mistymoncur.blogspot.com

Made in the USA
San Bernardino, CA
18 December 2018